DRENCHED

DRENCHED

STORIES OF LOVE AND OTHER DELIRIUMS

Marisa Matarazzo

Soft Skull Press
New York

Library of Congress Cataloging-in-Publication Data

Matarazzo, Marisa.
  Drenched : stories of love and other deliriums / Marisa Matarazzo.
    p.cm.
  ISBN-13: 978-1-59376-271-1 (alk. paper)
  ISBN-10: 1-59376-271-2 (alk. paper)
1. Love stories, American. I. Title.
  PS3613.A823D74 2010
  813'6—dc22
                            2009041152

Cover design by Silverander Communications
Interior design by Elyse Strongin, Neuwirth & Associates, Inc.
Printed in the United States of America

Soft Skull Press
New York, NY

www.softskull.com

CONTENTS

PART 1

PART 2

PART

1

Deliquesce

OUR LIAISON. One summer long. It ends when I break the building. I meant it to impress her. And cool her, in the heat. Grievously I'll never know if it does. Because she disappears, washes away, gone. Vapor.

Meeting:
She's with a traveling group of acrobats and trapeze flyers and flexibles that bend their bodies in extraordinary and unnatural ways. This is because of their childhoods. They did gym when they were kids. They stretched and lifted weights. Held themselves suspended between rings on chains. Spent their whole youths hurling their small, tight bodies off vaults, through air, spinning.

She is the strongest and most delicate-looking woman I have ever seen. Her torso: compact, muscles like cables wrapped in skin. Her hands: smooth and pale and straight fingered. Glimpsing them, I wish I had a fever. She would press her hands to my forehead and my temple. Her face: soft cheeks over strong bones. Blue eyes—deeply blue, like paint-tube colors. They are cerulean. But they sometimes change—azure, cobalt, ultramarine. Long black eyelashes she flaps open and closed, a little slowly. On purpose she does this, maybe. Blinks slowly with her lashes like that. Because it makes me feel as though in my body, in the space of my torso, is a large empty bottle. Its belly in the place of my belly. Its neck in the place of my neck. And my head is gone. She blinks her eyelashes and wind howls across the bottle mouth.

We meet on the beach. Men with big trucks chug into the parking lot, unfold equipment, stab stakes deep into the sand, click and drill, stretch tarp taut. The troupe follows and arrives in a sleek black tour bus. The doors *fiss* open, and out they tumble, onto the sand. They spot one another for twists and flips in the sky. I am sunbathing. I sit up and watch. Her troupemates run at her, leap into her interlaced fingers braced across her flexed thigh and bent knee. She ejects them backwards and high into the sky. Up there they roll and turn and look like swimmers in the yellow sunlight. I notice her forearms. On the pale inside part where the blue vein scrawls close to the surface, she has tattoos. One per forearm. From my towel I can make them out. They are sailor tattoos. Vintage-looking women in heels, hose that stop with garters at the thigh, panties. They are topless. They stand on her wrists, on toe, backs arched. Flirty and sexy posture. I stare at her arms. I esteem: tattoos are permanent. There through death.

I stare at her whole self. From her steady feet on up to where the sun winks from sprigs that shoot from her short and wavy hair. I stare her up and down and admire how she launches the tumblers. In my chest opens and swells the space that longs. I stare.

She notices me and looks away and then looks back and then away and then back and smiles and dusts sand off her thighs and looks at the ocean and looks at the tent being pupped and looks at her mates and looks back at me. I still stare but feel safe because they are putting on a show even if they are only practicing, and it is my job to look. But I am looking at her, and she notices and waves me over. I put on my shorts and tuck my wallet and keys under my towel and walk over. My face is hot. She asks me if I want to try, and I imagine myself in the air and then snap-necked upside down in the sand.

"No thanks," I say.

She says, "You should."

I say, "No thanks, I'll die. I'm afraid I'll die."

She says, "Seriously, you won't die." And then she blinks kind of slowly.

I believe her. So I back up in the sand and run at her. She heaves me high into the air and I know what it's like to do a somersault, so I do one in the air, backwards. She catches me, easily. I don't know how. I am short of breath and my heart is beating. I feel it thud hard in my hips and in my throat and against the top of my head. My hands are locked around the back of her neck. My butt is slung between the flexed muscles in her arms. She sets me down and says, "Go again?"

I say, "Yes." My face flushes and there is the smell of the ocean in my nose, the salty damp of it in my lungs. I back up and run at her again.

She tosses me higher, and the other beachgoers look to see and go blind watching me up there, backlit by the sun. And here I am again, my hands around her neck, my body braced by the two sexy girls on her forearms.

We do this all afternoon. The rest of the acrobats get bored and leave for the hotel. The sun goes down and streaks the sky violet and carmine and butter. Seagulls gather on the wet sand. Thin layers of ocean and froth rush and suck their pronged feet. They squawk. She comes home with me.

We sit on the couch.

"Can I kiss you?" she asks from over there, her pretty face cushioned in enormous pillows.

I say, "Yes, uh-huh," or maybe just nod while my heart charges at my ribs. I think it will knock clear into her while we kiss. Thump against her chest. Make her mistake its beat for her own.

We kiss long. Hours. They pass quickly. Then we are dizzy and wobbly and blissed out. She stays.

Proof:
We fall in love. In these ways:
1. olfaction
2. protraction
3. bathtub

1.

The smell in the air—the breeze blown through our bedroom window. We make bedroom curtains ourselves. Gauzy soft silk, white but sheer, we buy it in the fabric district downtown where the buildings are tall and the homeless are everywhere. We take the silk home. Hang it in our bedroom window in my apartment where we live together—my first time living with a lover, her fourth she tells me, but I won't think too hard about that.

This window catches the sunlight and the hot draft off the street. Amber and sooty. Plus the smell of jasmine from the hills, exhaust from cars, and dirt from all over. Mixed together, the waft is very romantic. It charges the air in the bedroom so the skin on our faces and our bodies hums with an awareness of something. Like when you're a teenager and you dream about how your life might be, and you sense, somewhere deep, mostly in your groin, that your life just might turn out that way—the way you'd like it.

In the mornings in the bed, with the breeze and the light like this, we listen to slow music rich with ladies' voices and cello. We lie on top of the covers, no clothes. And the nice wind waltz from behind the curtains pushes on the hairs on our arms. Blows her smell across my face. She smells like bay leaves and mist. The sunlight rolls out from behind the curtains, tumbles, fades. Rolls out again.

We feel things rising in our chests. Breathing each other like this and looking over into the face of the other coaxes and fluffs this rising thing. Puffs it large so it presses out against our ribs and up into our throats, and while people don't often feel the same things at the same times, I think we do. We smile and sniff and laugh a little, which starts to look like crying but doesn't feel like crying. Her eyes are ultramarine. I hold out my arms and stretch out my hands and fingers to touch her face, and it's like these arms and hands are not my own because I can't feel them because the feeling swelling in my chest has cut the circulation to my arms, and they are heavy and almost numb, and there is her skin beneath the pads of my fingertips. I breathe deep, and the feeling is better than holding a sleepy baby in your arms and sniffing the sweet smell from the top of its head.

2.

Some days she teaches me how to stretch. I'm on my back, on the floor. She takes my ankles and places them on her shoulders. My calves against her chest, my butt between her hipbones. She leans her whole body into the backs of my legs. It hurts and my legs don't bend back far. But we do this often and in two weeks I get good. She folds me in half. My nose touches my knees. Then this thing: nose to my knees, and I grab my ankles with my hands and stiffen all over. She lifts me at my waist and by my legs and picks me up. I stay firm, a folded person like a bundle of firewood in her arms. She is so strong. Sometimes she tucks my rear into the crook of her right arm and scoops my legs and head and arms in her left arm and she pretends I am a giant machine gun. She takes me onto the balcony and makes shooting noises.

"Deadly fire from the bottoms of your feet!" she shouts. She picks off planes in the sky. We shoot down so many planes.

"Imagine the sad families," she says. "So many dead relatives."

The stretching lengthens my spine. I've grown three quarters of an inch.

"Only in my torso, though, not in my legs," I tell her.

"Torso's more important," she says. "It's where everything important is. Good to give it more room. Legs just keep you up," she lies. She has very long, muscular legs. They do a lot.

3.

She props her ankle on my shoulder and shaves her legs. She shakes the razor under the water in the tub. Dark specks float from it to the surface.

"I was going to be a synchronized swimmer," she tells me.

"When?" I ask, watching her body in the bathwater.

She says, "When I was a kid. Before I took gymnastics I was on the synchronized swimming team for toddlers." She takes her leg off my shoulder and places her other ankle on my other shoulder. Squeezes liquid soap in a line along her shin. She smears and lathers it.

"I liked it," she says. "Then I found I like falling through the air and into nets better." She drags the razor over her calf. "Faster movement over greater distance," she says and looks hard down the skin road she shaved into her soaped leg.

"I could work in your show," I say. "I could lie on the ground beneath the trapeze," I tell her. "Naked," I say. She laughs and looks up and her eyes are azure. "Instead of a net it will be me," I tell her. "I won't catch anyone. I'll just get crushed, naked. By acrobats who fall."

She shakes her head, smiles, blinks slowly. Her eyes, cobalt. In my chest and stomach, howling. She swishes the blade in the water. Then drops the razor in the tub. *Cloomp.* She starts to reach for it, but instead scoops up a handful of water and splashes it up my arm, across my forehead, over my chest.

"Feels good, huh," she says. She pushes a handful of water through her hair. She stands. The water level drops. Naked, dripping, looking very tall in front of me. I grab her thigh, squeeze it all the way around with both hands. My thumbs meet, tucked high up near her crotch. She is warm.

Other:

When she is not practicing with the troupe, we walk around. We wander the cheap shopping street near the apartment looking for a French bakery I remember being there. We can't find it. We walk with coffees in white paper cups. She brings the coffee to her lips, sips from it. I spy the lady on her arm. Midsip my acrobat glances at me from the corner of her eye, winks slowly. There's the howling. I feel light. I sink my cheek into her shoulder.

These times with her. I have loved them.

When the weather turns too hot, she complains. "It's killing me," she says.

AFTER THE preceding three, but before the end, there is *Preparation*: It is early. She's out. Practicing with her troupe. Sun's just risen and already it's hot. Has been hot for days. Sticky, wet heat. I work in the bedroom. The walls are painted aquamarine, oceanic blue. We painted them this color directly after our first make out session, the night she moved in.

She said, "Cool blue makes me limber." She asked, "Can we paint the walls blue?"

"Sure," I said. So we did.

Today, a big tub of shower putty by my foot, a steel spatula in my hand, I focus on the line in the angle where the wall and floor meet. With my fingers I scoop rubber putty from the tub and smudge it between the baseboard running the perimeter of the walls and the hardwood floor. It gives like dough, but is stickier. Gluey. I press the steel spatula into the clump and drag it along the line. Dirt and grit from the floor roll under the blade and mix with the putty. The steel spatula scrapes the surface along the drag and makes small ding sounds at the end of each stroke. I scoop more, push it in there, white out the dark crack between the wall and floor. All four around, pushing putty, smoothing it with the spatula. The thin cracks alongside the window where the frame meets the plaster wall, I fill them. Around the window parts, the gaps between the panes of glass, designed to be separate so they slide open and closed—I seal them solid. Shut and airtight. Crouching over the floor, I fill the pencil lines between the slats in the wood. Fill three small gouges—two from furniture and one from when I dropped a hammer.

Working around the bed and the desk and the bookshelf and the dresser, I streak the dark floor with white putty, sealing it clean. The sun shines through the small skylight in the ceiling. I'm sweating beneath my shirt. I putty the space between the door and its frame. Fill in all around the hinges. I heave handfuls at the gap between the door and the floor, glopping out the space. Then up, where the ceiling meets the walls. I climb on the dresser and fill the line between the crown molding and ceiling. Then I climb onto the bookshelf, then onto the desk, then the bed, reaching above my head, stuffing all cracks high up. Steel spatula, chalky plaster walls, gooey putty. Nail holes and nicks are plugged. The entire bedroom is pasted shut. I stand and look at the aquamarine walls, now streaked and splotched with shiny white putty rubber. I stack a few hardcover books on the desk, climb on top of them. Reach the ceiling. Unlatch the skylight. Flip it back on its hinges. Out of the skylight I climb into the white sun. Stumble onto the roof, blind. I walk the length of the apartment, but on top of it, squinting. Soft tar sticks to my sandals. I trip on the garden hose coiled neatly near the ladder leading down to a fire escape. I climb down the ladder, drop onto the fire escape, return to the hot kitchen through the window.

SHE IS gone long, practicing through the night. Rehearsing in the dark to beat the heat. This is what she tells me. I believe her. I sleep alone. Just before dawn I climb back to the roof, drop into the bedroom to test. The putty is dry. Up, out, and into the heat again I find the hose. Unwind it and insert it into the room through the skylight. Twist the knob all the way strong. Crawl back in to the kitchen through the fire escape.

Later, she returns. Shiny, breathing hard. Two acrobats passed out during practice. The news says old people and children are dying. We make love in the living room, in front of the fan, on a sheet on the rug, sweating so much we leave stains in the shapes of whole bodies.

Presentation:

"Follow me," I say. I go to the kitchen, exit out the window, onto the fire escape. She squints hard, shades her eyes, climbs up after me. On the roof the tar paper blisters. We step slowly across the top of our apartment. Our sandals rustle and crunch the fine gravel littered across the roof. I lead her to the skylight.

"I smell water," she says. We stop at the skylight. Stand over it. The burbling is loud.

"What's this?" she asks smiling. Her long lashes are wet and sparkling with sweat. She smudges her forehead with the back of her arm.

I grin at her, hold out my hand. She takes it. I drop headfirst through the skylight into the bedroom. She follows.

The room is filled with water, floor to ceiling. Our bodies slippery, salty sweat washed over in cold water. We float still for a moment, suspended, in the middle of the room. Arms out, legs apart, like skydivers. We feel the cool. Her hair is like dark anemone, swaying.

I bend and dive into the mattress and kick across the room. The sheets on the bed float and tangle. We swim from wall to wall, knocking into the floating alarm clock and hat rack. Pens and pencils drift in front of our eyes. Our clothes are blousey and stretched and billow after us. Wall to wall, kicking off, then gliding across, bodies buoyant and turning in space.

We stand on the chest of drawers, press our noses to the ceiling, suck breaths of air. Dive down again. She pulls books off the bookshelf. We watch them roll, spill open. The pages flutter. Flying fish.

She swims to the floor, graceful like a seal. She looks up at me, smiles, waves in slow motion. I swim over her, my hair out, seaweeding slowly around my head, into and out of my face. I can feel the sun through the skylight illuminating the surface of the water behind me.

The room swells. It bulges fat, ripe with water. The water begins to cloud murky, muddy. First closest to the walls, creeping toward the center. The putty holds strong, but the plaster is dissolving. The window creaks. The glass spider webs. Sharp snapping sounds echo through the water. We swim toward the floor and try to stand upright by flapping our arms, pushing the water above our heads to get our feet on the floor. Her right foot touches down and the floorboards give beneath her sandal. Her foot slips down into the soft split in the boards while chords of silver bubbles stream toward the ceiling from her nose. Water whips into a small cyclone in the hole in the floor. It pulls her leg deeper into the hole. She is half calf into the floorboards, but yanks her leg up and flaps at the water hard, with her arms. Her calf and foot reappear. Her sandal is missing. Flushed down the hole.

The glass in the window bursts out with a sound like *choot!* Milky blue-tinted water gushes from the window frame. I imagine shards of wet glass crackling in the sunlight as they tumble and fall to the walk down below. Shatter into bits with the crash of the wave.

The walls give. Chunks of plaster and dry wall in the shapes of states blast from our bedroom, pushed by the surge to the street outside. The floorboards give. So much water. More than I thought could fill this room. More water.

It takes us. Our floor caves into the apartment below. We fall with the water and follow its sweep. Sloshing from our blue room, into our downstairs neighbor's bedroom. His stuff is ruined. I glimpse his eyes; they're huge. His yelling alternates loud then sputters drowned and muffled. We flood his hallway. Feet and more feet deep of water. Me on my seat, she on her back, we ride the tide through his hall, out his back door propped open in the heat, down stairs, and into the street. The heave carrying our soppy bodies splits at the trunk of a tree growing from the apron of grass in the sidewalk. The rush of water slipping me along tapers thin, and I slow to a stop on the asphalt. Her current is strong. So much water. It carries her down the road. Her sleek black tour bus is idling at the corner. It shines bright and oily in the sun. I watch her wash across the street, her knees tucked close to her chest. Her sally subsides. The door on the bus hushes open. She spins slowly on her back as she comes to a stop. She steps gracefully up from the spin and in one smooth movement lifts herself from her back to her feet and onto the step entrance of the bus. She shakes her body. Drops of water whip from her hair and her fingertips, diamonding in the daylight. She ducks into the bus. The door hisses and vacuums shut. I watch it pull away and lumber down the avenue. Sun blazing. The bus shrinks small and miragey. She is gone.

Sense:

Every day gallons, pounds, miles of water evaporate from seas, lakes, rivers, pools. Different volumes of water evaporate off different bodies at different rates, depending. What determines what body of water evaporates at what rate, at what time? Hydrologics. The water cycle. There's solar radiation, so water turns to vapor. Under conditions of extreme heat, there's sublimation. *Poof!*— from ice to gas, solid to beyond—just like that. Molecules disappear into the sky, serve time as clouds, and return in various forms. Snow, sleet, frost, rain, fog. The wispiest of mists is called virga.

The human body is composed of 80 percent water. I weigh 109 pounds. That is 87.2 pounds of water. My acrobat weighs 124 pounds. That is 99.2 pounds of water. More water than me, but she is taller and stronger. Her water stretches from her feet on the earth up toward the sky.

The average unit of time a water molecule will spend in the atmosphere before precipitating back to ground is nine days. It might return as dew or downpour. I could wait nine days. But the likelihood of those molecules homecoming to that same location of evaporation is too slim. Consider jet streams, the rotation of the planet. Virga reevaporates before it even touches ground. And when the hydrogens and the oxygens clump and hit heavy, slicking the streets and eroding the hills, there is always runoff.

THESE THOUGHTS I think, they do not help. In my heart, an aneurysm. A fluid-filled sac, soused milky blue, cerulean. The walls of my arteries go runny.

Hotmouths

ESPITE THE complications, they kiss constantly. She can hardly stop herself, she loves to kiss him. His rose-quartz teeth taste like maraschino cherries. It's the red flavoring of her kidhood and erupts memory fireworks in her mouth.

His teeth are polished and pink and flecked with minerals. His lips are pale and match the flesh of the rest of his face. When he smiles they pull back taut and white, revealing two straight rows of rose-quartz teeth—pink like organs, crystalline like ice.

His teeth get hot. When he is pleased, the rose quartz rises in temperature like the hood of a car in the summertime. He sleeps with his mouth open, to let the rose quartz stay tepid in the event of a pleasurable dream. Sometimes in the night, on the couch, The Girlfriend watches him sleep. She sucks wintergreen hard candies. She blows wintergreen breath into his open, sleeping mouth. She imagines his rose-quartz teeth steeled cold and frosty. Wishes they could be that way.

When he kisses The Girlfriend, he is pleased. His teeth roast and scald the backs of his lips and his tongue. He's grown used to this and callused inside and around his mouth. But not The Girlfriend. She winces and whimpers at her blistered lips and tongue but loves him all the more. They kiss in bursts, pull away often to sip cool aloe juice. He bares his teeth; she sprays them with the water spritzer the mother uses for ironing. Then they dive into each other's faces again until the smell, taste, and sting of seared flesh force their heads apart.

THE GIRLFRIEND has no hands. She lost both of her original hands in ceramics class halfway through her junior year in high school. She'd thrown a Mother's Day vase. Students were not allowed to use the kiln. It was an old kiln and unsafe. They were instructed to leave their pieces on the steel table in the drying kiosk. After school, in the dark, the night janitor, a large old man who once worked in an open-pit mine and was accustomed to danger, would put the students' pieces in the kiln. The Girlfriend didn't want to wait. She went in during lunch. No one was around. She placed her vase on the big spatula and pushed it into the kiln. But she didn't push the spatula in straight, and a corner of it caught and knocked out the metal post that propped open the sliding door. Heavy and iron and hot, it slipped like a guillotine onto The Girlfriend's wrists. It split skin and muscle and bone. Severed, her hands fell into the kiln. The vase was destroyed. The heat partially cauterized her stumps, and she was rushed to the hospital where they stitched up the gaping parts, shot her with antibiotics, gave her a drip and then pills for the pain. Extracted from the kiln a day after the incident, The Girlfriend's hands were baked black and hard and small.

The Girlfriend survived with stumps for an entire summer. Instead of making her get a real summer job, the mother signed her up to be a counselor in training at the sleepaway camp on the small island off the coast. The mother suggested The Girlfriend take the summer to relax, to grieve her hands, to accept her stumps. On one condition: "NO boys, NO funny stuff," the mother commanded, her face a block of cement. "NO hanky-panky bedtime nothing. None of it." She and The Girlfriend stood in the kitchen. Sun shone through the stained-glass window above the sink. The light through the blue sections of glass looked like water. In contrast, the mother's face and big hair loomed red, her eyes black. "Don't even think about it." The mother spoke deliberately. She spun her car keys around her finger before catching them and pointing her finger between The Girlfriend's eyes. "Not at your age," she said, "not *until.*"

The mother has convictions. She aggressively imposes them on her daughter. She doesn't scream. She hardly raises her voice. However, the mother has a way of not yelling that, to The Girlfriend, is louder than trumpets and garbage trucks and space shuttles returning to the atmosphere. "Okay!" The Girlfriend wailed as she scooped the straps of her duffel into her elbow pit, marched it to the driveway, heaved it into the back seat.

AT CAMP, she windsurfed every day. Because she couldn't paddle out, she dropped onto her board from the end of the dock, rigging up far beyond the breakers. She attached a chest hook from her life preserver to the boom. She leaned the weight of her body against the blow of the wind and raced handless across the ocean. To tack she locked the boom in the crook of her elbow and swung it around. Like a do-si-do—The Girlfriend and her windsurfer—hooking elbows, swinging to the right, swinging to the left. She led the sail and its big white board over the chop and the waves.

She met Rose Quartz in the ocean. He repaired buoys. It was a stormy day. The ocean surged and cracked like slabs of granite colliding and crumbling. The Girlfriend cut across the jagged water, ignoring the red flag warnings flapping from the lifeguard stands on shore. She could hardly see. On shore, the rest of the CITs organized the campers into a game of military hide-and-seek. They did this during foul weather, when the ocean was too wild for sports. Campers imagined themselves guerilla soldiers. They dove behind bushes and crawled silently through the mud and brush behind the cafeteria. They always made The Girlfriend keeper of the torture chamber. She had to inflict the torture of knocking captives in their eye sockets with her stumps while they screamed. Once, a weak girl threw up. The Girlfriend hated the game. On this particular day, she refused to play. Instead, she careened across the frightful sea in that stern storm until she smashed into a buoy. The board broke into foam and fiberglass shards that thrashed in the churn, knocked into her head and shoulders and back. The sail flumped onto the surface of the water and was sucked under in a wash. The Girlfriend lunged onto the buoy. Locked her elbows around its neck, wrapped her legs around its base.

Rose Quartz was manning the Buoy Damage Station aboard a nearby offshore oilrigPLUS. An orange light went off on his console indicating a collision and possible damage to Buoy Angustia located several degrees north and east from here and there. Rose Quartz took a breath, pushed his chair away from the console, grabbed his wet suit from the hanger on the wall. He suited up, checked the air pressure in his tank, attached his lean tool kits to the slim compartments on his calves, hustled to the diving stage, fingered on his fins, rolled backwards, and dropped into the donnybrook sea.

Beneath the surface, the ocean felt tame and huge. Rose Quartz flapped his fins and watched sea particles glint in the sun that fought through the chop. He approached the buoy and checked its underside. It was mossy and barnacled, but undamaged. He broke the surface of the water with his head to examine the exposed body of the buoy, and he saw thigh. Then buttocks in a bikini bottom, torso in a life vest, and back of a head of wet blonde hair. He removed his respirator and yelled, "Hey!" He laid his cold hand on her cold thigh. The Girlfriend's scream blew away in the wind as she tried to scramble higher up and over the buoy. No hands to grasp it, she hugged the buoy, clamping tightly with her biceps and forearms. But the sea shoved her and she slipped.

Rose Quartz kicked up next to her, said hi, grabbed her in a lifeguard tow, and swam her to shore. He laid her on the damp sand. They both panted. Rose Quartz smiled, exposing his teeth. Pink teeth. Immediately The Girlfriend wanted to touch them with her tongue. Sweet, she imagined they would be, like Life Savers. And they were smooth and flat and comforting like ocean glass beneath his pale lips that looked kind of smeared.

She wanted to kiss him. She didn't even think about it. It was an impulse that slid up behind her in the swash of a wave. She found herself closing her eyes slowly, lifting her mouth toward his. Maybe it was the rescue, the waves, the rain, the wind, or the tilt of her chin, but Rose Quartz felt it too. He moved into her lips and kissed her.

This was The Girlfriend's first kiss. She'd never even played those games at those parties in middle school, afraid the mother would somehow know and blow out The Girlfriend's skull with the sledgehammering blasts of her voice. But something about this moment, about this kiss, pinned The Girlfriend up against a door in her mind: On this side, kissing on the beach like Ferris wheels and cotton candy and hot oil and red meat. On the other side, the mother and her vocal chords and pointer finger. This kiss here, on the sand in the ocean's slobber, braced the door shut. Sealed it briefly, air- and sound-tight.

The Girlfriend imagined right—his mouth was sweet. Like the strawberry sauce she ladled on her waffles when she was a little kid. She had nails and knuckles, whole digits and palms, could lift a ladle and pour. She ate with her hands and licked her fingers.

They kissed deeper, tongues and grunts. Rose Quartz's mouth felt warm. Then his mouth felt hot, like holding your hand too long over a candle—burning hot. Too hot. It hurt The Girlfriend. The pain distracted her from the kiss. In her mind she stepped out of his embrace and away from the door. Immediately, it was nuked open, the mother's voice mushroom clouding The Girlfriend's encounter. "A stranger? A STRANGER!" she heard the mother say. "You can't kiss strangers on the beach!" The Girlfriend flinched and cringed, broke from his lips. She lifted her hand to her head to try to dull the explosion. But she felt only the nub of her wrist on her eyebrow. She opened her eyes and saw Rose Quartz staring at it. She dropped her arm. He watched it hit the sand with a thunk. The wind picked up. She shivered, despite her still warm and honeyed mouth. He put his hand over her wrist, cupping her stump. This, to The Girlfriend, felt very private. "Are you okay?" he asked quietly as the wind flicked and the sky grew darker. Goosebumps rose up her arms. "Are you cold?" She watched his face watch hers. They fell hard for each other.

CAMP ENDED and The Girlfriend went home. For back to school she got clamp attachments for her stumps. They suffice as relatively opposable thumbs and forefingers. Rose Quartz stays on the rig but swims ashore on weekends to meet The Girlfriend. It's not too far.

The Girlfriend is in twelfth grade and desperate to get out. "It sucks," she tells him. "It sucks so much."

Rose Quartz, being older and calm says, "Yeah, baby, it really does." He removes her clamps, holds her stumps, slowly kisses her lips.

Rose Quartz's teeth make their relationship complicated. The Girlfriend's mouth has taken on new shapes. Blisters harden her lower lip while scald scars crack the line of her upper lip. The weird ashtray girl from her chem class stopped her in the hall and asked her, seriously, if she had started boxing. The Girlfriend hunched over like a fighter and held her arms up, protecting her face. The girl saw the stumps and clamps up close, floating before her eyes. The girl gasped audibly, and a look crawled across her face that made The Girlfriend feel so uncomfortably understood, she got nervous, dropped her clamps to her sides, turned, and took off to the parking lot where she could gaze at a slice of the ocean through the fence and some hills and trees. She smoked cigarettes and thought of Rose Quartz.

She thought about his age. He is older. He is twenty-eight.

Which feels astonishing to The Girlfriend. Like he knows what it is to be in deep adulthood. He doesn't live at home and hasn't for years, and his waterproof wallet is thick with cards and slips and money he's earned. And while she would never consider going to prom, if she did she would bring him as her date, and the music would veer and crash to a stop as they passed under the ballooned archway, and everyone would freeze and stare and marvel that the no-hands girl has got a much older boyfriend who works out at sea and is even a little older than the cute English teacher everyone is in love with. Additionally, and secretly, she keeps a hot spot in her mind where she is quite aware of what the mother would think of this relationship. This awareness is thrilling. It is terrifying. It all makes her time with him feel wondrous.

And without him she feels dumpish and glum. She is suffering from monumental boredom, except for on weekends, which are okay, just because of him.

"I AM MONUMENTALLY BORED!" she shouts from the shore during the weekdays, her face red and wet. She hopes the sound travels to Rose Quartz, out tending to his console.

"SAVE ME," she sobs.

Maybe Rose Quartz can hear her. And being a man and liking to save things, namely her, he makes short lists in his head: cigarettes, barbecue beef, beer. He thinks of things she likes. On land he buys her rich cigarettes from Europe and takes her out for barbecue beef and beer at Plum West.

ROSE QUARTZ and The Girlfriend hide in The Girlfriend's basement and kiss heavily on the couch. They start slow, try to pace themselves; the Girlfriend's lips are suffering. She has scabs and sores—cracked and hard, fresh and soft.

"Kiss only my mouth," she tells him. "I have no hands," she says, "I can't afford burns all over my body."

Rose Quartz nods, says he understands. He tries. But sometimes he slips. Kisses her neck, ears. They'd quit the kissing altogether and try other things if they could, but they can't. The Girlfriend and Rose Quartz can't cut to anything beyond kissing due to the Rule of the Natural Progression of Things. The Girlfriend was raised to think she believes firmly in this. The mother planted it fixedly and fertilely in The Girlfriend's mindsoil. It pollinates all her thoughts. The mother also speaks of it from time to time. Loudly, into The Girlfriend's ears it goes. The mother has dogmatized the rubric: kissing comes, but eventually, only after hello and goodbye hugs have been thoroughly exhausted. And it is not until kissing winds down to its natural end—marked by marriage or, the mother has conceded, attending a prestigious college and dating an equally prestigious gentleman student with a big brain, good job right there in the future, and a proposal on the tip of his tongue—that it is acceptable to move beyond kissing and into something else. The next level.

"You can move to the next level in college because that's where you will find your husband. But until then, you are not *allowed* to move to the next level," her mother has said. "At your age kissing is tops. The limit." She straightened her back and elongated her neck, accentuating her height over The Girlfriend. She raised her eyebrows and spoke slowly, suddenly gypsy-like. "And don't do too much of it. Because I'll know. I'll know what you're doing," she said. "Don't bother sneaking around." The mother's words were like cannon fire blown demolishingly into The Girlfriend's ears. And from the rubble, she didn't know how the mother would know, but the thought of it—of the mother knowing how to somehow know—made The Girlfriend gasp for breath. It drove her to the basement where she withdrew into the couch and curled beneath the colored light that beat through the long skinny window. Shades of red and orange and mulberry paraded over the top of her head, across her arms, over her thighs. They toppled and fumed over the rug.

In addition to her opinions, the mother is a stained-glassiere. Every window in the house, even the basement window, is one of hers. They are very colorful and without recognizable imagery. Abstractions in Stained Glass is what the mother calls them. Shafts of colored light fence across carpet and furniture all daylight long. To stand in the living room in front of the big window at noon is kaleidoscopic. The window's called *A Map of the Whole Wide World* because that's what The Girlfriend called it when she was a little kid, because that's what she saw when she looked through it, although there are no such recognizable bodies of land or placements of water. But looking at it felt like peering over the earth. It's the mother's masterpiece.

While she can't quite articulate it, The Girlfriend has a vague notion of the idea that everything from the outside world—the light that feeds the planet—is interpreted for her through the mother's interpretation of it in these stained-glass windows. The Girlfriend has a dim awareness that this interception influences her own perceptions. She's not conscious of the details of this arrangement, but she is often overcome by a roaring sense of resentment.

This drives The Girlfriend to do things like smoke. To squeeze the butts of her favorite European cigarettes tight between her clamps and suck hard. She cracks the stained-glass window above the basement couch, watches the smoke from her cigarette chuff through the colored light. Watches it become red and orange and mulberry plumes twisting above her head and out the window. She blows out gusts of tobacco like she is hailing a ride with a whistle. She also lies. Despite the mother's fusillade of threats about *knowing*, The Girlfriend musters the sand to take that chance. She tells the mother she is spending weekends in the basement because it is there that she can finally concentrate and get some work done, "Like apply to college and everything!" she screams at the mother.

Fridays and weekends, she stealths around, heart pounding—scared and angry that the mother might somehow know what she is up to. She disobeys this much, but it is not easy for her. She's not that kind of girl. She gets nervous. Nights leading up to her

Rose Quartz weekends, she sleeps barely, can't seem to manage the calm to gentle into her pillow. And when Friday slips into evening, she keeps very quiet, careful that the mother doesn't hear her creep out alone or return with Rose Quartz. The one smudge of luck for them: the mother likes to go salsa dancing. She goes every weekend, stays out late.

THE DOOR separating the basement from the backyard is locked with a latch. The Girlfriend easily flicks it up and open, pushes it bodywide, scoots out. She wears sneakers and jeans. She carries a towel under her arm and walks fast to the shore as night falls over Friday. Sometimes she jogs. She arrives at the ocean just a little bit sweaty. The salt on her upper lip stings. She watches for Rose Quartz's long, wet-suited body to slog backwards out from the waves. She listens for his large slapping fins on the wet sand. On his back, a waterproof rucksack with a change of clothes.

The first kiss out of the ocean is the best. Rose Quartz is so cold, it seems to last forever. The Girlfriend runs at him and jumps. Hooks her elbows around his neck, locks her clamps together between his shoulder blades, squeezes his hips with her thighs. He holds her up. Pulls her against him. One arm around her waist. The other under her butt. Her clothes get wet. They breathe and stare into each other's eyes for a thick moment, then dig in, lips first. The Girlfriend and Rose Quartz make sounds like things are delicious. His mouth broils hot.

Seawater, saliva, and maraschino cherries. The Girlfriend licked red Ring Pops from the snack stand at the field by the airport. Age eight, she'd watch her best friend from down the street play Little League. He wore cleats and stirrups and whomped at the ball. One time he saw her naked, when they were ten. She made it happen on purpose. She changed with the door open so he'd see her when he got out of the bathroom. He saw her, nude, except for one leftover ring pop on the middle finger of each hand. She screamed and leapt behind the door. She made like it was an accident. Days later, on the way to school, when he was still alive, she told her dad about it. Even at ten she figured that the mother would shriek and trounce if she heard *naked* and *boy* in the same sentence out of her daughter's mouth. She wondered if her dad would react similarly. She told him that the neighbor had accidentally seen her naked because she forgot to close the door because she forgot he was over. Her dad nodded and said, "Hmm." He adjusted the radio, rested his hand on the gearshift, drove too slowly for the freeway.

Rose Quartz and The Girlfriend devour one another. Ocean drips from Rose Quartz's hair. They kiss and kiss. The furnace of his mouth rages. The Girlfriend's lips sizzle. They stop.

Burned, dizzy, beaming, The Girlfriend walks with Rose Quartz. He holds her clamp and they meander through the sand. His wet suit squeaks when he walks. At the public showers near the restroom by the parking lot, Rose Quartz peels off his wet suit, hits the steel button, steps under the water. The water is cold, but he takes it without flinching. He smiles into it. It washes over his mouth. He rinses the ocean from his hair and body. He wears small, tight trunks.

The Girlfriend watches his body. Water breaks over his shoulders and slides across his chest and stomach, flattening his dark hair straight down. She can see all the muscles in his legs, even though he's not flexing. She considers him almost naked, except for the trunks. She stares at his chest and his stomach and his bathing suit and his legs, and for a minute she remembers her hands. She can feel the feeling of holding his face in her hands. Her fingers are splayed. His right ear tucked between the index and middle finger of her left hand. His left ear tucked between the index and middle finger of her right hand. His earlobes touch the soft space in the V between the two fingers. She slides her hands over his neck, onto his shoulders. She presses her fingertips into the saucers above his collarbones. Slides her palms over his chest. His nipples trace a line through the center of her palms straight up to the tip of her middle fingers. Over his stomach, she wants to stop. Lay her hands flat. Feel his stomach rise and fall with his breath. He breathes. She moves her hands over his hips. The sharp bones like picture frames in the center of her palms. With one finger she can pull down the front of his shorts. With another, trace the line separating tanned from pale skin. She pushes her hand down into his trunks. Her whole hand pinned against him by the elastic in his waistband, he is warm and soft and not soft and in her hand that has fingers that move and hold him. She can hardly breathe. Rose Quartz holds his wet suit to the showerhead. Water charges against it. Sounds like screeching brakes. Startled, The Girlfriend looks away. Notices the sky above the waves is pink.

The shower stops. She gives Rose Quartz the towel. He pats his face with it and takes it to the bathroom to change. The Girlfriend moves so she can see inside the bathroom. Rose Quartz is not in a stall. He changes near the sinks. His back is to the bathroom door. The Girlfriend watches him change. Spies his naked rear. And maybe a little more, for just a second, as he lifts his leg to step into his pants. Before he zips up, The Girlfriend steps away from the bathroom door. Wanders toward the parking lot.

He catches up to her with a squeeze. "Hi, baby," he says. He is clothed and handsome. He puts his arm around her. She tucks her clamp in his back pocket. They walk to Plum West.

They sit at the back of the restaurant, behind a plant. Rose Quartz orders beer—a large one with a glass so he can share with The Girlfriend. "You're contributing to the delinquency of this minor," she says and smiles awkwardly, trying not to split her scabs. Then, "Look how fast I can drink it," she whispers, carefully puckering her lips around the straw. She drains the glass into her mouth. He smiles. He takes a sip from the bottle. Beer steams from his lips as he swallows, giving away his desire.

"Do you know you taste like maraschino cherries," asks The Girlfriend, "when we kiss?"

"I didn't know that," he says.

"You don't taste them?"

"No."

"What do you taste?" she asks.

"Your mouth. And my mouth."

"But what does your mouth taste like to you?"

"Just my mouth." He picks up a fried wonton strip from the plastic bowl on the table, places it between his teeth, crunches it, and smiles. "Did you know that a Shirley Temple made with vodka is called a Young Adult?" Rose Quartz asks.

"I didn't," replies The Girlfriend.

"I learned that in the military," he says. "Special forces."

The Girlfriend gently licks her lips. The acidic taste of a fresh burn seeps into her mouth. It tingles like she's touched her tongue to the prongs of a nine-volt battery. "If your lips still scalded and split and bled like mine," The Girlfriend says, "when we're kissing, we could be like blood brothers . . . or . . . siblings. No. Sort of . . . I mean—" she gets jammed up. Flustered, she stops speaking.

"True," says Rose Quartz, "but more like blood lovers." He smiles and his eyes glitter. "Not lovers *yet*, though." His beer wets the flat, scarred blot of upper lip that The Girlfriend finds particularly soft. "Maybe soon, though? Lovers?" He looks expectantly at The Girlfriend.

Nervous, she laughs, knows what he wants and suddenly feels the clobber of the mother's fist against the door in her mind. She looks down at her placemat, feels her forehead go damp. She reaches her clamp into her pocket and removes a pack of cigarettes. Pulls out a single cigarette with one clamp. Takes it by the butt with the other clamp and places it between her lips. She leans toward him. He lights it. She can smoke in this restaurant; the owners don't care. She fills her lungs. Feels the blood pump from her heart into her face. The waiter brings two plates of barbecue beef. The Girlfriend sucks deeply once more and extinguishes the cigarette into the red plastic ashtray. They eat. He with chopsticks, she clamps a fork. She asks Rose Quartz questions about some things she's been wondering.

"What happens during other times," she asks, "like when you're alone." She pushes a tangle of barbecue beef over the Plum West insignia on her plate. "What happens with your lips when they get hot?"

"What do you mean?" asks Rose Quartz.

She leans across the table and speaks quietly. "Like when you're not with me and let's say you think of things," The Girlfriend's cheeks grow damp and pink. "And those things make your teeth hot—what do you do then? If I'm not around? And you're on the rig. And I'm at school. And we can't kiss?"

He smiles wide, his scars stretch white. He holds up a hand and slowly wiggles his fingers like he is casting a spell. "Oh, I've got hands, see." He shrugs. Looks at her for a beat.

"But you, baby," he says, shaking his head, "what do you do?" he asks. He takes her left clamp, kisses it.

The Girlfriend looks at him and blinks. "Nothing," she says.

AFTER DINNER they walk around town. They go to the boardwalk pier. They like it there. They stand in front of the saltwater taffy store and watch the mechanical taffy puller in the window. Smooth and continuous and to a mesmeric rhythm, it squishes and stretches and squishes and stretches long satiny legs of taffy. The Girlfriend stands close to Rose Quartz, leans her cheek into his chest. He holds his arm around her like a cape. The steady mash and pull of the taffy is quietly seductive. Their breathing lengthens, aligns with the rhythm of the taffy puller. Their faces fog nostril tufts against the glass. The tufts steam thick and fade and steam thick and fade at exactly the same time. The synchronization is exhilarating. They stand until the ache in their lips is echoed longingly beneath their zippers. They look at each other wolfishly.

"Should we head home?" The Girlfriend asks.

"Good idea," says Rose Quartz.

They hurry from the pier, across the big traffic street, through the neighborhoods, across her backyard, and in through the basement door. The couch is in front of the TV.

The Girlfriend and Rose Quartz hit the couch. It can take up to thirty minutes for Rose Quartz's teeth to get hot enough to scald. Usually the first thirty minutes of every kissing session are great. Once his teeth reach their burning point, the temperature plateaus. It can be brought down with aloe juice breaks and water spritzes and thinking unpleasurable thoughts, but once peaked, the teeth fire hot again, in shorter increments, with even less stimulation. It takes a whole sixty-minute make out break to bring his teeth back down to bearable. The Girlfriend and Rose Quartz play the TV loudly to drown out their noises, in case the mother's listening. They flip to news programs for the cooldowns between kissing sessions. They click over to music television while they near swallow one another. Until her lips roast raw.

The Girlfriend thinks she is probably becoming a really good kisser. Rose Quartz holds her face. Tucks his fingers into her hair. Pulls away just far enough to focus on her eyes. They stare at each other. Breathing fast. The Girlfriend's lips and tongue frizzle. The scabs split. They kiss harder.

She is seven and eats a red-flavored Popsicle before bed. She unwraps it and touches her tongue to it. The tip of her tongue sticks to it as though it were a lamppost in wintertime. She plucks it off. The Popsicle tears a sliver of flesh. Out blops blood. She swallows it, then dabs the tender tip of her tongue against the back of her front teeth and tastes more blood. She goes to bed afraid she will bleed to death in her sleep.

They pull away, eyes crossed, lungs heaving. The Girlfriend's mouth is bloody.

"You okay?" asks Rose Quartz.

The Girlfriend nods. "Blood," she says and sips some aloe juice from the straw in her glass.

"Yeah," says Rose Quartz. "You need to stop for a bit?"

"Yeah," she says.

She presses the buttons on the remote with the tip of her clamp, finds the news channel. Rose Quartz focuses on the TV. Listens closely. Shakes his head at the injustice in the world. The Girlfriend lifts the spritzer from the floor by the couch. Ice cubes knock around inside it like the marble in a can of spray paint. He turns to face her. He bares his teeth. With one arm she holds the bottle against her breastbone and with her other arm, she depresses the spritzer trigger with her wrist. She sprays his mouth with cool water. They watch the news, spritz, chat softly.

The Girlfriend is curious about things girlfriends are curious about. Curious about his life before he knew her.

"Say," she asks as icy spray swooshes from the plastic nozzle, "are your calluses calluses simply because you live your life with your hot teeth? And you're just accustomed to them?" Water drips from his mouth to the front of his shirt.

"What do you mean?" he asks.

"Like, probably I'll get calluses eventually," she says, "from kissing you." The spritzer squeaks when she presses the trigger. "And your calluses have gotten tougher since we've been kissing, right?"

"Yes," he says and rubs his hand over her hair.

"So did they ever get tougher any other time?" She spritzes him. Lights and darks from the TV flash across his wet face. "From kissing?"

He pats his mouth with the sleeve of his shirt. He smiles shyly at her. "Yes, baby," he says. "Of course."

"Right," she says, quietly. She turns to watch the news. A woman with perfect hair introduces a clip. People on a road are wrapped in sheets and lifted onto gurneys. "Like a lot?" The Girlfriend asks. She digs the tip of her clamp into the cushion of the couch.

"What do you think is a lot?" asks Rose Quartz.

She looks at him. Feels embarrassed. He is smiling sweetly. She doesn't want to say out loud something like, "I don't know. Two?" She doesn't want him to know that her lips have never blistered from kissing anyone else. Even anyone with regular teeth.

"I don't know," she says. "Never mind."

He refills the glasses of aloe juice. For him, for her. He looks at her. He pats her forehead softly with the tips of his fingers. The muscles in her face relax.

They watch the news for an hour. His teeth drop to regular temperature. Then they start kissing all over again. And stop and start and stop and start, all night long. And they do it all again on Saturday.

On Sunday night, just before parting at the shore, they'll kiss ravenously against the lifeguard tower. In the dark. Under the moon. Waves crash and salt the air.

A MONDAY morning, in the kitchen before school, the mother mentions the TV. "You say you're working on college applications," says the mother. The Girlfriend hears the roar of leaf blowers and lawn mowers in the mother's voice. "But I can hear that TV on all weekend. How can you work with that TV on?" She takes a swig of coffee from her commuter mug. "You can't focus like that. No more TV when you're working. Got it?" Motorcycles and big rigs and stadium sound checks boom in The Girlfriend's ears. Then she notices the mother staring jaggedly at her lips. The mother steps toward her. "What the hell's happened to your mouth?" The Girlfriend feels the mother's voice shatter the helmet of her skull. She feels suddenly very aware of the scabs on her lips—dry and tight. Of the raw flesh just beneath her nostrils—wet and tender. She stares at the mother and blinks twice. She drops her head, tries to cover her mouth with her clamp. She decisively plows past the mother's question.

"I can focus better with the TV on!" The Girlfriend screams.

"Part of my brain shuts it out so the rest of it can concentrate!" The Girlfriend stabs a bagel with her clamp. Storms out of the house. Huffs to school, the bones in her body rattled and already aching for Friday.

TEACHERS AT school notice The Girlfriend's burns. Her college counselor calls her into a meeting to ask where she is applying, because the office has not received her PPAFs, preliminary plan of action forms. Rumor has it the counselor was in a bad relationship with a bad man when she was young. Supposedly he tried to make her eat a hot coal. Her lip looks normal from everywhere but up close. The Girlfriend notices a small bump of healed-over skin on her lower lip when she stands next to the counselor's desk.

The counselor tells The Girlfriend to have a seat, asks her her plans. The Girlfriend tells the counselor she wants to go nowhere. She looks out the window toward the ocean and tells the counselor she wants to work on an oil rig.

"Oil rig," echoes the counselor whose eyes wash up and over The Girlfriend's clamps and stumps and linger on a fresh burn on her upper lip.

"How are things at home?" the counselor asks.

"Fine," says The Girlfriend.

"How are you finding school?"

"Boring," says The Girlfriend.

"Mm." The counselor stares at The Girlfriend's mouth. "So . . . you been getting in fights?" she asks gently, a little laugh.

"Hm?" The Girlfriend turns to look at the door.

"You look a little banged up," she says motioning to her lips and pointing out the burns on The Girlfriend's ears. "You want to tell me about anything happening at home?"

"No. Nothing happens at my home."

"Okay," says the counselor. She straightens some papers on her desk. Picks up a pen and bites the cap. "How are the boys? Do you have a boyfriend?"

"Yes." The Girlfriend locks eyes with the counselor.

"And how's that? Are you good to each other?"

"Yes." The Girlfriend scratches the back of her neck with her clamp.

"Okay." The counselor pulls at the collar of her sleeveless blouse. She stretches her arms behind her head. The Girlfriend's eyes drop to the counselor's armpits. They are perfectly smooth. Shaved clean. Not even a razor bump. "Do you have any questions about any of that? Boys or anything?" the counselor asks.

"No."

The counselor rocks slightly in her desk chair. "How have you been adjusting since"—she motions to The Girlfriend's wrists— "ceramics class?"

"Fine," says The Girlfriend and clanks her clamps one against the other. Sounds like cutlery. She hooks her backpack with her arm, stands, slings it over her shoulder.

"I gotta go to fifth," she says. She steps toward the door, looks at the knob.

"Okay, well, get those forms in." The counselor walks to the door, gives the knob a twist, pushes it open. The Girlfriend turns and leans against the door. She slides her backpack against it on her way out. The counselor leans into The Girlfriend and stops her before she can exit into the hall. The Girlfriend freezes, feels her face get very warm.

"Listen. Don't let anyone push you around. If something hurts, that's no good." The counselor is earnest and pale. The Girlfriend looks into her face, pinches her eyes into slits, steps away, and walks quickly down the hallway, out the door, through the student parking lot, past the smokers she sometimes smokes with, around the bushes and the hedge and the fence, on to the main road. She skips fifth and takes a bus to the shore.

She cries at the ocean. Glimpses the oil rig through the fog. He's stuck out there. He gets weekend leave, but is contracted there forever. He'd been in the military, and when the government sent him to the desert to fight a war for stupid things, he objected. Went so far as to gargle with gasoline to prove his point. Then he lit a lighter and blew gas-bomb fireballs from his mouth. He set several bunks ablaze which, his superior informed him, would cost good taxpayers major money. He also scared a few of the men in the barracks. His mouth bombs didn't harm Rose Quartz on account of his particular mouth, but the government determined his behavior made him unfit for combat. As punishment, they committed him to a life of oil-riggery. "They're dirty assholes," Rose Quartz told her, "but not without a decent sense of irony."

Today on the beach, The Girlfriend misses his hot mouth. Wonders what he is doing right now. Hopes he's thinking of her. She sits in the sand watching the waves pile high, block out the oil rig, then tumble flat, revealing it like a surprise. She smokes. Recalls what he said about the Rule of the Natural Progression of Things. He told her it doesn't have to be that way. She explained to him she knows that's true for some people, but for her, it's what her mind has learned. He told her authority's tyrannized her mind and, in turn, her actions. He told her authority tyrannizes his actions, keeping him out on the rig with only weekend leave, but not his mind. He told her, his mind's his own. "Most people in charge are wrong," he spoke softly to her from the couch, "the mother's got your mind now," he told her, "but you might get it back."

In the math and science part of her brain, she understood what he meant, thought he made sense. But the sense of it did nothing to reorder how she'd been reared to think she had to behave. His words did not undo for her the Rule of the Natural Progression of Things. But she did enjoy the soft vibration of his voice, can still feel it now. Like a song to drift into.

WEEKDAYS, ROSE Quartz mans his console, wanders the rig. This particular oil rig not only mines crude oil, but because it's an oilrigPLUS, it's also a multifunctional industrial complex. There's a plant on the rig where large corporations outsource the manufacturing of goods. Passing by the plant part of the rig, Rose Quartz notices new activity. He presses his face to the wide window overlooking the processing procedures. They are making something. Red dust is dumped in one end of a series of stainless steel tanks. It whorls into a drum of liquid and is boiled. Red translucent bubbles riot at the brim of the vat. And there is sound. Like voices humming over the intercom. The voices are distorted and muffled by the machines but continue slow and whispery. Rose Quartz can't pick out exactly what they are saying, but the arrangement of inflections—the pace and cadence of whatever it is they're saying—enchants him. Like cool feathers stroking his face and neck. They circle down his chest, over his loins, down his legs. He listens and looks hard at the boiling red. Briefly imagines his face plunged into the cherry foofaraw. He wonders if that is how The Girlfriend experiences his mouth. He wishes it weren't so permanently so. The boiled dust, now syrup, is channeled into another tank. Those voices resound across the floor, bounce off the steel, rile the air with an urgency. His attention is amplified, his nerve fibers feel shuffled and splayed against the glass.

From the end of a wide pipe, tiny clinquant red beads waterfall into another vat that funnels them into transport gutters on the other end. Those voices rise and fall and zap Rose Quartz in the chest and in the crotch. He rounds the wall surrounding the plant floor and peers through another window. From here he can see the control booth and the window into it and in it the source of the sound, maybe. The glass is tinted, but he can make out the silhouette. Looks like the shape of a man and a woman. They seem to share a chair at the desk. A microphone points at them from the desk. She is sitting on top of him, then he on top of her, then back. The silhouette suggests they might be lovers. Their limbs and parts shift and fit together like tessellations as a coo rumbles over the intercom.

"Why don't you go mind your console, son." The rig boss startles Rose Quartz from behind. He stands so close, the brim of his hat rustles Rose Quartz's hair. Rose Quartz skits and swats the back of his head. He catches his breath, composes himself, and asks, "What's being made in there?"

Chin up, legs apart, looking intimidating, the boss waits several beats before slowly saying, "Some sort of something."

Rose Quartz gets the sense he shouldn't ask more, but he is impassioned by those voices, drunkish. "What is it?"

The boss pauses and breathes. He squints. Says, "Some kind of novelty treat or something."

Rose Quartz can tell he is lying. He doesn't think the rig boss would outsource his plant for anything as stupid as candy. But he plays along. "Any samples?" he asks.

"None," says the boss. His voice drops an octave. "Now get on back to work."

"Who's outsourcing?" Rose Quartz asks quickly. He notices the boss's eyes dart the way of the window, at the shape of those lovers doing their love talk.

The boss swallows, clears his throat, pauses like he might not tell. Like he might, instead, bash Rose Quartz's head against the window. "Target," he says.

Rose Quartz believes this. He looks intently through the window. They've done stuff for Target before. He's seen the president of Target power up to the rig in a large black yacht with mirrored windows all the way around. The president of Target wore black wrap-around sunglasses indoors and out, smoked cigarettes from a long gold cigarette holder.

The sight and sound of those lovers is a lot. Roused by what's happening in there, Rose Quartz's wits are scrambled. He feels like he does with The Girlfriend. Like there're carnival rides pinwheeling in his chest and in his pants. His teeth simmer.

"Go now," the boss says like he's loading a shotgun to blast between Rose Quartz's eyes.

Fire mouthed and head spinning with images of The Girlfriend on the couch, in the sand, his memory of the weight of her in his arms, he is overcome. He agrees to get back to his console. Would like very much to get away from the rig boss. Would like to swim to shore in one smooth stroke, take The Girlfriend there on the wet sand.

He keels away from the rig boss. Wends his way down a spiral steel staircase to a lower deck beneath the plant. He stumbles the gangway surrounding the underguts of the plant. They pump and gurgle and hiss to a rhythm of working hard. Collection vats gather by-product from the production above. One such fills with some kind of semisolid. It is white. It curls out of an emission pipe and winds into the vat like soft-serve ice cream. It riffles, slowly and evenly filling the drum. It strokes Rose Quartz's attention, like the taffy puller he and The Girlfriend get lost in on the pier. He can still hear the lovers on the loudspeaker above. What they are saying is completely obscured down here, but Rose Quartz is tuned to their drone, feels the vibrations of their voices through the metal deck, down the steel railing. He thinks more of The Girlfriend. He is hot mouthed and hungry in a whole-body way, like the entire surface of his skin were mouths, chewing. He wants to strip off his clothes and step into the vat full of white cream, lower himself to his neck, jerk off down there, immersed in the drum. He checks for the rig boss, sees him nowhere. He climbs up and over the railing, drops into the plant guts.

His skin alight with whatever it is dynamizing the air, he undoes the first few snaps on his shirt, pulls the rest up over his head and tosses it to the floor. Breathing quickly and unbuckling his belt, ready to dive into that drum—he spots a pair of industrial rubber gloves, like big hands lopped from a big person and chucked between pipes. The feeling he's got in his body and the sight of those gloves, like severed hands, plus the lovers' droning updeck, plus the undulant disemboguery calling him into the vat—an idea unfolds and stretches wide in his head. He snags the gloves. The rubber is thick and strong and keeps its hand shape when he holds them. He dips one glove into the collection vat, fills the fingers, palm, wrist with the stuff from the pipe. It scoops like heavy gravy. He dips and fills the other. Hands full, he shimmies back over the railing and hustles to his office. He hangs the full gloves from cable clamps, sits back in his chair, feels certain whatever's in those gloves will dry just right. Feels something unbuttoned in his chest.

MEANWHILE, OVER on land, things go bad. The people in charge step in. The mother received a call from the counselor who mentioned missing forms, her daughter's interest in some oil rig, a boyfriend, the burns. Upon recognizing that she is not being obeyed, that her daughter is behaving contrarily to the ways she was raised, the mother reacts.

The latch is removed from the basement door and in its place: a greased knob. Greased knobs on all the exits inside the house. It's Friday evening, the mother's not home, and The Girlfriend can't leave.

On the rig, the heavy gloves sag from a cable in Rose Quartz's office. He checks on them. What he'd gathered in them has dried stiff and in the hand shape of the glove. He takes them to his console, clears a space to work. He peels the rubber glove from the solid inside it. The hands are bulky and man-size and feel like dense plastic. With a carving knife, he whittles them down. Her image perfectly detailed and always in his mind, he tapers the hands in proportion to The Girlfriend's body. The substance is bright white like a bleached bed sheet. He details the creases on her palms with the knife. He smoothes her fingers and the flesh of her palms with fine sandpaper and gives her slender, manicured nails. At his window the rig boss appears.

"What you got there, big guy?" Rose Quartz's boss says through the screen.

Rose Quartz startles, jerks to hide the hands, then blurts, "I'm making hands."

"Hands, huh?"

"Yes," says Rose Quartz, feeling foolish.

"Sure you are, champ, good for you." The boss adjusts his hat. "What you gonna do with them?"

Rose Quartz dusts the whittled hand debris from his desk. "I'm giving them to someone."

"Right." The boss clears his throat. "Everyone needs hands," he says under his breath. He looks down at his clipboard, indicating business. "Everything running smooth over here?" he asks.

"Yes. Just fine," Rose Quartz tells him.

"Good." He flips through pages on his clipboard. "What're you making those hands from?" he asks, not looking up from his paperwork.

The pulse in Rose Quartz's neck throbs. Protective of the new hands, he leans over his console, covers them with his own hands, coughs, and says, "Just some kind of plastic." He shrugs, "Recyclable."

The boss raises his eyes up from his clipboard, missiles his gaze at Rose Quartz. "Where'd you get it?" he asks.

"Get what?"

The boss cocks his head, squints his eyes. "Don't be an idiot with me. Where'd you get the material?"

"On shore," Rose Quartz lies. "At a hardware store."

"Oh yeah?"

"Yes," says Rose Quartz.

"Is this your shirt?" asks the boss, pulling from his jacket Rose Quartz's blue work shirt.

"No," Rose Quartz says, breathing slowly and calmly.

"No?"

"I don't think so."

The boss sighs like he's got no choice but to hurtle his fist into

Rose Quartz's face. He pauses, gathers himself. "It's got your name in it."

Rose Quartz swallows. "Huh," he says. "Weird."

"Where you been lately," the boss asks flatly, like he already knows the answer. "Not seen you around on the weekends."

"I go to shore." Rose Quartz smiles. "I've got a lady."

"Right, fine," says the boss. "Nice for you. You got an ol' lady."

"Not really. She's young. And lovely." Rose Quartz grabs a gear rag from the floor by his console. He quickly lays it over the hands like a tablecloth, sits back in his chair.

"Really." The boss shifts his weight from one thick leg to the other. "So I hear. Young's the word on the boat, my friend."

Rose Quartz had mentioned The Girlfriend to a few of the guys. Gossip, he realizes, travels fast among shipmen. A sudden seasickness rises in his throat.

The boss squints at him. Flexes his jaw. "How young, son?"

Rose Quartz blinks at him. "Excuse me?"

The boss steps away from the window and enters Rose Quartz's office. Rose Quartz stands, steps in front of his desk, blocks the new hands with his body. The rig boss pushes his broad chest into Rose Quartz's space, leans into him, and speaks from the back of his throat. "Listen, asshole," he raises his thumb to count one, "stay out of the kiddie pool. I don't need the coast guard or any human-itarian-children's-rights-group bullshit calling attention to my rig and coming on board here to bust you and then fuck my shit up." He raises his pointer finger to count two. "And stay away from my plant. Keep away from the processing, and if I find you anywhere near the emissions," he tilts his head, lifts his eyebrows, "your little lady"—he pauses—"won't ever see legal." His thumb and pointer finger make a pistol shape. He points it at Rose Quartz.

Rose Quartz's mouth drops open. His throat clicks with the start of a word, but the boss cuts him off: "I'm having you trans-ferred to the Arctic." He hands him an envelope of papers. Rose Quartz opens and scans the pages. It is a government order.

"Pack your shit," continues the boss. "You leave in the AM."

Rose Quartz stares at him. Feels the boss's words corkscrew into his earholes, loosening and upturning the matter in their way, tunneling directly to his brain compartment lodging love for The Girlfriend, sounding alarms of panic and rage.

"You got that?" the rig boss asks, puffing his shoulders wide. He turns and glides weightily away from him.

Rose Quartz feels deaf and sick. He has trouble breathing. Like his lung sacs are fattening with blood or water. His cheek, just below his right eye, twitches rigorously. He watches the rig boss walk away along the outer deck. Rose Quartz could tackle him over the railing, take him overboard. Drown him. Drown with him. He breathes deliberately, forcing air into his chest. Tries to calm down. Tries to register the smells of the ocean. Kelp. Fish. Drilling mud. Exhaust.

He turns to the hands, uncovers them. Rose Quartz shuts his eyes and holds the hands in his hands, like he is shaking them. They are stiff and small and pretty. He squeezes them hard. Rose Quartz is not *so* much older than The Girlfriend. He is eleven years older than The Girlfriend. He recognizes that the years between seventeen and twenty-eight are long ones in this culture, he gets that. But in eleven he finds a number that feels especially right: the one-one of it, the two of the sames that make a prime. He likes to think that contributes to the true love of them. He thinks the people who make the arbitrary rules in this world are assholes; imposing some rules, breaking others. This unfairness tastes as familiar as milk. He squeezes the acrylic hands, until the sound of the rig boss's words quits his mind and all he can hear is the cold echo of his grinding teeth.

OVER ON land, out of breath, clamps greased up from clawing at the knobs, and night falling fast, The Girlfriend considers *A Map of the Whole Wide World* in the living room. It is dark now; the sun has set. The Girlfriend worries that Rose Quartz has swum ashore and not found her. Not on the sand or by the showers or near the bathroom. She worries he's left, returned to the night sea. She misses him meanly. *A Map of the Whole Wide World* window seems less imposing in the smaller hours, without the light of the planet burning through it. The Girlfriend considers launching her foot through the glass. She feels very right to wreck the window, given the way the mother has trapped her indoors. On the other hand, it's the mother's favorite thing, and she made it. The Girlfriend's split down the middle: her left side in deference to the mother, her right side in honor of freedom and justice and Rose Quartz.

On the rig, Rose Quartz links the fingers and places the hands in a cigar box that was once stuffed with fine and illegal Havanas—one of the perks of the rig boss's dealings. Rose Quartz places the box in his waterproof rucksack, looks out at the ocean and sky, both turning the darks of a deep bruise. He worries The Girlfriend's left the beach already, he won't find her, and tomorrow he'll be headed for the Arctic. He suits up quickly, flaps his fins viciously through the sea.

The Girlfriend kicks her foot through the glass. The window crumbles clear out of its frame, cascades across the lawn in a mess of battlemented shards. The Girlfriend crunches across them, particles like jewels shingle from the legs of her jeans. She stops on the sidewalk to shake the glass from her hair. She removes her socks and shoes, knocks them clean. All the way around her right ankle, the skin is serrated.

Nearing shore, Rose Quartz catches a high night wave and rides it into the sand. He rises from the froth, dark and shining. The Girlfriend lives sexily in his mind. He made love to her the whole swim over. His teeth smolder as he trudges from the surf. He has the rubber rucksack in hand as he sploshes backwards in his fins. The Girlfriend is not on the beach by the lifeguard stand. She is not by the showers or by the parking lot. His rucksack tucked tight under his arm, his fins hanging by their heel straps from his fingers, he treads down the beach toward the big rocks and shore caves and the docks in the bay. He pauses by the craggy stone caverns glowing ghostly in the moonlight. Compelled, he pokes his head into a grotto and The Girlfriend gasps. She is sitting in a stroke of light. She is waiting for him. His teeth swelter volcanically at the sight of her.

Her eyes are large and red and puffy like her mouth, the rest of her face waxen. Her shoes are off and one foot's bare. She clamps a sock around her bleeding ankle. He sits on the cool sand in front of her. In his wet suit he bends like a tough swath of elastic. A dark crab ticks across a hunk of rock by his head.

"I got locked in," she says and swallows. Then, "because she's found out." In her skull, The Girlfriend's brain feels like it's swelling and contracting in time with her breath. There is a quiet composure in that rhythm. It keeps the door to the mother's room in her head shoved shut.

Teeth still seething, he doesn't want to talk about the mother, his transfer, or what he's now afraid is their inevitable end. He removes the cigar box from his rucksack. Rose Quartz hands it to The Girlfriend with his mouth wide open and his lips pulled back. He keeps his eyes on his lady, but tips his head from the cave toward the ocean to catch the cool breeze on his teeth. She unfastens the lid, flips it back with her clamp. In the box The Girlfriend sees the hands, folded and gleaming. She catches her breath. They are more beautiful than any human hands she has ever seen. They are more beautiful than the hands sculpted by the Italians she learned about in art history class.

"I made them," says Rose Quartz.

The Girlfriend feels warm. Her throat swells thick and her temples ache. Her heart beats fast, shaking her guts loose. She feels like her stomach might split open and all her important organs might spill out onto the blanket. She leans into Rose Quartz and kisses him with more tender ferocity than she has ever felt. His teeth sizzle her in seconds. Their lips pop and sputter and sting.

Rose Quartz pulls his face away. Their lips peel apart. He takes her
by the wrists, removes her clamps. He takes the right hand from
the cigar box and holds it to her right stump. He puts his mouth
on her wrist and bites down. He works his way around her wrist,
like he is chomping on an ear of corn. With each chomp he leaves
one hot rose quartz tooth embedded in flesh and new hand.

Sixteen upper teeth join The Girlfriend's right stump to her
new hand. He takes the left hand and does the same. Gnaws
deeply, all the way around. Sixteen lower teeth join The Girlfriend's left stump to her new hand.

The Girlfriend now wears two exquisite rose quartz bracelets. She moves her hard hands slowly through the ocean air. She
admires the crystals sparkling smooth in the light from the moon
and the few lights from the dock. The ocean crashes black and
white behind her wrists. She forgets to breathe. Rose Quartz puts
his hand on the small of her back. Her lungs shudder awake and
suck in a gust of salty air. She taps each individual tooth with
the tip of her finger. She touches her stiff hands to her face. She
touches Rose Quartz's face. He smiles big, without teeth. His
pink gums are smooth and healed clean.

She kisses him again. She never imagined kissing someone without teeth. She feels like her face is going to fall clear through his.
And this is new: no teeth in his mouth, his mouth doesn't burn.

But this: her wrists blaze hot. And the maraschino cherries?
She tastes them faintly. Just an essence in the back of her throat.
Heat moves up her arms, pumps through her veins like a flu shot.
She is twelve, her head down, slurping red Jell-O from a bowl
after the funeral. They dropped her dad deep into the earth.

Their faces are wet and slippery. The Girlfriend's wrists beat
warmly, but without pain. Rose Quartz pulls her closer and shifts
her onto her back. He kisses her neck. His toothless mouth no
longer sizzling, so they don't stop kissing. This is new. He lifts
her blouse, kisses her stomach, unbuttons her blouse.

Then this: The Girlfriend freezes. She pulls away, out from under him. Pulls her knees into her chest. No burning teeth, and she is thrown. She feels quiet, shy, and nervous. She stabs the sand with her fingers, leaving sets of marble-sized holes.

The Girlfriend hooks the handle of her purse on her stiff finger and sets it in front of her. She pushes it open and with both hands scoops out a pack of cigarettes. She pushes open the lid to the cigarettes, but can't remove one. She taps Rose Quartz's shoulder and holds out the box. Rose Quartz plucks a smoke from The Girlfriend's pack. He wedges it into the crevice between two new fingers, lights it for her. She brings her stiff hand to her face, drags from the cigarette, exhales, and maneuvers her hand away from her face.

Rose Quartz's mouth feels imploded but his chin is high. He's proud of his gift. And his hands on her make him want her more than ever. He takes her cigarette, extinguishes it in the sand. He leans into her for more kissing. The Girlfriend notices that without teeth to brace his lips, his lips feel especially elastic. They pooch out to deliver kisses, but swing in deep to receive them. The rhythm of it is like rocking, or bobbing. She imagines this might be what it would be like to make out with a wave. She likes it. They both get into it, again. Rose Quartz leans into her. The Girlfriend's wrists sting hot. Rose Quartz pulls her closer and shifts her onto her back. Gets her shirt all the way off this time. The Girlfriend stiffens again—this is kissing beyond the parameters they've always stuck to so diligently. A piece of her mind creeps away from the kissing and imagines the mother behind the sand dune near the caves. She imagines the mother biting off grenade clips, spitting them over her shoulder, and chucking the grenades at the lovers. And here is Rose Quartz, his body on her body, his mouth no longer roasting. She has her arms around him. He moans.

Then this: her fingers curl and grab a fist full of his hair, pull.

Rose Quartz stops abruptly. The hands let go. Rose Quartz

sits up, takes her wrists and holds the hands up, in between their faces.

"What was that?" he asks.

"I don't know," says The Girlfriend.

"They moved," he says.

"I know," she says, staring at her new hands.

"Can you move them?" he asks.

"I don't know."

"Try," he says, his voice tinged with panic, his lust lost in the sand.

She flexes her memory of moving her hands. The veins stand out in her wrists. "They won't move."

They sit for a moment. Something urgent throbs in the air between them. The Girlfriend, startlingly aware of her missing top, hooks it with a finger, stuffs her arms in the sleeves, crosses her arms to keep it closed. She feels discomposed and skittish. She glances at her new hands. Rose Quartz rubs the tuft of hair on the back of his head. His scalp there is tender, proof that those fingers moved.

"Do you think it's the kissing?" he asks.

"You think it's the kissing that does it?"

"I don't know," he says.

"Me neither."

"Maybe we should try all that again," suggests Rose Quartz.

"More kissing and things?"

"Yeah," says Rose Quartz.

So they do, and despite their nerves and distress, they get into it again, as always. The Girlfriend feels his weight on her hips. Rose Quartz's breathing quickens and his hips press heavier. The Girlfriend's wrists fire hot while Rose Quartz's hips begin to rock. He reaches between their bodies and pulls at the buttons of her jeans. The taste of cherries rolls slowly in the back of her throat.

Then this: Rose Quartz moans and The Girlfriend's hands claw the wet suit on Rose Quartz's back. The Girlfriend freezes and looks over Rose Quartz's shoulder and across his back. Her hands are balled into fists. She screams. Rose Quartz pushes himself up and stares down at The Girlfriend.

"What?" he asks quickly, his chest heaving. He is upright on his knees. The Girlfriend is eye level with his weight belt. His tight wet suit seems much much tighter. She thrusts her hands between them. The Girlfriend wiggles her fingers in front of his face. His eyes focus, register the movement. The color falls from his face and the wiggling stops.

Startled and a little bit scared, he says, "Move them again."

The Girlfriend tries. "I can't."

Her bracelets are cool in the breeze. Rose Quartz stares at the hands. The Girlfriend is out of sorts. She remembers her hands, remembers what it feels like to have them—to touch and pick and clap, and these are not they.

One more try. Rose Quartz unzips the top half of his wet suit. He peels it off of his arms and chest. It hangs upside down and empty around his waist. He takes The Girlfriend's hands by her wrists and brings them to his face. He presses them into his cheeks. He closes his eyes and runs the hands down over his chin and onto his neck. He breathes deeply. He pulls them over his chest and across his stomach.

Then this: his lips pull into a smile and the hands soften and splay over his skin. The fingers fan and press as he directs them across his flesh. The Girlfriend's wrists sting hot. The taste of cherry syrup arrives without memories and gurgles at the base of her tongue. The hands slide lower. They stop at the buckle on his weight belt. With all of her fingers, nimble and shining, she removes his weight belt. He lays back and kisses and licks the soft palm of one hand and pulls it beneath his trunks. The palm presses firmly and the fingers curl around him. Her eyes bulge wide and she sips short breaths in shock. He maneuvers her wrist.

He moves her new hand and its firm grip quickly and then faster while he looks toward the sky and his whole body springs taut. His hold on her wrist makes her arm go numb. His body shudders and his breathing staccatos. Then he slows her hand down, slowly, then slower. He wheezes loudly into the ocean air.

Sunder

MY HEARTMEAT was sodden and sore. My hand to my chest, I pressed hard, hoping to keep the muscle from ablating into my lungs. I left the soaking rubble of our blue room and before the officials could arrive—the landlord, the damage assessors, firefighters often show up for floods—I turned my head and nailed my eyes to that last point in the road where her bus was and then wasn't. I plucked that point from the horizon, put it in my mouth, bit down. Felt it snap and crumble, gristle down my throat. I moved far away.

I felt cold and gruelly for a long time. Shaky, thin. I tripped on steps, bumped into furniture, bruised everywhere, shopped for food and forgot to put it in the refrigerator. Left it.

I could sit on the couch. A different couch. Not the couch whose pillows poofed around her face, framing it in my mind. This one was short and stiff. Unsoft pillows stuffed with something like gravel or teeth. My back straight, head balanced on my neck, my palms on my thighs, I sat. Like the story of the drug kid in high school who, after a bad trip, was convinced he was a glass of orange juice filled to the brim. He couldn't move, afraid he'd spill. I sat like that and practiced not thinking about my acrobat. I got good at it in a way that folded pleats into my brain so my thoughts bent and zigzagged to avoid her. And while dodging her, they crashed into a daggered voice that grabbed and shook them by the collar, urged them to urge me to keep away from people, keep alone, don't try that again. I listened. Yes, yes. Good idea.

Everything was sad. A dog barked somewhere in the apartment building: sad. I slugged along the boardwalk of the beach near my new home: sad. Drunks slept on benches: sad. Old women sold beaded bracelets and hair clips from blankets: sad. Sand sculptors fashioned mermaids, pressed seashells onto their sand lump breasts: sad and stupid. I saw a man wearing a mask, making masks for a bunch of kids. The masks fit their faces perfectly and they jumped around: sad. I watched sadly. The mask maker noticed. He blinked at me through the eyeholes in his mask then pushed it up and into his fluffy hair to reveal his face. He smiled at me: so sad. I turned and walked away.

Everything else was scary. So when one day I got a knock at my door, I jumped. Thought not to open it. I'd moved to a dicey neighborhood. Only a few weeks prior a solicitor had come by, said he was selling meats from his van. Would I like to take a look? Or he could bring some in, shave off some prime slices in my kitchen. My eye in the peephole, I shouted through the door, "No thank you!" The meat man's eyes withdrew into his face, his lips shrunk into a narrow line, his jaw flexed, his neck and forehead flushed. On the news thereafter, I heard several reports of door-to-door murders.

Then a new knocker, and I froze frightened on the couch. I remembered I had mace in my purse in the kitchen. Wondered if I should make a dash for it. I couldn't move. But the knocker knocked more, and knocked gently. Soft wraps. Not like the meat man. Not danger knocks. It could be a neighbor kid, I worried. In trouble, even more scared than me. I unfroze. I slid from the couch and slithered toward the door, worming slowly to keep the floor from creaking. On the other side of the door I heard whispering. Not from a kid. A man whispering. I pressed my ear to the crack between the door and the frame, reached above my head, checked the bolt, quietly slid the gold chain into its lock.

"Hello," he breathed, "excuse me."

I peeked through the window by the door—through a corner slice of glass between the pane and the blind. I glimpsed him. He held a thing in his hands, was pitched toward the peephole, was whispering into it. He had blond curly hair cut round and loose. The sun shone behind him, glinting the ends of his hair, haloing it around his head. I got a good look at his face and felt a single electrical poke prick my chest. I felt the fluid in my heart sputter as it pumped and squirted blood through its loosened parts. I recognized this man. He was the mask maker from the beach. I ducked away from the window, cupped my ear to the door.

"I have this—" he murmured. "Something I'd like to show you."

I considered crawling away from the door, hiding at the other end of my apartment, hoping he'd leave. He would eventually leave. But I didn't move. I kept my ear there.

"I made this," he said softly. "It fits your face. It's your face."

I peeked back through the corner of the window. I bumped my forehead into the blind. The blind clanked the glass. He heard the clunk, looked down, dropped to a squat to meet my spying eye. I steeled stiff all over.

"Hi," he whispered loudly. He smiled. His smile was warm. I felt it radiate on my one eye beaming him through the glass. He held up the thing in his hands so I could see it. It was a mask. Two of his fingers poked through the eye socket holes. "This is yours. It's for you." He said it like a secret. "It's you." I looked hard at it. The mask face sort of resembled mine, I guessed. The chin and the cheekbones reminded me of mine.

Through the closed window he tamely explained that he saw me at the beach and molded it from his memory. This felt very sad and very scary. Then this: The two sensations collided in the wet wreck behind my ribs and my sound mind, I'm certain, was knocked unconscious and drowned because when he said, "You should try it on," and looked expectantly through the glass, I pulled away from the window, stood, unlatched the chain, flicked the bolt, twisted the knob, and opened the door. He stood languidly in the jamb. His eyes flashed in his face that was roundish, and looked so kind that the illogic of dropping my guard and letting him in felt immediately and unexpectedly fine.

We shared a grapefruit in my kitchen, and later I pressed my face into the mask he made while he held it with both hands. I leaned all the weight of my head into the mask, into his palms. He held me upright for ten minutes. I felt the heat from his hands seep through the plaster and warm my cheeks. When I lifted my head, it felt empty and light. A salty breeze could have blown off the ocean and passed clear through my forehead. "Nice to not hold up your own head for a while?" he asked as my pupils pulled his face into focus.

It was. And suddenly I felt: not sad, not scared. Like someone was lifting me up from underneath my arms. Big hands against my ribs, catching me in my armpits, light as a baby, tilting me toward the sun. I had to catch my breath, like babies do, napping, when their whole bodies puff and shudder as they pass from one chapter of sleep to the next.

Still, he sensed that I was wary and weary and deep in the habit of sitting moveless and alone on my couch. So for several months, this mask maker practiced patient wooing. He showed up at my apartment between 12 and 3 AM, when the asphalt in the road reflects the streetlights like a wet sponge. He brought my mask, fixed it to my face, held my masked face in his hands while the slackened sections of my heart reattached maybe, slightly, slowly. I remembered the daggered voice and its wise recommendation, but I liked not sad and not scared so much. I rejected the voice. I named the mask maker My Love. We went around and we did things.

There were a few things he really liked:

1. The Shave

When I shaved my name into the hair on his stomach. He had some hair on his stomach, which surprised and frightened me at first, but turned sweet when I noticed it glint goldy like the curls on his head. My Love howled at the tickle of the blade. I told him tenderly to shut up. Then My Love fit his body next to mine and we sunk together like some taffies I left on the dashboard when I first learned to drive.

2. Calcutta

We went on Sundays to a neighborhood we called Calcutta. It was busy and trash blew along the sidewalk and clung to our calves as we walked. Poor people and their kids begged for change. Babies were pushed around in small shopping carts swiped from the Save More. We bought pineapple chunks stabbed onto big toothpicks. We ate them. A small dusty shop sold herbs and oils. My Love bought several paper bags and glass bottles full. He'd cook and combine them, decant the concoction into a little red vial. He'd daub it on his wrists, the sides of his neck. I found my face in his neck often, breathing. And when he'd drive, I'd take his wrist and sniff whenever he didn't have to shift.

3. Grapefruits and Lager Beer

Grapefruits, preferably yellow, rated high on his list. And lager beer. I could never remember the difference between lager and ale and the other kinds. A liquor store in Calcutta sold big boxes of lager *and* fresh yellow grapefruits from a wooden bin. As we drove, they'd jiggle in the trunk of the car.

4. My Feet

He bit my feet. I wasn't sure if I liked it or not. I think I might have hated it. He'd suck a whole toe into his mouth and chew hushedly with his front teeth.

MY LOVE and I were tide-pooling behind the local energy plant when we found our place together and moved in. Beneath an eroded dune behind some tall and fat rocks we spotted an O-ring sticking up out of the sand. We pushed aside piles of sand, swept with our hands and uncovered an iron manhole. Instead of the Department of Water and Power's initials raised up on it, branded onto the middle of the manhole was a big dollar sign: $. We levered the manhole open with a scaffolding pole that we found by the plant trash, and beneath that manhole, down in the earth, was an abandoned bomb shelter.

The bomb shelter was deep and cylindrical, like a long canister shoved far into the ground. A fire pole ran from the floor up to the edge of the manhole opening. A chain ladder hung from the opposite edge down. The manhole cover could be opened and swiveled aside from inside by a beefy steel latch that I imagined might be used on tanks or submarines.

We measured the circular floor with a broom—an average-sized broom with straw brush teeth. It was almost ten brooms across. There were amenities already installed—a kitchenette complete with a cabinet, icebox, sink, tap, counter with a very old but func-tioning hot plate. The bomb shelter was wired with electricity and outlets and a small shower and a toilet and plumbing, which we were grateful for. The toilet was positioned up against the curved wall and was exposed, so we fixed a bent rod in a wide U above the toilet and hung a shower curtain for privacy.

We pushed a small foam futon through the manhole and cackled over the hole when we heard it *boof* onto the concrete floor. It was our couch and our bed. We found a folding table above ground and lowered it by rope through the manhole. We did the same with a bench to sit on when at the table. We set up the table and bench in front of the kitchenette. We lowered down a lamp. We lowered groceries and ice. We swept and scrubbed. And this: we found a secret in the cabinet, underneath the shelf liner. We found dry and yellowed pages of poetry written by, we guessed, the original owner of the place. From his poems we learned that he'd been a banker. He wrote a lot about money, which he sometimes called *cabbage* or *lettuce* or *kale*. He wrote about sadness and called his *funebrial*. He wrote about a lady and his love for her was *mutineering*. She didn't love him back. He *hired mourners* to wail on his behalf, but it didn't make him feel any better. He *avouched* to never love again. I thought his poetry was okay. The avouchment line strummed the tendons beneath my skin, thrummed a tune that rocked me uneasily. It's what I'd heard sitting on my couch in my old place. It's what that sharp and pointy voice in me urged after my acrobat left. Then this mask maker came along and I hushed it quiet. And then, in that kitchenette underground, I wondered if the banker-poet ever did that too—if he ever shushed aside his avouchment. Or if he'd stuck to his agony his whole life long. I remember not knowing which was better—to stay pained for the duration, or to trollop elsewhere, if just for the diversion. This moment of not knowing dizzied my understanding of my love for My Love. Unplugged a drain and swirled my acrobat through my system. She circled my heart. I felt its parts undo where they'd felt done up by My Love. I lost my balance and fell into My Love, thudded into his chest, knocked my focus off her. I stuck it sturdily on him. On the bomb shelter. On the brittle pages of poetry. We held the pages carefully. My Love said he felt shy reading them, like he was spying on someone's mind. But I assured him our poet-banker was probably long dead and isn't it lucky and strange to hold the thistledown of his life? To be regardful of his life and death, we tucked the pages back under the liner on the shelf in the cabinet where we found them. We keep our cans and jars and bags and boxes on the other shelf. And to avoid my own unrest, I made a point of never reading them again.

All moved in and My Love snapped a picture of me sliding down the fire pole—back arched, free arm whooping above my head. This was my second time living with a lover. I didn't ask him what time was his.

IN THE bomb shelter we got to know each other better, and it turned out My Love was a little broken, like everyone. He was tortured by an incident that played on a loop in his mind. Before I met him, he worked as a developer at a big corporation. He wore white shirts under white coats and used tools like pipettes and microscopes and lasers and various plastics and liquids and wires, and in the hallways on his floor were industrial showerheads that could beat hazardous chemicals from the skin in the dangerous case of contact. So one day, My Love was walking home from work when a sad man on the eleventh floor of a building jumped. My Love was below, walking, walking, *boom*—he was whacked in the chest and knocked to the ground by the falling man's heel. The man splashed into the sidewalk and died. When My Love sat up, he noticed that the bottoms of his feet and the bottoms of the dead man's feet were touching. The impact had knocked off both pairs of shoes and pressed their soles against each other. My Love said that if he shook his feet just so, his and the dead man's feet would clap. This made My Love think of applause. He thought of Olympic scorecards. He wondered how the Eastern European judges would score the fall. He imagined he was Eastern European. Finally he thought he would give the man a very low score, lying there bent and bloody, his teeth tossed like confetti all over the sidewalk.

My Love told me it was this series of thoughts in those few seconds that undid him, gouged him with chiseling and unending guilt.

"Why so guilty?" I asked, not getting it. "What'd you do bad?" We were lazing on the futon in our bomb shelter.

"Two things," he explained. "I heard the whizzing sound of his body before I knew it was his body, so I stepped out of the way of the sound. And the man crashed to his death. Then, in my mind I made a joke, pretending I was a large gray judge."

"Hm," I said, still unclear about his torment. Because I would have stepped away from a disturbing sound in the sky. And would likely have made a mental joke about the tragedy. Probably something awfully unfunny about the suicider's shoes or socks. "I don't get it," I told him but noticed the pain in his face, and it made me sad and scared and I wanted it gone.

"You don't understand," said My Love. "First, I think I could have saved the man. I could have caught him, maybe. Or better broken his fall." He sighed. "Then when I didn't, I could have at least been respectful of his death. But I did none of it." And after the incident, My Love felt so bad he couldn't sleep, eat, work. He quit his job. Took up mask making at the beach. Hid his face.

My Love's history and his big anguish made me think of two things.

1. About making jokes during painful times:
When I was little and my mom was around, we watched TV together, sunk into the giant beanbag chair in the living room. Once we saw a special on lady criminals who were caught, convicted, locked up. Their mothers had to visit them in the brig. Had to talk to them on telephone receivers and through thick, wired glass. The orange of their daughters' jumpsuits cast shades of illness across the mothers' foreheads and necks. Through the telephone receivers, the inmates and their moms talked about plain and boring things, but all the while, in those mothers' faces was defeat—ripe and odious. There were their daughters—shackled convicts.

I was eleven and felt heat rise off my mother's cheeks. Intuitively I knew my mom recognized something in those TV mothers' faces, could harmonize their feelings with her own. On the big beanbag, under a blanket, my mom's bulk against my hip, my side, my shoulder, I sensed that in my mother's mind she was imagining me—at some obscure point in the future—one of those jail girls. My mother was looking into that doom. Then it was too much. She broke under the weight of it and made jokes. Poking fun at the jumpsuits, the hairdos, the fat warden in the corner of the screen. The jokes weren't funny; they were skittering and thin and popped across the coffee table like ping-pong balls. But they relieved me because in that moment—young and thought-free as to how my life might unravel—I was strangled by fear. What if I went rotten? What would my mother think about me if I got crooked and got caught? Because it seemed possible. Anything is possible. What if I were to wind up in jail? And so I said to my mother, "It's good you can joke about this." I smiled and nodded, "Daughters." I pointed at the screen, "And jail."

My mom turned to me with a face like a bag of sand and said, "Yeah, well it's better than killing myself," and turned back to the screen. It left a puddle of acid bubbling around a steel shard in my stomach.

I didn't tell My Love this story.

2. About not saving lives:
There was a kid in the public pool one summer. The pool had a tiled fountain in the shallow end. Kids climbed on the fountain, tried to plug the spouting hoses with their fingers, mash the water back with their palms. One day, the shallow end was crowded and a kid younger and smaller than I slid from one of the fountain's ledges into the open water. The shallow end was still deeper than this kid was tall. I was sitting on the side of the pool, feet dangling and dipped. I watched the kid's head slip beneath the water. Submerged, his body remained vertical. Through the ruffled pool surface, I saw the kid's legs kick small and fast. His arms were above his head and his fingers broke the surface and flapped and flicked like bugs' wings. He couldn't swim. All his quick pumping and flapping did not push his body high enough. His nose and mouth and eyes remained underwater. None of the summer people around the pool noticed. I watched, and like wheels screaming into collision across a highway, a voice tore through my mind: *That kid is drowning.* I watched. The power went out on my instincts to respond to *move!* and to *help!* Later, when the

adults noticed and they removed the kid from the water, his skin looked wet and soft as toothpaste.

When my parents kicked a year later, I thought it was because I let the kid die. This thought was torturous. So I hid it from my consciousness. Wrapped it and bagged it and taped it and dipped and dried it in cement and tossed it and sunk it to the bottom of a sump in the back of my mind. But My Love's story gravedug it up and unplanted me. I didn't mention any of it to him.

SHORTLY THEREAFTER, and very unexpectedly, My Love's haunting reared into reality when a subpoena arrived in My Love's PO Box from a lawyer working for the falling dead man's family.

The envelope torn open, pages shaking in his hands, My Love read and said, "They're suing me."

Like My Love, they—the suicider's family—thought My Love was somehow, somewhat responsible for the death. Because, they said, he participated in a failure of action: My Love was stunned too still by the violent connection to up and scream and flag and rescue in the final flash of the jumper's life. So the family considered My Love an accessory to their loss. I didn't think they had much of a case, but My Love buckled at the news. He slapped his hand across his heart. "I can't bear it," he said.

A grown man. I didn't know what to do. His torment steamed from his skin, dampened the air. I was inclined to suggest he shred the document and close his PO Box. Then drop by that law office and slug that lawyer for being ridiculous and idiotic. Then change his name and hide out down in the bomb shelter. Then practice not thinking about any of it. I liked to think not thinking about things works. I liked to think not thinking about things works better than it does. Because, quietly, down there with My Love, sometimes I thought I could smell my acrobat on my hands. And swinging around that fire pole challenged gravity in such a way as to flash her face across the backs of my eyes. To squeeze them shut only tightened the focus, defined the picture. I'd shake my head, her face stayed. I tried so hard not to wonder where she was. I'd breathe slowly, notice the limp chug of my heart.

My Love said the letter presented two options: appear before the lawyers and the family for a series of official proceedings, or pay a settlement sum. It was long with zeros and commas. He crumpled onto the bench. "I can't face them," he cracked. He laid his head on the worktable. His arms and hands and fingers sagged toward the floor.

"Come on," I said, "come here." I tried to change the subject. I took him to the futon. Unfolded it from couch to bed. Kissed and held his face. Pulled his shirt over his head, his pants from his legs. Then mine too.

We were sweaty and tired and splayed like starfish on the futon that had traveled across the floor and was pinched between the frosted plastic shower door and the curved wall of the bomb shelter.

SHORTLY THEREAFTER that, we stumbled upon a solution. It sprung from a tray of Jell-O that, after we'd unknowingly invoked some kind of love wizardry while preparing it, turned very un-Jell-O-like. Became something else completely. Something intoxicating.

"Hungry?" asked My Love.

"Yes," and the niceness of lying there in our bomb shelter felt rich. We climbed from the futon, leaving it out of place and where it was. We put on underwear only. We dazed to the kitchenette. My Love removed a box of red Jell-O from the cabinet. I put water on to boil. He put a bag of sugar on the table. I got the measuring cup. He placed a baking tray next to the sugar on the table. The water boiled. I unplugged the hot plate. My Love poured the water into the glass tray. A sploosh lapped over the lip of the glass, spilled from the worktable onto the concrete floor.

It splashed our feet, stung and burned. The water banked around his toes. His big toe, I noticed—and in a sudden burst, adored— was the shape of a rattlesnake's head. I scooped and poured a cup of sugar into the water in the tray.

Our faces in the steam above the tray, I smelled his sweat and my sweat and sugar and water and noticed My Love's features in a particular way. His face in that moment, its specific shape and size in space, met and matched their opposites in me. Like separate parts clicking to lock together. In that moment I felt especially taken with him. And in me burst a love dam. And in him too. And the deluge came in the form of a Wish List, which we gushed all over each other. And it was like an incantation that spunked the Jell-O with unexpected and spectacular properties. Our Wish List was the heavy syrup of love talk—a little embar- rassing to someone not involved maybe, but all hot sauce to us at the time. It went like this:

We were belly to belly. I sat on the edge of the worktable. My legs were wrapped around his waist, my chest pressed to his chest, my chin hooked over his shoulder. He had both hands free behind my back. I heard him tear the Jell-O sack open, then I heard the wet mizzle of the Jell-O dust flurrying into the water in the tray. We'd just sexed, but in me still bucked a lickerishness. I leaned into his neck and whispered up into his ear, "I wish I could shave the hair off your head and tongue the stubble across your scalp." I stuffed my fingers deep into his curls.

He pulled my hips firmly against his and breathed into the top of my head. "I wish I could vaporize you in a humidifier and breathe you to the bottom of my lungs," he whispered back.

"I wish my shoulders were diving boards and the suicider fell on me, not you, and touched down on one of the boards and sprung high up over the surrounding buildings," I pulled down the front of his underwear, "then swan dove perfectly and splashlessly into the community pool on the other side of town," I told him.

His shoulders relaxed while his abdomen flexed taut, and he pressed his hips harder against mine and said quietly, "I wish your mask was your actual face and flesh and was connected to the rest of your body and I could step into it and wear it and it would fit me," he pulled at my underwear. "And I could feel what it is like to be me as you, walking around." He tugged the waistband below my butt.

My face in his neck, My Love's hair crossed into my eyelashes and the tip of my nose pressed softly into the grooves of his ear and I could smell his smell. He smelled like ginger and licorice and lemons. I said, "I wish you were married and I wish I were married and down here's where we would meet and hide and sweat at each other and touch, and each stroke would be a volcano blow between us, underground." He yanked my underwear down my thighs and directed himself into me, but just the tip. It was one of the moves he liked to do. I liked it too. The muscles in my stomach and my butt and my center sprung tight and bated. He pulsed his hips. My breath shrunk to a fist and pounded the back of my throat. His pulsing and my breath Morse-coded my words, but I managed out, "I wish I had ten good hearts and could pluck them from my chest and plug each onto your fingers by my aortas"—it was difficult to speak—"and like big heart thimbles, they could beat on your fingertips and you could touch yourself." I felt the blood in my neck cook the surface of my skin. I pushed my fingers deeper into his thick hair and felt the size and shape of his skull. He continued with his move—just the tip, shallow but fast. I felt the skin across my body and the skin across his body pull tight as a blister and our breaths just about stopped until the move was too much and we broke and we knocked hard into each other against our worktable that creaked and jostled. A coffee can of supplies near the edge of the worktable vaulted to the floor, scuttled across the cement. Eventually we slowed and stopped. Then we clung to each other. And I had the sense that something had occurred between us. More than more sex, an event of love—one of those throned moments lovers flash to when remembering the gilt of a relationship. I felt drunk on it.

"Mmm," he moaned over my shoulder, "red." It vibrated through my lungs. I unhooked my chin and removed my hands from his hair and leaned back and looked at his face. His eyes were bright and glassy and reeling. His nostrils and eyelashes twinkled rouge with Jell-O dust. I looked over my shoulder and saw the Jell-O tray. It was red. And bright and translucent. And completely full—not a drop spilled. I wanted to stick my finger in it and lick it. I twisted to face it. My Love adjusted himself out of me. I felt my breath fall back into place. I pulled my underwear up. I stood facing the tray on the table. I pointed my fingertip at it, poked. My fingertip bounced off the Jell-O. I looked at My Love. He poked it too. His finger bounced back, left no dents or even prints. I slapped the slab in the tray and my whole hand bounced and slung back. The slab trembled, didn't bruise.

"How's that?" My Love asked.

"It's firmed?"

"Firmer than firmed," he said. "So quick. And without refrigeration?"

We stood blearily side by side, staring at the Jell-O in the glass pan on our worktable.

"Peel up a corner," he told me.

I spatulaed my fingertip into a corner, inched up and pinched the slab, peeled away the whole sheet in one smooth and satisfying lift, like pulling a bumper sticker from its glossy backing. I held the sheet between our faces. It ungled and shook, and through it My Love's face smeared stretched and long then smushed blobby and back. He waved at me from his side of the Jell-O, and his fingers whipped skinny and crooked. He laughed, mouth open, no sound, and his teeth looked like they were dripping from his nose. My Love over there, his underwear white and full and tight on him.

From the supplies tossed across the floor My Love grabbed a

pair of scissors, returned to the Jell-O sheet. The scissors flashed on his side of the Jell-O and a thick ribbon of red fell from the sheet and bounced on the table. He picked it up, dabbed it on his tongue, tasted, thought, sniffed it. Thought for a moment more, about what I didn't know. Then he cut the whole sheet into strips then across into smaller pieces and placed them back in the tray. He crossed the bomb shelter, dug into a small box of his things on the floor on his side of where the futon was normally positioned, extracted his red vial of perfume oil. He unscrewed and dripped a few drops onto the Jell-O pieces in the dish. The whole place smelled more like him. He stirred with a spoon. The Jell-O broke into baby beads. They were perfect tiny shiny red spheres. I stuck my hand in and swished my fingers around. Felt like when I was a kid and unzipped the beanbag chair and swum my hand around in the Styrofoam pellets.

"That looks good," said My Love, and he stuck his hand in too. We squeezed and fingered around and felt the beads slip between our digits. We pulled our hands out, the beads clung to our flesh as though static held them there. My Love wiggled his fingers and the beads stayed. He drew his mouth wide, laughed. He licked the length of his pointer finger and cleared it of beads. His face grew flush and his eyes wet and he took me by my wrist and steered my hand into my mouth and I cleared three fingers.

I felt my heart spring high into my throat and press low into my abdomen like it was a folding cane for the blind bent tight in the center of my chest and suddenly flicked long. My head swooning heavily on one end, my groin anchoring heavier on the other. I looked at My Love and I looked at the beads and I looked at the bench by the table and each look overlapped the last, but My Love's face was the main image that glowed bright-est even when I looked around at the dark wall of the bomb shel-ter all the way up to the manhole with its sunlight ring around the seam. My Love and me and our Wish List and our Jell-O. We'd made something. The air tickled my skin, especially at the center of my chest. From the center of my chest, it felt like things were growing. Like cords or elastics. They sprung and reached and stretched and met the same things from his chest. They tangled together and pulled our bodies close. They were taut and vibrating and how can I explain it? We had invoked a love pitch that hummed between us. I felt dizzy and delirial. My Love blinked tipsily at me.

We killed the lamp and lit a few meek candles, so all was fairly dim. What felt like filament between our chests flexed long then shrunk tight as our bodies distanced and returned. We pulled back the curtain and twisted the knob to all the way hot and slipped into the shower. Through the ripples in the shower door, the candlelight eked and mingled with steam, aerating the space with gold vapor—like how you'd imagine warm, calm, and hidden places under waterfalls. It was misty all around the arched chute of water. We stood in and out of its pelter, glistening at each other. My Love pressed his wet body against mine and the areas beneath all of my skin felt hollowed out, unloaded. And the skin keeping my shape felt permeable, so that his touch passed through me. My head felt like bubbles. We swayed.

WE CALLED the beads The Floodgates of Love. The Floodgates of Love make you feel good. They take the love experience and set it on fire, burning away the two-bodiedness of lovers. This fire is a desire and symptom of the Love Instinct. When you think you are in love and there is your lover, whose breath smells like sea salt and whose hands are large and soft, and you kiss and touch and make love and feel as if your skins should mesh—not keep bodies separate but mix like sea does with sand at that moment when a wave purls away from the shore and for seconds leaves a spongy sheen across the flat, wet beach—this fleeting fusion is a Love Instinct. The feeling occurs from time to time, in the beginning madness of new love. One day it wears off. But The Floodgates of Love kick up and sustain that feeling. Who knows

why or how? Not me. But while making them, we whispered that
Wish List of wet and quenching things, like an incantation, and it
is my belief that the thaumaturgy of love, which I invest in heavily, had everything to do with it.

We recognized that we'd made something special. So we
devised a plan to earn some dough to handle the lawyers. We
submitted a proposal to Kelly Green, the president of Target, to
enlist the corporation to manufacture The Floodgates of Love.
One meeting with some Target representatives and a sampling of
the product—the samplers went wild, besotted with The Floodgates of Love. I'd never seen office people so happy and writhing.
They shut down early for the day, phoned lovers, grabbed more
samples, left to play. The very next day we heard that Kelly Green
was interested in working with us.

We couldn't tell if Kelly Green was male or female. In my life,
I've known both kinds of Kelly. My Love only knew one Kelly
and she was a girl, but he'd heard of boy Kellys. And our relationship with Kelly Green was limited to mail correspondence only.
Kelly Green's letterhead read Kelly Green, President & CEO,
Target Corporation, on three separate lines at the top of the page,
superimposed over a bull's-eye. So we couldn't ever determine
the sex, but the business went like this: We signed a contract
allowing Kelly Green to purchase the conceptual rights for the
product. Kelly Green booked a plant, processing vats, and had
a line fed from the manufacturer of Target-brand gelatin desert.
Working with Jell-O brand would have required an additional
contractual relationship and a smaller cut for us. Then the ingredients in My Love's cologne oil were isolated and examined (by,
it turned out, the company My Love used to work for. "Imagine!" whooped My Love when he saw his former company's logo
in the correspondence). The ingredients were deemed nontoxic
and shipped to the plant. All was go, and My Love and I received
several checks from the Target Corporation. My Love flipped and
forwarded them on to the offices of the suicider's lawyers, and

by the peaceful look on his sweet face, I was convinced that his terrible experience was shrinking small and blippish and into the night behind him.

THE MANUFACTURING plant was on a rig in the ocean—a large, ocean-lining multifunctional industrial complex that produced items for companies like Target and even mined oil. On the first day of production, we were invited to the plant, ferried out to sea. The rig manager gave us a tour of the complex. We noticed that the processing center was equipped with a loudspeaker and sound system. We inquired about the decibels that could be projected over the vats and were told a number and I turned to My Love and his eyes went distant into thought. Then his eyes clicked back and he nodded his head, said that number seemed fine. Fine enough to convey our Wish List over the loudspeaker during the powder-melt phase.

"Because that is the thing that brings The Floodgates of Love to life," I explained to the rig manager. "The essential step that makes The Floodgates of Love *The Floodgates of Love.*"

"That so?" he said, looking bored and smug. He lifted his hat and pushed sweat from his forehead with his forearm. I didn't like him. But he showed us the control room with the audio equipment. There was one window in the room overlooking the vats, but it was narrow and the glass was darkly tinted. I asked the rig manager if he wouldn't mind leaving us alone for a bit, so we could Wish List it over the loudspeaker. He frowned and looked impatient and reluctant and stepped away for a moment and made a call on his waterproof phone and returned and rolled his big head on his thick neck and cracked it loudly and sighed and said sure, that'd be okay. He told us Kelly Green told him to honor our requests that day. New clients get a special day. Whatever we want. So on that first day of production, we did our thing in the privacy of the control room. The machines pumped and roared and the whole rig smelled like licorice and lemons and ginger and sugar and grease and oil. And it crossed my mind that our gush was no longer just between us, and I briefly wondered if the rig manager could hear us and if it might make him groan and uneasy—listening to lovers oozing love talk. Then it recrossed my mind that I didn't give a shit. And at the end of the day, we were ferried back to shore—hot, bothered, full up on the harmonics of us.

Weeks passed, another check or two arrived in the mail, but no request to participate in production. We got production status updates and learned that many units were being made—but without us. Without our Wish List. We sent a letter to Kelly Green inquiring when our personal services would be needed. When should we be available to broadcast our Wish List as the powder is mixed with boiling water?

We did not receive a response to our inquiry. But the product was being produced. The ocean factory out there was smoking and chugging. From the shore we could see it through binoculars. I got really irritated and perplexed and wondered how The Floodgates of Love were being produced minus the key ingredient. We submitted another proposal, this one full of all caps, insisting we be a CONSISTENT ELEMENT OF PRODUCTION. Kelly Green rejected this proposal.

IT WAS my idea to rent a boat. My Love rowed us rigorously out to the plant. His arms looked strong and lean, the striations in his muscles playing beneath his skin as he heaved and hoed. When we arrived at the rig, it was huger than we remembered. It was a steely piped skyscraper on the water, and our rowboat was a speck thunking against the crisscrossing beams sunk deep into the seabed. The first platform was like a high iron ceiling above us, the ocean our floor, and the dumb rowboat didn't catch anyone's attention. When the company had ferried us out, the rig manager dropped a bridge to let us on. This time, we were not expected. I shot a flare. We waited. Then stories above us, leaning over a railing and booming into a megaphone, the rig manager hollered, "What the fuck do you think you're doing!" and "Leave immediately!" I cupped my hands around my mouth and shouted, "We want on!"

My voice was nothing. The rig manager disappeared. Other workmen arrived at the railing, rolling an oil drum. They hoisted it up and over the railing above us. We watched it get bigger as it fell toward our rowboat. "Jump!" screamed My Love, and he grabbed my arm and we both went overboard as the drum crashed down. It busted our boat to pieces. We choked and splashed. Rowboat chunks like punched-out teeth batted around us. I was afraid a current would thrash me into a beam. The water was cold and oily and smelled like gas. I saw My Love's head on the surface, then he went under and popped up closer, and I lunged for him and I missed. Then two life preservers hailed down from above and landed in the froth and mess, and through his megaphone, the manager outshouted the fracas. I heard him clearly. "Go away!" he repeated, and "Don't ever return!"

We flailed to the life jackets, managed them on. My Love hooked his arm under my armpit and across my chest and kicked hard, away from the rig. Some distance from the plant he let me go. "Keep going," he gurgled. We swam. The shore looked like a paper plate tossed on the horizon. We swam toward it. I was sure sharks would eat my legs, stingrays would barb my lungs.

When we slapped the sand on the beach the sun was setting and everything looked blood orange, and all of me was cold numb. We lay in the slobber of the waves, breathing hard. My Love crawled toward me, pushed me onto my back, told me he was so happy we were alive. He took me in his arms and kissed me as the marshy breakwater moussed around our bodies. I was too angry and tired to kiss back.

Eventually we dragged ourselves from the packed wet sand to the dry moguls and on through it. I watched a tall, wet-suited man kiss a young crippled girl by the lifeguard tower. Squinting in the wind and from the corner of my mouth, I told My Love the world is a loathsome place.

WE RETURNED to the bomb shelter and slept for a night and day and night. When we came to, we made coffee and tacos. Stirring milk into our cups, I realized My Love had suffered another great trauma of things falling from above. Different, this time, was the intent. I asked him if he thought we weren't meant to be killed out there, by the oil drum and the shipwreck. He looked at me from the worktable and blinked and returned to shredding lettuce. I got the impression he didn't want to talk about it. I asked again. He sighed, said "Obviously not." His voice was soft. "We were tossed life *preservers*," he explained. "That rig manager was just trying to communicate his point."

"That he wished us dead?"

"That he'd prefer us alive. And away from his plant." The lettuce crunched against the cutting board.

"Because next time he won't toss life preservers," I said and watched My Love wince. He paused, wiped his hands, stepped toward me, put his hands on my cheeks. They were moist and warm and felt, as always, good. "That it's respectably best we don't return there uninvited."

"Respectably best!" It was like he shot me in the thigh with a nail gun. I removed his hands from my face, turned away from him. Then, to make a bad thing worse, My Love admitted he'd been in recent communication with Kelly Green, even before we boated out there. He admitted he gave the go-ahead to Kelly Green's request in one of his/her correspondences to change the name of our invention.

"Kelly Green has changed the name of The Floodgates of Love to Juicy Sweetheart Suckers," he informed me.

"To what?"

"Juicy Sweetheart Suckers."

My forehead and my neck and palms slicked hot and wet. "Say that again."

"Juicy Sweetheart—" he stopped. Looked at me carefully. I could feel the red in my face. I was so mad. The Floodgates of

Love, as a name, felt very good to me, very appropriate. The name suggested its effect on the consumer of the product—that when ingested, those floodgates will open and the ingester will drown in a superflux of love joy. *Floodgates* and *Love*—two key words, rightly descriptive.

My Love showed me the letter. I read it. Kelly Green cut the product into seven categories and distinguished each category with a color. Kelly Green wrote that *Buyers can select the love that they are in and purchase the respective color flavor accordingly. The categories to choose from: madly in, obsessive, lusty, long-term, puppy, codependent, desperate. Each category will be color-coded following the light spectrum ROYGBIV.* I didn't understand. What if categories overlapped? Was Kelly Green stupid? What did the light spectrum have to do with anything? Color flavors sounded disgusting.

"The Floodgates of Love are red. Only red!" I was shouting. "And they're not a category. They just are. They're just—" I lost my words. I stepped away from My Love, devastated that he wasn't protecting what we'd made together. I felt bits and pieces of us were being chipped at, chinked off, flicked onto the shining linoleum that slicks all of Target's stupid aisles. I blamed Kelly Green. I hated Kelly Green. I glared at My Love as he washed tomatoes. I put on my shoes. I grabbed my purse.

UP THE chain ladder, through the manhole, out of the bomb shelter, I charged to the local Target. I asked some employee in a red vest, "Where the fuck can I find Juicy Sweetheart Suckers?" The employee sent me to the candy section. The Floodgates of Love is not candy. In a point-of-sale display in the middle of the aisle I found Juicy Sweetheart Suckers. I grabbed the violet flavor in the violet packaging, marched to the checkout counter, threw the Juicy Sweetheart Suckers on the black rubber belt. "I'm paying for this!" I shouted at the red-vested cashier. She glanced at me, bored. "Okay."

Outside in the scalding sun, under giant red Target letters, I tore open the Juicy Sweetheart Suckers and tipped the carton of violet beads into my mouth. They were sweet and tangy and fizzing. I waited. They foamed on my tongue, seeped between my lips. I dribbled violet syrup on my shirt. I sucked, chewed, swallowed. Waited. Nothing. I saw a good-looking shopper pass by. I stopped him, asked him to help me out. Asked him to try some of this candy with me. I told him I thought he was so good-looking, would he mind? He was flustered and blushed. He smiled and blinked and stammered and then said okay. I loaded his palm with violet beads, poured more into my mouth. "Eat them," I said, mouth stuffed. "Look at me," I ordered. We chewed the beads at each other. His lips turned really purple. "Check your chest," I told him. He didn't get it. His mouth frothed. "Your chest! Do you feel anything in your chest!" He shook his head no. I pulled the neck of my shirt out and looked down into it and all I saw was my bra and my breasts and nothing felt like it was stretching out from my heart like it did that day in the bomb shelter. I looked at him and asked, "Anything?" And he said, "I don't know what you're talking about," and purple foam sponged over his chin. "Forget it," I huffed and turned and walked away. Feelings of thrill and bliss and brain-tipping passion swelled nowhere in me.

More evidence: In the parking lot a screaming kid and his mom passed by. The mother looked miserable. She dropped her Target bags, scrounged through one of them, pulled out a package of blue Juicy Sweetheart Suckers. She ripped it open, handed it to her bawling kid—to a little kid!—saying "Here, here, Christ, but you still have to eat your lunch." The kid's face was wet and terrible. He poured blue beads from the carton into his little fat hand and pushed the heap of beads into his wailing mouth. He chewed and cried, and blue foamed all over his mouth, and he ate more and cried harder. These were not The Floodgates of Love. I was furious.

Back in the bomb shelter, when My Love mentioned that my lips and my teeth and my tongue were purple, I didn't respond.

I scowled and felt an igloo of ice bricks whiten around me. He looked nervous. We'd never been in a fight before. I wondered if he wondered how our fights would go. He went to his bag of stuff and returned with the mask he'd made for me the day we met. He smiled and asked if I wanted to try it on again. "No," I told him. I sat on the bench, leaned an elbow on the worktable, breathed slowly, decided I didn't want to fight. Decided instead to calmly tell him about my plot.

"Kill Kelly Green how?" he asked me.

I didn't know yet for sure but thought anything would do. "We could build something explosive," I said, "and we could launch it over there, onto Kelly Green. With a catapult or something. We could build a catapult."

"I don't know," said My Love, "I think that's terrible." He looked pale and shaken and slipped to the futon and lay flat on his back and closed his eyes like he was trying to sleep. And for a twitch I wondered if I shouldn't blow this place up too.

A DIM and viral worry—what had been soft and plinking notes easily unheard, very ignored, now sounded deep and round and echoed through my bones—that maybe My Love and I were not what I'd hoped. Only a small section of my mind was available to that idea, and I had to try hard to sort through it. I thought: Maybe My Love was more evolved than I—a better person, disinterested in payback. Or perhaps he was just more pansyish and damaged because of the falling man. I knew that turnabout isn't always fair play, especially when it means murder. But I was certain that there are things that should be done when some person who owns a lot of things—like a whole Target empire, which brings fairly to poorly made items to the not-so-flush public—tries and succeeds in sucking the heart and soul out of an invention that I believed was 100 percent heart and soul and utter and miraculous love faith. Kelly Green's heart-and-soul sucking was what could be called the commodification of the spirit. I explained to My

Love that the phrase was Latin, and in ancient times such acts were punished. A whole army of fighters with flashing breast-plates would sit on a perpetrator—the perpetrator would be the conglomerate, I explained—that captained the commodification. And the perpetrator's bones would burst beneath his skin, and he would die of marrow poisoning in his blood. "It was an ugly but necessary death," I tried to convince My Love.

"It's like the lawyers who look at precedents," I told him. He rolled over on the futon and looked at the floor, at a gray dust pile we'd missed brooming. He rolled back over, sat up, aimed his gaze right at me.

"I don't think we can make a precedent argument about this," he said and rose and got the broom and pushed the lump of dust into the dustpan. It left a ridge of debris, so he brushed it from another angle and into the pan. "There are things that don't deserve murder," he said. His voice was smooth and sincere.

In that moment, I understood: He wouldn't help me assas-sinate the president of Target. This truth came slowly and delib-erately and whacked me upside the head, flattened the back of my skull like a slab. I saw something plainly: We couldn't go on together. Between my ears alarmed the shrill call of something like train brakes, but very far away and constant. A long, drawn, deafening squeal. My Love met my eyes. He looked curiously at me for what felt like a while. I thought maybe he could read my thoughts across my face. He propped the broom against the edge of the worktable, dropped the dustpan, came toward me, picked me up like a sack, carried me over to the futon. He put his nose to my head and smelled my hair. We toppled onto the bed, in a lump, tight and soft. Our noses made faint whistling sounds into each other's ears.

This felt nice and then was crushed under the crash of some-thing loud inside me. It said *go*. I pulled myself out from his arms and backed away from him on the futon. I kneeled, ready to speak. Nothing came out of my mouth. Like a dry wooden doorstop was wedged between the two pipes in my throat. Inside me I heard the thing again, and louder. It brayed *GO!*

I backed up off the futon. "You won't kill Kelly Green with me," I managed to say slowly. My sound came out crumbling and brittle. "On account of your history, I know you can't." A long time throbbed in the air.

"I need to go do it," I said, the focus of his face drowning behind tears piling high against my eyeballs. His lips drew tight in his face. They made a straight line. He couldn't look at me.

WE KISSED a lot on the way to the train station. The kisses were sad. Everything else was scary. I had my suitcase packed for Kelly Green. Kelly Green was going down. Kelly Green was going downtown. I repeated this in my head.

When the train pulled away from the platform, it was night, the sky was dark, the city outside the station lurched and shifted with the breaths of one million people. From my ribs to My Love's ribs I felt those tugging things. The elastics that stretched from each of our chests and tangled together when we ate The Floodgates of Love. Now they strained tight and thin, their knots stringent and small, their gum feathering. When the train rounded some bend along a river just out of town, the elastics snapped. They flung furiously back to their points of origin. Mine smacked and shook my body meanly. Pieces of bone broke from my ribs and felt like they entered, murky, into my bloodstream. My Love—I didn't imagine the sting he buttoned under his coat as he walked from the station in the cold.

Fisty Pinions

RONNIE SCARTOON loves Ashlyn Aschenbecher, the girl with the glass ashtrays for breasts. For ash. For fists. FOREVER!

IT'S BEEN glass ashtrays since high school for Ashlyn Aschenbecher. In the eleventh grade her parents died. They were vacationing on an island. They loved snorkeling. The one day they left the water for land, they hiked to the top of a volcano. Dad lost his footing; mom was holding his hand. They fell into the hole, knocked into jutting rocks on the way down, melted in the lava at the very bottom. Ashlyn Aschenbecher got the call at her grandparents' house. She wept and slept facedown in her bed for four days, her head feeling full of hot rocks too heavy for the mattress, the box springs, the floorboards, the cement, the continental crust, the upper mantle, the mantle, the semirigid inner mantle, the molten outer core, the iron and nickel inner core of the earth. The rest of her body felt like cotton. When she got up, she washed her face, borrowed the car, and bought two clear glass round ashtrays from the smoker's store. She took them back to her grandparents' house, her new home, and got started with the double-sided mounting tape. Four squares of tape spaced evenly at twelve, three, six, and nine on the flat face of the bottom of each ashtray. She mounted the ashtrays to her chest over her very small, very flat breasts. She stuck them bowl side out, cigarette grooves facing into the world. Her nipples were mashed flat. Beneath the glass they can look like coins. Like bottle caps.

She wears ashtrays every day. She does not bathe with them. When she removes them, she does so carefully, with baby oil. She sits in her closet, on a towel, has always done it this way. She douses a cotton ball with baby oil and squeezes. Oil goes in the slim space between the glass and her skin. Her skin gleams glossy, the glass smears smudgy. She twists slowly until the adhesive loses its grip, fails. One breast, then the other. Because she rotates the ashtrays each time she adheres them—adjusting the placement of the mounting tape on her skin clockwise, one hour ahead with each adhesion—her bare breasts, from years of ashtrays, have developed tough, pink-callused circles around their circumferences. In the center of the circles, her nipples appear like bull's-eyes. Straight on and bare, her breasts look drawn on, illustrated in pink marker on the flat paper flesh of her chest.

She sleeps in ashtrays five nights a week. On the two ashtray-less nights, she lies on top of the covers. The window cracked, fan oscillating, or space heater humming if it's cold, she tunes her attention to her chest and dozes off, aware of atmosphere on her unglassed breasts.

For exercise she does shirtless push-ups, going all the way down with really nice form so that the ashtrays clunk lightly, but evenly, on the floor. She does four sets of twenty. Around fifteen of each set, her muscles burn and shake. She powers on. At the end of the sets, eighty perfect push-ups, she rolls onto her back, a bit sweaty. She lights a cigarette, smokes, ashes into her breasts. Breath recovered but smoky and her sweat dry, she extinguishes her cigarette into one or the other ashtray. She cups it, stands, clomps to the sink or the trash, leans over, empties.

When out and about, the contours of her ashtrays are visible through her shirt: hard ridges, smooth curves. Like gears or machine parts.

RONNIE SCARTOON is Ashlyn Aschenbecher's admirer. She's liked her for years. They went to the same high school but were not friends. Ronnie Scartoon always wanted to be her friend because she liked Ashlyn Aschenbecher's face and dark hair, the tilt of her green eyes, her delicate and pale body and the little muscles in her arms. And the ashtrays were transfixing. Ronnie Scartoon wanted to *know* Ashlyn Aschenbecher, the girl in high school who wore glass ashtrays for breasts, tray side out, under her clothes. And then naked in the locker room, before and after gym, changing proudly, nipples flattened like photos in a frame. Ronnie Scartoon found her mesmerizing and felt certain a friend like Ashlyn Aschenbecher would make the sad, wet bread that is high school better.

Ronnie Scartoon liked to be around Ashlyn Aschenbecher—to stand or sit near her. For example, on the bleacher behind her during assembly. One bench up, Ronnie was only a foot or two from Ashlyn. Ronnie watched the back and top of her head, stared closely at Ashlyn's part, which was usually on the right unless she shook her fingers through her hair, and plates of it flipped to the other side or settled evenly on both, leaving a part in the middle. Ronnie noticed Ashlyn's scalp, at her middle part, was paler than her right-side part. As the student body president made announcements about the upcoming dance concert and food drive, and the drill team bounced and did the splits for the basketball team and the football team, Ronnie wondered what kind of products Ashlyn used in her hair. It was so satiny. And it smelled always like cigarettes but also like apples.

At the end of assembly, when everyone would shift and lurch from the bleachers, and Ronnie'd lean forward to grab her back-pack from the foot gutter between the benches of the bleachers, sometimes she'd lean very close into the back of Ashlyn's head. Close enough to stick the tip of her nose into Ashlyn's hair. It felt slippery and cool. Ronnie could blink and comb a few strands through her eyelashes. Once, Ashlyn noticed and swatted at the back of her head. She clocked Ronnie across the bridge of Ronnie's nose. Startled, Ashlyn turned around to see Ronnie, very red-faced, holding her nose. Both girls said "Sorry!" at the same time. And Ronnie pointed at her bag and said, "My backpack," trying to explain. Ashlyn said, "I thought a spider dropped into my hair." Then she laughed. Like thick suds in the tub, her laugh bubbled high around Ronnie's neck, puffed beneath her earlobes. Made Ronnie's face warm. "I didn't mean to hit you," Ashlyn said. "Are you okay?" Ronnie noticed a faint dimple in Ashlyn's chin that the yearbook photographer had failed to catch.

"Yes," said Ronnie, feeling illuminated by Ashlyn's face. She took her hand off her nose, checked her palm. "No blood." She smiled and shrugged at Ashlyn. Ashlyn looked at Ronnie for what felt to Ronnie like a really long moment, then Ashlyn bent down to grab her own bag and slung it diagonally over her shoulder. The strap crossed Ashlyn down the middle of her chest, pinning her T-shirt to her breastplate, dividing the space between her ashtrays. Ronnie's eyes dropped to the ashtrays—distinct curves and shallow grooves under Ashlyn's shirt—then back up to Ashlyn's eyes. Ashlyn smiled at Ronnie, waved a little, and filed down the bleacher lane with the rest of her row. This was their major encounter in high school. Ronnie thought about it often. When they'd pass in the hall, they'd smile lightly at each other, but they'd never talk.

Ronnie Scartoon continued to sit behind Ashlyn during assembly or at a neighboring table during lunch. Ronnie usually sat in a crowd but kept her attention flexed one table over, on Ashlyn Aschenbecher, who often sat alone, read, did homework. From the corner of her eye, Ronnie Scartoon would watch Ashlyn Aschenbecher. Notice her thin arms sticking out from the loose sleeves of her T-shirt. She wore the softest-looking T-shirts. Old and worn into silky tissue. They were just right with jeans. They hung on her ashtrays like they were relieved.

After lunch or sometimes between classes, Ashlyn Aschenbecher would slink beyond the student parking lot and smoke with the boys in the long black coats and that scabby-mouthed girl who lost her hands. Ronnie Scartoon would pass by, making her way to her car like she'd forgotten something and really needed it, just to catch another glimpse of Ashlyn Aschenbecher. This time, maybe, with a scenery of bushes growing up a wire fence in the background behind Ashlyn's body. Or that time, sitting on the bumper of some kid's parents' station wagon, the other student smokers drooping like laundry, around.

Occasionally Ronnie Scartoon thought she might like to kiss Ashlyn Aschenbecher. This thought felt like falling. She'd take a deep breath, grab a railing or a desktop or steady herself against a wall, look down at her shoes, register their placement on the ground. Say to herself: *Those are my shoes, they are on the floor. Those are my feet inside my shoes on the floor.* Then she'd try to think of other things: *Available in the cafeteria are pizza bagels! And the frozen yogurt is fat free!* But there is Ashlyn Aschenbecher, up and striding toward the vending machines.

Ronnie Scartoon decided she could think it'd be nice to maybe just hold Ashlyn Aschenbecher's hand. Maybe hang out with her one day. Maybe watch a movie while the rest of everyone was at school. Ronnie Scartoon thought they could rent one. And watch it in Ronnie Scartoon's room. In her bed. With chips, cheese and crackers, grapes, iced tea. Ronnie made good iced tea.

But Ronnie Scartoon never invited Ashlyn Aschenbecher over. She couldn't manage the guts to speak to her. Then they graduated, and each went elsewhere.

THE NEXT several years of Ashlyn Aschenbecher's life were roughly punctuated like this: She went to college, mixed cocktails, drank them fast. At parties, she walked shirtless through hallways, from bedrooms to the bathroom to the keg and back. She smoked two cigarettes at a time, ashing one into each breast, and making little messes because her ashtrays—adhered to her chest and not in natural ashtray position unless she is flat on her back—do not effectively catch and contain ash. When standing, sitting, moving about, ash flicked at the ashtrays tends to sprinkle down Ashlyn Aschenbecher's front, settle on her belt loops, dust the floor.

This toplessness and her ashtrays made her popular, not in the Greek party circuit, but at moodier black-nail-polish parties in attics and basements around campus. She spent many nights in dorm beds fitted with black sheets, red light bulbs glowing from desk lamps without shades, boys with long silky hair.

One who marked his forearms with sets of parallel knife strokes, like pink bar codes, painted around her ashtrays with dark watercolors. Indigo and slate and earth against her pale skin. He outlined the glass rounds and painted a clasp just below her breastbone. From the tops of the ashtrays he painted shoulder straps in little curlycues. "Like lace," he told her. The brush was smooth and cool and wet. From the side of one ashtray, under her arm, across her back, under her other arm, to the other ashtray, he swept a thick strap and in it detailed loops and petals, stems. "Flower pattern," he whispered. It made her calm and drowsy. She closed her eyes. When he finished he lifted the window to invite the breeze, took both her hands, held them up. She felt the paint blow cold, then shrink dry and tight. They shared a smoke in his room. Tried, but not very hard, to exhale out the window. He looked at his painting, her ashtrays, her nipples pressed flat like poker chips. They ashed in her breasts. Only during careful moments of vertical stillness could she, or a lover, smoke and flick in quiet precision so that the ash piled neatly on the curved glass. Two dark snowdrifts against her chest.

After college, Ashlyn Aschenbecher inherited her parents' house. When she returned, everything was as she'd left it. Only very dusty. So she dusted and scrubbed, moved back into her old bedroom. Left her parents' stuff as was.

She dated an older man. He was her high school English teacher. He took her to a cocktail party at his work, her high school. "No ashtrays tonight," he pleaded. "Please," while they readied to leave. She looked puzzled, then glared at him. Shook her head. Kept the ashtrays on.

He took her to a faculty party—a picnic on the sports field where the teams played during the week. There were all her old teachers and some new ones she didn't recognize. The old ones recognized her by her ashtrays. She wore a bustier top. The top drawstrings were strung tight and tied in the center of her chest, exposing the top quarters of her ashtrays. Black lace-up bustier with two glass crescent ashtray arcs plus black skirt and heels that sunk deep into the lawn, with former teacher at former high school—she felt uncomfortable. She should have rethought her outfit. Worn something with a collar. Or a pair of long pleated shorts. Or the flattest shoes. Or perhaps she shouldn't have come. And she was not accustomed to worrying about such things. So she drank cocktails at the open bar, lots of them. She placed her stir straws in the pocketed space between the bustier breast cups and her ashtray bowls. By night's end, she'd collected many straws, wore them proudly, could have been an emergency supplier of red cocktail straws to drinkers around the world. She decided to talk to all her old teachers.

She chatted with them on the big lawn as the sun set, slurring about old times. She smoked her cigarettes and ashed into her breasts. Her fingers cocktail thick, she flicked messily against her chest, sooting her shallow cleavage, blitzing small holes into her top, melting straws so they bent and drooped, crippledly. Her former French teacher, accustomed to drunk and smoking French people, gaped in horror at Ashlyn Aschenbecher as she drawled on about how she doesn't even mind reading white subtitles on French films because she regularly understands the French versions of many of the white words that get blotted out against the bright parts of the screen. "Like against all the naked flat asses of the French actoresses," Ashlyn Aschenbecher said. She said, "Thanks, *merci*. For the language instructions, lady. *Madame. Mer*fucking*ci beaucoup*."

In the morning she woke up next to the English teacher. Her ashtrays were on the bedside table. Alarm clock, cup of water, aspirin, ashtrays. One, two, stacked. Mounting tape yellowing. On her chest, her adhesive spots, tender and red. This had not been a night she'd intended to be without ashtrays. He'd removed them while she slept. She left.

RONNIE SCARTOON thinks often of Ashlyn Aschenbecher. Wonders about her. What is she doing? What is she like? If she saw her again, would Ronnie's rib cage crack open, bust through her chest, and reach out for her?

So, eight years later, Ronnie looked her up, found her address, went to the supermarket near Ashlyn's house. Meandered the parking lot, wandered the grocery aisles, hoped to run into Ashlyn Aschenbecher.

Three days of this: then, by the sushi counter at the end of the long case packed with shaved ice and pink shrimps and gray shrimps and white halibut steaks and some heavily draped dusky-colored other fish, Ronnie Scartoon sees her. She is holding a small container of pickled ginger. She is watching the sushi chef in his blue and white cotton headband roll rice. Still pale, still thin, her shoulders pointier, maybe. Her hair longer and darker than Ronnie Scartoon remembers. Still shiny. And beneath her tank top, ashtrays. Her tank top stretches tight across them. They are like small, shallow drums.

Ronnie Scartoon remembers once when she was a kid, she swung on a rope tied to a tree branch that stretched out over a lake. At the very end of the swing up, when she was like an extension of the branch, her body out in the air, looking straight up at the sun, she let go. She hung in the air like that, many feet above, for a fraction of a second, then fell. Through the air, flat on her back, into the lake. The water's slap scorched her skin, spanked the wind from her lungs, burst rumbustious green bubbles from her nose and her mouth. Then the big sound of her heart. Not beating, just one long, loud boom: This is what it is like to see Ashlyn Aschenbecher at the sushi counter in the supermarket.

Ronnie Scartoon turns and examines the shrimp through the case. Lays her hand against the cool curve of the glass. A thin fog outlines her palm and fingers. She removes her hand, leaves a sweaty print. She looks at her shoes. Steps one in front of the other. They click softly on the linoleum. She crosses thirty-two tiles. Stops. Breathes. Looks. Ashlyn Aschenbecher is wearing brown boots with worn and pointed toes. The cuffs of her jeans break just past the ankle of her boots and drag lower behind the heel.

Now, with a little age, a little time, and what seems like this miraculous opportunity she would deeply hate herself for passing up if it passed her by, Ronnie Scartoon finds the courage to talk to Ashlyn Aschenbecher. She says, "Excuse me."

Ashlyn Aschenbecher looks over. Her eyes are large and dark green and tilted like Ronnie remembers. Her face slightly sharper angled than in high school; the groove in her chin maybe a bit deeper. Her lips are glossy. Ronnie Scartoon sweats from her pits and her palms. "I think we went to high school together," she says.

Ashlyn Aschenbecher tips her head to one side, squints her eyes, looks, smiles. She has very clean-looking teeth. She frowns, breathes, unfrowns, smiles again. "I remember your face," she says, from the back of her throat.

And there is light powering through the long windows near the cash registers, and the fluorescent lighting lining the ceiling hails down over the entire supermarket and bounces back up off the plastic floor squares, and there are loud fast knocks from the sushi man chopping on his block, and Ashlyn Aschenbecher is in front of Ronnie Scartoon saying a sentence and remembering her. Ronnie Scartoon feels like her hair is on fire. She manages to open her mouth and joggle out: howareyouIcan'tbelieveitI knewIknewyoufromsomewhereyoulikesushi? And in it to win it, no time to lose, Ronnie Scartoon suggests they get sushi sometime, she knows a great place.

Ashlyn Aschenbecher says, "Alright." She drops the ginger and a to-go container of sushi handed to her by the chef into her grocery basket on the ground near her feet. She is also purchasing soy milk, croissants, canned coffee, a stubby bottle of port wine, and light beer.

"Okay," Ronnie Scartoon says, fortified by Ashlyn's positive reaction. "It'll be fun to catch up."

They make a plan. Ronnie offers to pick her up. Ashlyn Aschenbecher writes her address on a napkin from the counter. It is the exact address Ronnie Scartoon already has. As she walks away Ronnie Scartoon foams things like: great fun I'll see you then super! take care. She finds her car in the parking lot. The metallic fleck in the blue paint on this sunshiney day is gorgeous.

DINNER AT the sushi joint and Ashlyn Aschenbecher has a voice like the sexy ladies in the movies. Maybe from smoking. Maybe she doesn't sleep much. Ronnie Scartoon once read that the old black-and-white lady stars would wake up every morning, light a cigarette, suck a long drag, push their faces into their pillows and scream at the top of their lungs. But then Ronnie Scartoon also knew a five-year-old whose voice rumbled like a movie star's, and she was only five. So here's Ashlyn Aschenbecher talking, gravelly, to Ronnie Scartoon, over sushi, about her job once as a phone sex operator. She did it for two days. Day one she read from dirty magazines and sample copy supplied by the company, but they bored her, so the next day she made things up. And because she was one of the girls they got when they requested someone bossy, the callers usually asked, "Whatta you gonna do to me?"

And then out growls her voice, "'I'm going to take you to the

fucking ocean,'" she says. "'I'm going to sit you in the sand.'"
Ashlyn Aschenbecher leans across the table and looks at Ronnie
Scartoon like she means it.

"'I'm going to sit you facing the fucking ocean,'" she continues, talking into her hand like her thumb and knuckles and pinky
are a phone, "'the waves crashing and smashing at your feet and
spraying all over your face. I'm going to stand in front of you,
put my hands on your shoulders, and leapfrog, pantyless, over
your head.'"

"Really?" asks Ronnie Scartoon, tickled.

"Yes," says Ashlyn. "The first guy I said this to was foreign and
didn't catch *leapfrog-pantyless* and he stopped me and said, 'What
you say?' And I told him to shut the fuck up I'm talking, but after
that, I would say it really slowly." Ashlyn Aschenbecher grabs
Ronnie Scartoon's hand across the table and grumbles, "Leap.
Frog. Panty. Less." She lets go and leans back into her chair and
says, "Then I'd say, 'And if you got a big nose or a high pointy
forehead, you might get caught on me as I'm going over. But I'll
keep going, taking your head with me, stuck in my stuff. We'll
crash into the sand. You on your back, me on my face. But I don't
love that—falling on my face—and so I'll kick my legs up off of
you, like a karate queen. Spring to my feet. I'll shove you upright,
with my elbow or my knee or the side of my foot. And I'll take
my position kneeling behind your back.'" The waiter appears.
Ashlyn Aschenbecher stops talking. Both women stare up at him.
He asks how things are going. They say fine.

"Great," he says. He clasps his hands together in front of his
chest and nods his head. The women watch him. He nods more.
Stops. Inhales. Pivots on his black loafers, turns, marches toward
the bar. He leaves snow and wind and now all the hairs on their
arms are up and alert. Ronnie Scartoon leans in closer.

"So," Ashlyn Aschenbecher whispers and continues with her
story. "I would say, 'From behind, now I bite the back of your
collar and tear your shirt off. The fucking ocean moves closer.

Soaks your feet and your legs and your belt and now, your pants are dark but the seawater is warm and so is the mild wind. I come around the front of you, grab you by your dirty ankles. You're a bad boy.' We had to include certain phrases," she tells Ronnie Scartoon and takes a sip of beer. "Three phrases. You're a bad boy, and my pussy is something. Gushing, dripping, hot, wet, hot and wet, screaming—something. And finally, I'm not done, I want more of you. This keeps them on the line longer."

Ronnie Scartoon is enchanted. Ronnie Scartoon thinks Ashlyn Aschenbecher looks amazing saying her phone sex because Ashlyn Aschenbecher is delicate in a way that makes her look like a fragile person. She also has the distracted look of a thoughtful person, like a favorite art teacher. And then there's her voice and the things she says, and her ashtrays. Ashlyn Aschenbecher lights a cigarette. "This is a patio, right?" she asks Ronnie Scartoon. "I can smoke here, right?"

"Sure," says Ronnie Scartoon. She watches her smoke. Ashlyn Aschenbecher squints when she inhales. A busboy approaches the table with an ashtray. As he places it near her beer, Ashlyn taps his hand, tells him, "That's okay. No thanks." He stops, surprised, smiles and nods his head, yes, and sets the ashtray down.

Ashlyn Aschenbecher says clearly, "No thank you." She hands it to him. He smiles and nods his head again and points at her cigarette. "I know," she says and puffs out her chest, showing the grooves and outline of her ashtrays through her shirt. He looks at her breasts. Frowns. Doesn't know what he's looking at. She pulls down the neck of her shirt, reveals two glassy rondures, boobs smashed beneath. He backs up, giggles nervously. Nods, backs up, shrugs, nods, leaves.

Ashlyn Aschenbecher looks at Ronnie Scartoon. She rolls her eyes, sips from her cigarette. "You want one?" she asks Ronnie.

"No thanks," says Ronnie. She looks at the ash growing long on the cigarette. Ashlyn Aschenbecher takes another drag, pulls the neck of her shirt out and down. She ashes into her left breast.

Takes another drag. Reaches her hand deeper into her shirt, stubs out the cigarette, flicks the butt into a potted plant near their table.

"You don't keep the butts in there?" asks Ronnie, meaning in her shirt with those ashtrays against her breasts.

"Never," says Ashlyn.

"Oh," says Ronnie. And she becomes aware of this sensation: Talking to Ashlyn Aschenbecher is like taking a hot tub deep in a cave. Private. And warm and wet and simmering. Bubbles snarling from jets down below, raucousing the steaming water. Suddenly, Ronnie wants to do things. There is one sip left of her beer. She sips it. Now it is gone. Maybe if they were not in a restaurant, or maybe if Ronnie were a different girl, Ronnie Scartoon would stand up out of her chair, lean over the small table, grab onto Ashlyn Aschenbecher's ears like handles, pull her face up toward hers, and kiss her.

Ronnie Scartoon squeezes a soy pod and pops a bean into her mouth. Ashlyn Aschenbecher bites the ends of her chopsticks. Ronnie Scartoon clears her throat and says, "Then what do you do to them?"

"Sorry?" says Ashlyn.

"The men on the phone at the ocean?" Ronnie pauses. "You'd grab their ankles—"

"Oh," says Ashlyn. "Yeah," she remembers. "I'd tell them—" she pauses. "Right. I'd say, 'I grab you by your filthy ankles,'" she begins again, slowly. "'I swing you around so your back's to the waves, and I shove you on your ass into the frothy bawling fucking ocean. Your whole body as stiff as your fat dick, I'll paddle you like a surfboard into the breakers. Me on your chest, my boobs slapping your face, your cock poking between my thighs, my arms pushing the sea out of the way. Ocean water sloshes us all over. We penetrate waves. Seawater juices us everywhere. I paddle hard, and you float like an ocean liner, like a motherfucking sex ship yacht titanic dream cruiser, past the surf and out into the calm of the great fucking ocean. And in the middle of the sea, your prick is huge like a fucking lighthouse on your body that floats like the island of incredible fucking. We float and fuck. You are a motherfucking sex machine island lighthouse fucker. And we fuck and fuck and fuck. My pussy is rhapsodic, streaming, frenzied.'" Ashlyn Aschenbecher smiles wide, winks at Ronnie Scartoon, continues, "'And when your giant cock cums, the explosion is so colossal that I am blown to a billion little hot fucked bits shot high in the sky. My cummed-over, demolished pieces rain down on the surface of the fucking ocean and become potent vivacious sex food for the fish. The fish gorge themselves on my ravaged chunks made bionic by your cum. They grow mighty, magnificent, full of vim and verve—the strongest fish in the fucking ocean—and you are their leader. And when they swim up onto your bobbling nut bag, they change form, into sexy beautiful mermaids. They slink onto your island and you fuck them forever!'" Ashlyn Aschenbecher puts a whole salmon roll in her mouth. Chews. Says, chewing still a little, "That's about where I'd wrap up. I'd have nothing more to offer after that."

"And the callers?" asks Ronnie Scartoon.

"Well," says Ashlyn, swallowing, "I only got to do that story twice. The first time was that foreigner and he tried interrupting me a bunch of times to tell me to tell him I'm spanking him, and I said, 'Shut up or I'll drown you,' and at the end of my story he said, 'Lady, what's the fuck?' I hung up on him. And you're not supposed to do that. The whole charge for the call can't be rung up unless the caller hangs up. But then another call came through. I did the ocean thing again. Then I got fired. Our phone calls were occasionally monitored to assure quality assistance. My manager called in from the big office and said they wouldn't be forwarding any more clients."

"I'd call you," says Ronnie Scartoon.

Ashlyn Aschenbecher pauses, briefly. She looks down at the crab roll on her plate. Solid white like clay, outlined in orange, packed in rice, rolled in brittle black seaweed. "Okay," she says, rosy. She lights another cigarette. Offers Ronnie one again. Ronnie takes it this time. Ashlyn lights hers in the votive candle on the table. Passes the candle to Ronnie. They smoke. They don't talk. Ashlyn Aschenbecher ashes into her breasts. Ronnie Scartoon taps her ash onto the stones beneath her chair. She smokes it down to the filter. Ashlyn notices, leans forward across the table, pulls down the front of her shirt. Ronnie looks. The tops of the ashtrays catch the candlelight, and the down in there, inside her shirt, is dark.

"Put it out in here," says Ashlyn Aschenbecher.

Ronnie Scartoon looks into her shirt and up at her face and back into her shirt.

Ashlyn Aschenbecher says, "Go ahead."

Ronnie Scartoon leans out of her chair, reaches her cigarette hand across the table. She wants to keep her eyes on where she's extinguishing, she doesn't want to miss and put it out into Ashlyn's skin. But she also feels impolite looking.

Her hand disappears into the neck of Ashlyn's shirt. She goes ahead and looks, focuses on the ashtray on Ronnie's right. With Ashlyn leaning forward like she is, the ashtrays are practically upside down. Ronnie Scartoon presses the butt up into the ashtray. Ash falls into her hand and down the inside of Ashlyn's shirt.

Ronnie Scartoon withdraws her hand. She feels shy and light-headed. Her cigarette butt is stubbed short. The tips of Ronnie Scartoon's thumb and index finger are sooty. She tosses the butt into the potted plant. It lands next to Ashlyn's butts. Ronnie Scartoon sits back into her chair. Rubs the tips of her fingers on the thigh of her jeans. Notices her hand feels hot. She looks at Ashlyn Aschenbecher who is smiling, slightly, gently, lips closed, no teeth.

Ashlyn says, "What about you? Tell me something about you."

Ronnie Scartoon breathes deep and coughs a little. She sits up in her seat and tells herself: Say something good. She looks over at Ashlyn Aschenbecher. Her green eyes bright, her breasts like geometry under her striped shirt. Ronnie Scartoon's brain funnels inside her skull. She looks at the other diners on the patio. They are clinking and drinking. She tells Ashlyn Aschenbecher about the roach babies.

She tells her about the bad part of town where they lived when she was a kid, quiet and scary in the day, terrorizing in the night. A place where the bugs are lethal. Deadly cockroaches posture in the size and shape of soft babies, cooing and blinking and pumping their fists. "You see them in the streets—in gutters, in alleys, by trash bins, sometimes in your backyard, behind the garage. Fat babies, alone and abandoned in dirty spots," Ronnie Scartoon tells Ashlyn Aschenbecher. "You're drawn to them," she says, "A baby, you think. Pick it up. Save it." She shakes her head, "And then in your arms, when you bring the little baby close up enough to your face to smile and smooch at it," she looks seriously at Ashlyn Aschenbecher, "it turns into a giant cockroach, the size of a loaf of bread with yellow sac eggs gelatined to its belly."

Ashlyn Aschenbecher scrunches her face like food poisoning and looks skeptical. "I don't believe you," she says.

But Ronnie Scartoon tells her about the long cockroach legs. "Flailing in your arms, it pokes bits from its egg sac, and in single snap movements strokes your face with egg sac crumbles." She makes a claw with her hand and swipes the air.

"Sometimes it wipes crumbles on your lips, getting them in your mouth. Or," she says, "it slashes your eyes." She pauses and looks Ashlyn Aschenbecher dead in the face. "All this happens quickly, before you can scream and drop the giant roach that used to be a baby. But that comes next, fast," says Ronnie. "*Thunk*," she says and hits the table. Some sushis and chopsticks jump. "You throw it to the ground. And you had been a nice person who had wanted to help a baby, and now you are wailing. And then down plunges your boot or sneaker, or you might slam a brick on it if you're a lady wearing heels or sandals and don't want ooze on your foot. And you smash the thing, egg sac and all." Ronnie Scartoon lowers her voice, "Unless the roach gets the human first. If the sweet baby draws the human face close enough to it to switch over and bite it with its cockroach mouth. This stuns the human. Makes you pass out on the ground, out cold but alive. Then the roach snacks on your body and signals to other roaches. They banquet. Then lay their eggs in your ground meat. The person wakes later, chewed up, rotted out, stinging sore, and sick," says Ronnie Scartoon. "It's a very disgusting problem in that part of town."

Ashlyn listens quietly and asks, "What happens to the bitten people?"

"To remedy the attack," Ronnie Scartoon tells her, "most people take their own lives. If they can lift themselves up and drag themselves into traffic," she says, "they do. Lots of body parts on the roads around there."

"I'm not sure I believe you," says Ashlyn Aschenbecher.

Ronnie Scartoon raises her eyebrows. "I had to wear an eye patch for two months in the seventh grade after a roach claw scratched my eyeball." She pulls her lower lid down with her pointer finger. "See the scar," she says, "the yellow line?" She leans across the table, disfiguring her face like gum. "That's an eyeball scar from a time I tried to save a baby. See it?"

Ashlyn squints into her eyeball.

Ronnie says, "It's on the white part. A little down and to the side of the iris. My left."

Ashlyn Aschenbecher looks harder, asks, "Did you get stunned and chewed?"

"No, I got away," says Ronnie, very aware of how close Ashlyn Aschenbecher is to her face. Ronnie can feel Ashlyn breathe through her nose and exhale onto Ronnie's cheek and chin as she looks intently into Ronnie's eye.

Ronnie remembers being at an eye clinic, in the machine that held her face, stretched open her lids and touched a lens right up against the black part of her eyeball. The clinician was taking a picture of the inside of her eyeball to check for deep damage. Just as he clicked the machine he said, "Now I get to see all your thoughts!" A flash *poof*ed, bleaching everything in her skull bright burning white. She blinked, but didn't—couldn't, it wasn't possible to close her lids. She felt thieved of the privacy of her brain, robbed through her eyeball.

In this moment at this restaurant, Ashlyn Aschenbecher puts her hand on Ronnie Scartoon's jaw, her thumb curves around Ronnie Scartoon's chin. Her fingers are damp and soft and warm. She peers closer and harder into Ronnie Scartoon's eye. Ronnie Scartoon feels unfastened and suddenly protective of her thoughts. Scared that Ashlyn Aschenbecher might see into her eyeball and glimpse the picture in Ronnie Scartoon's head: Ashlyn tipping her mouth toward Ronnie's mouth, leaning farther across the table, tilting her head just enough, gently coaxing Ronnie's head in the opposite direction with her hand on Ronnie's jaw. And then, smoothly, their lips meet, and Ashlyn Aschenbecher's fingers slide beneath Ronnie Scartoon's ear, along the back of her neck, and move deep into the thick of Ronnie's hair. In Ronnie's mind, Ashlyn Aschenbecher kisses her. Soft-shell crabs' legs reach up from piles of rice on the table between them.

"I see it," Ashlyn says.

Embarrassed, Ronnie Scartoon squeezes her eyes shut, jerks away, sits back. She tucks her head and aggressively rubs her eyes like she's got a headache, nervous that Ashlyn Aschenbecher saw into her brain.

"Like a thick blonde brow hair," says Ashlyn.

Ronnie Scartoon looks up. "What?"

"The scar."

"Right," says Ronnie.

"Are you okay?" asks Ashlyn.

Ronnie Scartoon nods. Holds her breath. "Yeah. Yes. I'm fine," she says, trying to mean it.

"Does your eyeball scar hurt you?" Ashlyn asks softly.

"No, not really. It's old," says Ronnie Scartoon. She pauses, then, "Sometimes," she says, "I can feel it when I blink. When I concentrate. It's like a little rub."

Ashlyn Aschenbecher nods. They sit, uneasy. Ronnie Scartoon's mind is an empty can.

Ashlyn Aschenbecher asks, "Are we on a date?"

Ronnie Scartoon remembers being twelve. She stayed at her dad's for the summer. One morning he walked into her bedroom. She was asleep on top of her covers with her hand in her pajama bottoms. He woke her with, "What the hell are you doing!" Her eyes tore open on to his face, rumpled and red above her, and her sudden awareness of her hand in her underwear and the tone in his voice, and she felt mortified. Cankerwormed and crumbling. Ronnie considers excusing herself to the bathroom and leaving in her car. She considers saying, No, are you kidding? She looks into the tablecloth and breathes.

Ronnie Scartoon asks carefully, "Do you like dates?"

Ashlyn says, "Yeah. Mostly. Sometimes."

"This evening reminds you of one?" Ronnie asks.

"It does," she says.

"One you mostly like?" she asks.

Ashlyn smiles and slowly says, "Yes."

The candle flickering plus the dim patio lighting and the salty soft smell of soy sauce in the tiny bowls is delicious. Ronnie Scartoon remembers sleeping on a boat she snuck into by the docks, after the roach attack. She slept in it for a week, in her eye patch, feeling like a pirate, boycotting her mom until she agreed to move them to another part of town without roach babies. It was a small boat, but had a shallow underneath with a sleeping compartment positioned right up next to the hull, where the water slapped the planking. To Ronnie Scartoon it sounded like sleeping inside someone's mouth. It was the best sleep she'd ever gotten.

Ronnie Scartoon smiles at Ashlyn Aschenbecher.

The waiter brings the check in a black vinyl billfold. Ronnie Scartoon stuffs her credit card into it and hands it back to him. He disappears.

"Can I buy you a drink?" Ronnie Scartoon asks. And because it is good to vary locations on first dates, she suggests, "Somewhere not here. We can go to a different place."

Ashlyn Aschenbecher nods, says, "Yes." Then, "Let's go to my place. Have one there."

Ronnie notices the plants on this patio are loaded with flowers. She can smell them all around.

The waiter returns. Ronnie Scartoon tips and signs. They exit, walk to the car. Ronnie gets the car door for Ashlyn Aschenbecher. She walks around the front of her car, locks her focus on the parking meter across the street, frowns slightly, tries to appear distracted so that Ashlyn Aschenbecher won't know what she's really thinking, which is she just hopes Ashlyn Aschenbecher thinks Ronnie Scartoon looks good as she crosses in front of her car to get to the other side.

THE WALLS in Ashlyn's room are dark purple. She explains she's hardly changed her room since the eleventh grade, when she really liked dark purple, often imagined turning an eggplant inside out and sleeping in it. Ashlyn flicks on her desk lamp. The shade is blue, so the light is blue. Lamplight plus walls and Ronnie thinks it is a little like being underwater, or on the moon. Ashlyn leaves and returns with a glass and a short, fat bottle of port Ronnie recognizes from the supermarket. Ashlyn pours the glass full. She hands it to Ronnie. It is a thick and heavy one. There are bubbles trapped frozen in the glass. It was probably blown from a glowing orange blob on one end of a long tube, someone's lungs deflating on the other.

Ronnie leans against Ashlyn's desk. Ashlyn's room smells faintly of cedar. Ashlyn sits on her bed. Ronnie thinks of Ashlyn sitting on this bed in high school, while Ronnie sat on her own bed in high school, thinking of Ashlyn. Ronnie takes a gulp of port. She holds it in her mouth and sucks it through her teeth. It is sweet and leggy and tastes like it should be hot. Ronnie remembers gym and Ashlyn changing at her locker, the locker door wide open like an arm—out, extended, ready to greet and hug. Ronnie imagined the locker arm hooking around her shoulder, arcing slowly, getting hold of Ashlyn Aschenbecher too, and folding her into its scoop, closing. Shutting the two of them into the locker. *Clank, click*, dark. And there is the sound of their breathing in the long metal box. Their faces inches apart. Hipbones, thighs, knees touching. Ankles and feet tangled. And through the vented grill, three cuts of light.

Ashlyn Aschenbecher stands in front of Ronnie Scartoon, watches Ronnie Scartoon. She pulls her shirt over her head, drops it at the foot of her bed. There are ash stains in the folds. Ronnie stops breathing while an electric eel swishes around the back of Ronnie's skull, slides down the length of her spine, bites the meat between her coccyx and her pubic bone, firing crackling gold heat all the way up her back, through her neck, across her face, incinerating her scalp.

Ashlyn looks at Ronnie like she's been looking at Ronnie all night, like she hasn't just taken her shirt off. Her skin looks iridescent. The highlights on her shoulders and across her collarbone match the white reflections on her ashtrays. Ronnie notices the rings on Ashlyn's skin, through the glass, rimming the ashtrays. Darker in four evenly spaced spots. And her nipples, plum in this light, flattened like thumbprints. There are Ashlyn's ribs pressing against the backside of her skin.

Ronnie places her hands on Ashlyn's shoulders. Ronnie's hands fold over her shoulders. At her fingertips, Ashlyn's wing blades. At her thumbtips, the dip at the base of Ashlyn's neck.

Her face like a large leaf, Ashlyn looks at Ronnie and says quietly, "Make a fist."

Ronnie removes her right hand from Ashlyn's shoulder. Holds

it between them. Makes a fist, her thumb tucked deep into her fingers.

Ashlyn looks at Ronnie's face and then down at her fist. She says, "See if it fits."

She holds her right fist in front of Ashlyn's left ashtray. She pushes her fist into the ashtray. She presses her knuckles against the glass. The shallow glass wall rings her fist, pinches it lightly. Ronnie's fist fits snug. Ashlyn's nipple is behind Ronnie's middle finger. Ronnie thinks she can feel it. The ashtray gives a bit, into Ashlyn's breast, beneath the glass, under Ronnie's fist.

Henchmen

I AM VERY angry. A surprising, seething rage new to myself. A result of my unfixed, reconfigured heart? Maybe. Maybe the ravaging of the poor muscle in my chest has disrupted the distribution of natural chemicals carried through my bloodstream. From brain to body and back, maybe it has loused up the delivery of appropriate neurochemicals at the appropriate times. Tipped things inside of me and knocked me full of wrath. Maybe might have. Because I'm meeting a new shade of me. Hi, hey, hello, me. Ready to off Kelly Green?

My Love is not. He is forgiving and patient. He doesn't understand that certain things should never be messed with. He doesn't understand that if they are, retribution must be paid. So I left him. I left My Love to kill Kelly Green.

A sharp pain stinging deep in my chest, and on my skin, marks—small, short slashes vandalizing the flesh at my breastbone. What from? The Floodgates of Love twined My Love and me tightly. When I split on the train away from him, the splice snapped. My end hurtled back at me, lashed my chest, wrecked it further.

I rode far, exited onto the platform of the station in the town where Kelly Green lives. My Love, he is still somewhere. In the bomb shelter, maybe. Maybe he moved to a new place. Is making masks, sipping lager, eating grapefruit, smelling good. Somewhere. I don't care. We don't talk.

I am hiding out in places where I don't think I'll be found. I got two jobs, each under a different name. The other baristas at Starbucks know me as so-and-so. At Blockbuster I scare all the patrons when I shout, "Welcome to Blockbuster!" as they walk in the door. My nametag reads something else. No one knows my real name. Or that I changed it when I was with him. No one knows that in the pit of a bomb shelter by the shore, My Love and I, with contact paper, permanent ink, and a palette of off-whites, altered my state driver's license, my passport, and my birth certificate. We wrote my new name: His Love. Which became my real name, for a time. Which none of all matters now because My Love and I, we're done.

But recently, and quietly, I held my His Love documents up to the light, at just the right angle. I saw his fingerprints smudged into the sticky side of the contact paper pressed against my driver's license, my passport, my birth certificate. I peeled off the contact paper, looked closely at his prints—maybe a thumb, a forefinger. I considered keeping the contact paper. A memory of his fingertips. I stuck it to my thigh. Left it there for a day. Then yanked it off, threw it out. I shredded the remaining documents. Took the scraps, threw them out. No more His Love. I chopped my hair short. I bought glasses.

I work in Kelly Green's town. Because Kelly Green lives here, the Target in this town is supposedly the best in the world. It's cleaner and larger. The staff is happier and better looking. And it's stocked fuller than all the other Targets. If a person shopping at another Target in another part of the country wants something, and the Target that person is at is out of stock, it will be in stock at Kelly Green's Target. Why? To what end? Not for Kelly Green. There's no way Kelly Green shops at Target. Kelly Green doesn't need to save money by buying crap. I know this. I've seen it. I've seen Kelly Green. Kelly Green wears big, black, designer sunglasses with blinding diamonds set into the frame. Not available at Target.

Where do I stay? Kelly Green lives near a camping park. I stole some items from Target: a tent, flashlight, dust masks, bungee cords, sparkling wine. I camp in the park. When I'm not working or camping in the park, I stake out the Kelly Green compound. I hide in the mushroom field behind the site. Careful not to kick the big mushrooms that release spores that will infect my lungs— a terrible mushroom danger—I watch for Kelly Green through the binoculars that were My Love's and mine in the bomb shelter. I can see into Kelly Green's study.

Kelly Green appears slightly shorter than the average man, a bit taller than the average woman. Kelly Green smokes long, black cigarettes that are likely very expensive and definitely very rare because I haven't been able to find them at any gas stations, and they are not available at Target. Kelly Green smokes them from a holder that, from my vantage point, looks like it's high-karat gold. Probably is. Kelly Green has long, light brown hair and round shoulders. Kelly Green wears a nice coat that complements those big, black, diamonded sunglasses and the cigarettes in that holder. The coat camouflages the shape of Kelly Green's body. Kelly Green's walk is graceful and rhythmic like a ballerina or a cowboy. It's the confident and powerful walk of a rich businessperson. The sex of Kelly Green? I still don't know. I don't care. Kelly Green can remain sexless in my mind forever. That's good for me. In battle, its best soldiers don't know the personal details of their enemies on the battlefield.

There are a few important things I do know: At any moment, there's a strong chance I'll get snuffed out. Kelly Green has henchmen. They are after me. They are after me for two reasons: (1) They must kill me before I kill Kelly Green. Or maybe after I kill Kelly Green, whichever comes first. (2) They want The Floodgates of Love.

They are sly. They come to me in the disguise of dates.

How do I walk into their fields of view? I incriminate myself. What is the purpose of killing someone if that person doesn't know why you are doing it? This is why killers send death threats before acting on their hurt feelings. So the person getting the curtains closed on him or her will know it's because he or she fucked up. And he or she can suffer some remorse and regret over having fucked up because look where it got him or her: nearly dead. En route to being killed. That's what a revenge seeker wants. A revenge seeker wants the victim to know.

I launch a copy of the letter Kelly Green sent to My Love and me, back when we were still working directly with Kelly Green. It is the letter that ruined The Floodgates of Love. The letter that changed the name of The Floodgates of Love to Juicy Sweetheart Suckers and forbade us from whispering our Wish List over the loudspeakers during the final phase of production. I write "FUCK YOU" in blood pricked from my finger all over Kelly Green's typed text. Crush and wad the letter around a stone for weight so it sails solidly through the air. I chuck it into the window of Kelly Green's study. I am surprised by how good I feel about this.

1.

Tom, he is the first. With him I am on to nothing, don't notice clues when they appear. He picks me up after work. He takes me to a bar. It is a bar full of old drinking men. I have not been on a date in a long while. I am shy, awkward, distracted. I have murder on my mind. I look to the TV and watch the sports that play across it. I try to seem interested in the sports so Tom doesn't think I'm not talking because I'm shy and awkward and planning an assassination. We drink. I down my whiskey fast, order another.

During a commercial break, Tom says, "Would you like to meet my father?"

"Your father is here?" I ask.

"Yes." He takes me by the hand down the bar. Taps the shoulder of a man reading a paper and sipping from a snifter. "Meet my dad," says Tom. "Meet Thomas."

Thomas sparkles at me. "Well hello!" he says and shakes my hand. Tom excuses himself and goes to the restroom. I stand next to his father. Thomas smiles. He wears a fancy suit. His cuff links twinkle like the surface of the ocean.

"I like your cuff links," I say. The spice of his cologne claws the inside of my nostrils.

"Thank you," he says. "They are great indoors. Very romantic by candlelight." He smiles. His upper lip disappears into a line. Earlier I noticed his son's smiling lip does the same. "But in the sunlight," Thomas continues, "they are radiant."

"I'll bet," I say. I adjust a stool, arrange myself on the vinyl seat next to his, and while I generally don't enjoy talking to strangers, I try. "So," I say, "what's your job? What do you do?"

"I'm retired," he says and looks away for a beat. He turns back toward me and whispers, "And I write poetry."

"Huh," I say. "Great." I wonder for a moment if he's the banker who built the bomb shelter. This jerks a current from my heels to my brainstem, reminding me of My Love. Reminding me: My Love and I are over. I smack myself upside my head inside myself. Tell myself to remember. Over.

The father pulls his briefcase from the floor onto the bar. He snaps open the brass locks. The lid eases open. Inside there are only papers and a thing that looks like a holster. "Would you like to read some of my poetry?" he asks in a way that is kind of pompous.

"Alright," I say. He hands me several sheets of paper with stanzas on them. The paper is stationery—the kind made to look like marble. Paper decorated with varicose veins so it resembles expensive rock. Suddenly I do not want to read the poems. But he is right here and I can't fake it.

He writes gooily about some woman and some children. About

daughters. Interestingly, nowhere is any suggestion of his son. There are waterfalls. And sunsets. And sunrises. He is not the bomb shelter poet. And except for one line about feeding glass to someone who looked sideways at his boss, his poems remind me of greeting cards. I hate greeting cards.

Tom returns from the restroom. His father scoops the poems into his briefcase, snaps it shut, returns it to the floor. I shift quickly in my seat, cross my legs like a lady. The father and I, we act as if nothing happened.

Tom asks if we've been chatting.

"Yes," I say. "Getting to know your dad."

"What are you guys talking about?"

"Not much," I reply. "Mostly work."

"Did you tell him about Blockbuster?"

"Yes," I lie.

"Dad, did she tell you that's where we met?"

"Yes," he lies. Sometimes men tell women things they won't tell men.

We go back to our end of the bar. We drain our drinks and order more. Then drain, then more. I am quiet. I shouldn't get to know people; I'm about to commit a heavy crime. Tom tells me about himself. He tells me about the Asian girl in his sink. In his kitchen, he was boiling vegetables for a soup. He opened his freezer, scrounging for a snack. He found an open bag of frozen crawdads. He reached in to grab some. When he touched the crawdads, one moved. Tom withdrew his hand, and the crawdad climbed out of the bag and onto the freezer door and leapt into the green kitchen sink. Tom turned on the water to try to wash it down the drain because it reminded him of a spider, and he got scared. The water activated the crawdad, reminded it of its natural habitat. Fortified, it scrambled around the sink. Tom turned on the hot water, hoping to boil the crawdad to a steaming red. The water was not hot enough. He took the boiling vegetable soup from the stove to pour on the crawdad, but the crawdad grew, quickly. An immediate change, it grew into a small Asian girl, about four years old, in a blue and yellow one-piece bathing suit. She took the pot from Tom and poured the soup on herself, screaming and crying. Tom tried to get the pot from her, but couldn't. Couldn't touch the pale of her skin. He left the kitchen screaming, sat in the living room crying harder than came naturally. He moaned and ached, swallowed and gasped, like he was drowning.

"When was this?" I ask. I tip my glass back. The ice slides down the side of the glass and knocks into my front teeth.

"A few years ago," he says, slowly stabbing the ice in his drink with a small red straw. "It's happened to me a few times." He takes a long slurp.

"Oh," I say. "But did it really happen?" I ask. "Or do you think you imagined it?"

"It happened," he says and nods his head.

"Oh," I say. "But not for a few years?" We are date talking, chitchatting.

"No," he says. "Not since I started my current job."

"What's your job?"

He pauses, then, "I work security," he says quickly. He looks into his glass. "You?"

"Blockbuster."

"That's right. I knew that."

The bartender smiles as he pours drinks. The mound of ice in the well reflects in his glasses when he looks down to scoop. His face is large and round and flat. His face belongs to the man in the moon. He tops off our cocktails and winks. I look at Tom and blink slowly. I have had several whiskeys.

"You do any drugs?" he asks casually.

"No," I tell him and shrug.

He shrugs too and gulps most of his drink. The bartender in his straight slacks and soft shoes leans against his side of the bar and talks to some of the men down at the other end. He gestures with his hand and arm, in what looks like slow motion.

"Wanna see a card trick?" Tom asks.

I turn toward him. The room follows. My vision is a step behind the movement of my head. I say, "Okay."

He pulls a deck of cards from his jacket pocket. He juggles a whole deck between his sleek white fingers. He wears a pinky ring in the shape of the letters KGH. It reflects the candlelight on the bar. In these moments, his hands handsome and agile, I see the Three-Whiskey Gazelle. I haven't seen the Three-Whiskey Gazelle since the last time I was single. Before My Love. Before my acrobat. The thought of her ripples through me. She flips a somersault in my throat, plunges through my center, splashes into the bottom of my belly. I catch my breath and take a long pull from my glass and am quickly full and fat and smiley with the notion that drinking is so fun. I watch Tom's hands fondle the deck of cards while the Three-Whiskey Gazelle bounds across the soft dirt path of my mind. Its coat afire in the smoky reds of a setting sun, muscles shifting gracefully beneath its hide. Trailing after it like a kite on a short string is a sign reading GO AHEAD AND FUCK HIM! I sigh. Admire the gazelle. I excuse myself and go to the bathroom. Under fluorescent lights I try to pull my face together. Swab just below my lower lids with some toilet paper. Reapply lipstick. I breathe deeply. Waltz back into the bar. Tom's placed the cards on the bar top and is picking at a basket of popcorn. I elbow up close to him.

"You want to see the trick?" he asks.

"How about you show me your place," I say. My tongue is slow in my mouth.

I don't follow when, in his bed, he talks about "enhancing the experience." We are naked. I look him up and down. He is a long, thin, naked guy. The room sways. I am very drunk. His cheeks flushed, breath sooty with burnt popcorn, pasty with booze, he's climbed onto me. His face hovering above mine, he says, "You got anything, maybe, to enhance the experience?"

I struggle to pull his face into focus. I can't. It is too close to mine. "What?" I ask.

"Like. Enhance the experience," he says. "You know, turn it up a notch?" I think he is smiling. I don't know what he is talking about. "Do you have anything?" he asks. His voice is tight.

Because I am confused and want to stop with wherever this conversation is going, I say, "No," and pull him close to me. And into me. And he groans. No more talking.

IN THE morning his upstairs neighbors play music. I hear the muffled strumming of a guitar, maybe some singing. The sounds seep through the ceiling and settle onto Tom's bed like a mist. I breathe it in heavily, the tone of it drowning the sacs of my lungs. He is still asleep next to me. My head is thick, my stomach soupy. I lean over the side of his bed afraid I might be sick. Under his bed I see five handguns. Just there, under the bed, side by side on a towel. The air valves in my throat cinch shut. I slide from the bed, pull on some of my clothes, stumble to the bathroom. I throw up, quietly. I don't want to wake Tom and get shot. I don't leave, for fear I'll get shot. Panicked, I don't want to stay. Sick from the whiskey and now the guns, I stagger into the living room. I lie down on the couch for a moment, to gather my balance. I lean my head over the side of the couch. Sometimes blood in my head makes me feel better. I see a shoebox under the couch. It looks old. The edges are worn and the lid sags. I think maybe in it he keeps important things. Maybe another gun. But maybe Tom has a license for guns. He works security. He could be a nice, safe gun owner. I listen closely. I hear him breathe in the other room. It is the heavy breathing that means sleep. I carefully pull out the shoebox. Not even a scrap of tape to keep it closed. I lift the lid. Yes, indeed, the things of his life. I find a concert stub. An empty book of matches with a phone number scrawled across the flap, a flattened beer can, a train ticket, a glass tube and a sooty glass pipe, a class ring, yellowing pictures from his youth—he wore a T-shirt under his suit jacket to some dance. His date had curly bangs. In another, the most obvious picture in the world: He holds a big fish by its wide mouth on a dock in front of the ocean. I unfold a packet of papers. It's a contract. There's the red bull's-eye Target logo, bright and blaring. There is Kelly Green's embossed insignia right next to it. The blood in all my veins stops. I see Tom's messy brown signature. On the contract, there's fine print. I struggle to make it out: *In the case of accidental and/or wrongful death, injury, or threat to employer Kelly Green, members of the KGH are to avenge any losses incurred—physical, emotional, prideful, or otherwise—seeking terminal revenge on behalf of Kelly Green.* Tom signed his name in what looks like blood.

My mind is working slowly, gears muscling through muck. I fold up the contract, tuck it back into the box, lid it, push it back under the couch. I creep around. I find a slip of paper near his phone. I find a pen on his kitchen counter. On the stove is a large pot of water. Just there. I remember his story. I'd forgotten it, but now I remember. Might he have meant to boil it, dump it on me, scald me to a wet crisp before shooting me dead? Was that what that was about? I feel sicker. I jot a note—*Thanks for a super time. Forgot I have to work this* AM. *Will take bus. Sleep tight!* I creep to the bathroom, lick the back of the note so it sticks to his mirror. I exit swiftly.

In the elevator I sweat. I bolt to the campsite, booze fumes from the night before evaporating from my skin. I zip myself into my tent, terrified.

Do I run? No. Do I hide? No. Do I change my mind about Kelly Green? No. My resolve is strengthened. I proceed carefully, stealthily.

Night falls and I dart silently from campsite to compound. I lie low in the mushroom field, my eyelashes bent against the lenses in my binoculars. I look for Kelly Green. For Tom. For others. I spy none. I puzzle over my date with Tom.

Back in the bomb shelter My Love and I drew up a product description for The Floodgates of Love:

Once ingested, The Floodgates of Love take a body by surprise. They make every receptor cell swim to the surface of the water you feel like you've become. Your brain does not function like normal, though you are still safe to do things like operate a vehicle or heavy machinery. But it's not likely you would want to because it is like all of what is inside you—the parts that transition your insides to your outsides, to the air and to the world—all of that is engulfed with a feeling that is wet and humming. It is like you are that small town in Hawaii in the 1940s and the feeling is like the tsunami that swallowed the town whole. People got lost in that tsunami. They were sucked into the middle of the ocean with pieces of homes and stores and vegetation. But you are alive and in love.

This product description wasn't released with the product because the product released wasn't even our product. It was Kelly Green's Juicy Sweetheart Suckers. Its description written, no doubt, by copywriters from the Kelly Green marketing team. Because Kelly Green is a jackass who doesn't understand that one should never destroy then market something that two people create out of certain love. And for that and this fury in me, Kelly Green will pay.

But I figured something out. Tom was confused. The Floodgates of Love are not drugs. Not drugs. Do they feel like drugs? I don't know. I don't do drugs. But I have a hunch. Similar maybe to some drugs, they make you feel love-drunk and creamy. And radiant, and glinting, and magnificent. They blitz a fiery love fever through partners, but it's my bet they might also charge a single person with paroxysms of delight. So, the KGH, probably being members of Kelly Green's inner circle, likely sampled the real Floodgates of Love when My Love and I left leave-behinds after our initial meeting with, not Kelly Green, but several other Target representatives. They've tasted of and tumbled in the rapture of the true Floodgates of Love. Which are long gone now. And they want more.

2.

I meet the second at Starbucks. In line for coffee, some scruff on his face and smiling, he stares at me. I do not make eye contact. I never make eye contact. Especially now that I know they're after me. At the counter he orders a medium mocha with nonfat milk. "Three-o-five," I say after punching some buttons. He dips his hand into his breast pocket. I notice the flash of his pinky ring: three golden letters, KGH. I'm catching on.

"Your name?" I ask.

"Harry."

With a black marker I write Harry on a grande cup. He pulls out his wallet. Hands me five bills. Says, "Please keep the change." He smiles and walks to the other end of the counter. Eventually he gets his coffee. Dresses it with brown sugar and mocha dust. He comes back around to the register. "Excuse me," says he, "You have nice eyes." I look at him, then behind him at the other customers. I hope he will see me concerned about the other customers and he will feel uncomfortable and leave. He moves his head to catch my eyes and hold my gaze. "Would you like to go out sometime?" he smiles.

To go out, knowingly, with a henchman who's got a hit out on you. What do you do? I smile at him and say, "No, thanks, I can't."

He says, "Why not?"

I lie, "I'm involved."

He says, "Come on. It'll be fun."

And I say, "Okay." And I am surprised and fascinated by myself. In that moment I decide I am ready for the thrill of avoiding getting murdered on a date. I have not yet killed Kelly Green. Why? What am I waiting for? Quietly, in the dark of my mind, I think, perhaps, I am scared. And so I reason with myself: If I can avoid getting murdered on a date, I can certainly kill Kelly Green.

"When do you get off?" asks Harry.

"Six."

"How about I come back then?"

"Great," I say.

Harry smiles and exits. One of the other baristas, a really pretty girl who dates customers all the time, raises one groomed eyebrow to a point on her forehead and nods approvingly.

HE RETURNS at six. Takes me to the bar. The same bar Tom took me to. We pass from fading sunshine into smoky dark. My eyes adjust. The same men are here. I see the moon-faced bartender. "Hiya, Harry!" he says, scooping ice into a tumbler. He winks at me. "Harris," he says to one of the men on the stools, "Your boy's here."

Harris pitches himself forward energetically. "Hey there, Harry!" he says and takes a pull from his beer. He looks young. Younger than the other old men. Harry introduces us. I saw him here last time. He was a stranger then, and now we meet. Harris's handshake is rubbery like old celery. Beyond him I see Tom's dad, Thomas. We look at each other. His face changes not at all. I don't say anything. I keep my guard up. "Look at you!" says Harris. "I've got a girlfriend too, you know. She's taller than me. Pushing six feet." I consider telling him I'm not Harry's girlfriend. "Beautiful, she is. But won't come in the bar," he says and whaps his son on the arm. To the bartender he says, "Get these kids anything they want!" The bartender nods. Pulls a bottle of beer from the cooler, pops its top for Harry. He pours a tall glass of whiskey over ice for me, smiling—maybe because he remembers my drink.

Harry and I sit at one end of the bar, several stools and earshot away from his young father. Harry swigs golden beer. I notice he swigs like his father. Throws his head back and bares his front teeth. The beer gurgles past them and down his throat. We sit for a while, watching sports on the bar TV. Waiting for the alcohol to kick in. Harry finishes his beer. Orders another and a shot. "You want a shot?" he asks me.

"Sure," I say.

"Tequila?"

"Alright."

"I call it a beer and a bump," says Harry.

"That's fine," I say.

We shoot. And then again. I am surprised the henchmen are allowed to drink so much on duty. I am not allowed to drink at Blockbuster or Starbucks. They made that very clear in orientation. Harry's face now looks peaceful. He tells me a story. He tells me he had a child. No longer, but once he was a young dad. He had a girlfriend. She was young too. Both sixteen, unmarried with child, living in the garage behind his father's house. The baby was born with a condition. It was a miniature. A whole baby, but very tiny. It fit in the palm of Harry's hand. It hardly cried. It slept a lot and smiled. Its mouth was the size of an adult eyelash. Harry's girl took care of it mostly, for two months, before it passed away. The day it passed away Harry was in charge. His girl had to go into the high school and take her last test before she was officially considered educated enough to be through with school.

Harry washed his hands carefully and held the baby in his palm. He fed it a bit of milk through an eyedropper. He stroked its cheek with the very tip of his finger. The day seemed long; his palms grew sweaty. He didn't want the baby to bathe in its father's perspiration. He put it in his shirt pocket. It gurgled peacefully like it was relaxing in a hammock. Harry sat on his bed, listened to the traffic charge down the street outside. He fell asleep face-down. He woke and wrenched himself from the bed as if all the muscles were ripped from his bones by an electrical current. The sounds in the room went out of his ears and were replaced by a high-pitched, deafening hum, fear screaming through the rivulets in his brain. He swallowed. Checked his pocket. Pulled the little baby from its cotton den. It smiled. It was okay.

He was painfully careful with the baby for the rest of the day. Except when he misplaced it in his messenger bag. He was looking for a magazine and some paper. The baby slipped into the front zippered compartment. Again, the panic swept through him. This second time through his body, it felt like an illness. He emptied out his bag, terrified his baby had been stabbed by a pencil or keys. It slid out, smiling. Its legs shorter than half-smoked cigarettes, kicking. Scooping his baby into his palm, this time he couldn't swallow. His throat seized dry. His eyeballs burned dry. He sat quietly on the couch, sickeningly alert, holding his baby in his hands on his lap.

An hour before his girl was due to arrive, Harry fixed dinner. He fixed a pot of stew on the hot plate near the small refrigerator. He set the table with one hand. The other held his child. He ladled out two bowls of stew. One for his girl, one for him. Spoon in one hand, baby in the other, he sat down at the table and waited for his girl. He set down the spoon, picked up the remote, and turned on the TV. He watched the game intently. His baby shifted in his hand, slid into the bowl of stew. Harry didn't hear the dim splurch over the loud commercial break. Eventually he ran both his hands through his hair, massaging his own scalp. It had been a long day. It took a second for him to realize he had both hands free. The dread rocked through him for the third time. His face fell toward the bowl. He saw the back of his baby's head breaking the surface of the stew like a bump. He saw its small diaper floating like a potato. He lifted his baby out of the bowl. It had drowned.

Harry's face is twisted and red, thinking about his miniature baby. The man in the moon refreshes our drinks. Harry pours mouthfuls of beer between his lips. I glug too. I hate this story of his. It's gone into a spot in my brain where the volume is so loud. I feel a panic in me I can't squash. I wonder if it's my guts telling me he's going to kill me. He signals the bartender. More tequila in those little glasses.

I go home with Harry. He drives us blindly, pressing his palm to his shirt pocket, glancing down to check it. We arrive at his place, my sensibilities pitched and plunged in tequila and whiskey. We sit on his bed. I picture guns beneath it and am scared. Then a picture of his little baby in a bowl of stew sticks to my mindscreen and sweat slicks all my skin.

I watch Harry. He holds his breast pocket and shakes his head. He looks so pained. His story, his face, make me want to cut a tube from my brain matter—from temple to temple—and throw it in the ocean. He moves closer to me. Suddenly I wonder how he will try to do me in.

"I wish I could feel better," he says. "I want to feel better."

"I know," I say. I too feel disquieted. And in this state, in his room, by his hand, maybe I'll die.

I try to scope his room inconspicuously. I pretend to stretch so I can look around a bit.

"You don't understand," Harry snivels. "I need to change the way I feel on the inside." He smears his nose on his sleeve. "On the underside of my skin all over, I feel terrible." His eyes are bloodshot, his lips loose.

"I get it," I tell him.

He continues, "Do you think you could help me?"

"I don't think so," I say gently. I think I know what he wants. "I don't have what you want."

"Check your purse," he pleads.

"Un-uh," I shake my head and pat his face. The room rocks like a boat. "It's not in there."

"Please," he moans. He stands, takes my purse, empties it onto the bed. Lipstick, mascara, mints, Blockbuster card, a packet of Starbucks brown sugar, a tent stake, a ten and two fives, some change. No Floodgates of Love.

He drops his face into his hands, rubs his forehead, then lifts his head and steps toward the sliding glass door in his room. He flicks the lock, glides it open, exits onto a balcony, leans heavily against the railing. I follow. I lean also and peer over the thin beam. There is a pool way down there. It glows green below us. He is breathing loudly, staring into the pool. He could probably grab me by the back of my neck and flip me over this railing. This building is tall, we are high up. I might not make it into the water from here. I might break in half on the pool lip or crash onto those lounge chairs, then bounce into the pool, facedown. He could drown me to death. I step away from the railing, grab hold of Harry's hand, pull him back into the room and onto his bed. His face is still a wreck. I hold him. Then I take my clothes off. Then his.

IN THE morning his sleeping face looks calmer, finally. But I've got an anvil of fear crushing my sternum. The time has come, I am sure, for him to be a real henchman. A meek part of me wishes he would step on it—if anything, to stop the story of his drowned baby from whimpering through my mind. I hold my breath and shut my eyes and try to zip my brain silent and white.

We lie side by side in his big bed. I notice his bed is soft and fluffy. I don't think his comforter is from Target. It's like a cloud. It is too expensive to be from Target. I think Kelly Green must pay the henchmen well.

Harry wakes slowly and stretches his arms above his head. I am paralyzed. Probably he is reaching behind his mattress for a gun or maybe a knife. I gasp, but it is drowned in the howl of his yawn. His body contracts back to normal, and he looks at me and blinks. His eyes are puffy. In his hands, no guns, no knives. Perhaps he keeps them elsewhere.

"Are you going to blow my head off?" I ask.

"What?"

"Will you slit my throat?"

"What are you talking about?" he asks, the blankness of his face matching the pillowcase.

"It's okay," I say. "Never mind." He is a professional. He's going to get me, or one of them will get me, and it will be a surprise.

He stares at the center of my chest.

"What are these from?" He fingers the marks gently. They ache like a deep purple bruise.

"Ow," I say and steer his hand away. "They surfaced when I left."

"Left where?" he asks.

"Whom," I say.

"Left whom?" he asks.

"My Love," I say.

"Where's your love now?" asks he.

"My Love. I don't know. He's underground, I guess." I scour his chest. It is fairly hairy. His skin is obscured beneath. I touch the center of his chest, try to press aside some hairs so I can see if he's marked too. I think he might be. "How about you? How about these?" I ask, squinching at what might be marks.

He turns to me, narrows his eyes, and tightens his jaw, says "You know," then swats aside my hand. He looks away, folds his hands behind his head, broods.

Two things: One, I've made him mad. And mad might get me killed. Two, what is "you know"? Do I know? Does he mean I know they're from The Floodgates of Love? Is that what he thinks I know? I am thrown and panicky and unable to ask what he means. My mouth and throat and everywhere else in me feel packed with sand. I think, this is it. I hold my breath and watch him motionlessly from the corner of my eye. His hands remain behind his head. I still don't move. How does one prepare oneself for possible imminent and fatal retribution? I don't know. I imagine some might run. Steer clear of menace. Avoid potentially threatening situations. But I'm not doing that. Instead, I feel myself listening carefully to the air. Listening for the shift in the white noise—the warning that precedes danger. It is normal to step out of the way of a terrible sound. But what about listening harder, peering into it, scared and excited? What is it? How will it unfold?

3.

Number three's name is Dick. He finds me in New Releases. Asks me about a slasher film with a bunch of young, freshly scrubbed actors. I tell him I hate young, freshly scrubbed actors. He laughs loudly, slaps his knee. His pinky ring glints: KGH, yellow gold. I'm onto them now. He asks me out, I say yes. I'm feeling fatigued, always hungover, sexed-out with strangers. If I'm killed before Kelly Green at this rate, so be it.

Dick takes me to the dark bar to visit his father. His father has thick, hard hands folded on the bar top. His nails are opaque and dense. Limestone fingertips. I'd seen him here the other two times. These men, I think, are here every day. Dick's father drinks scotch and water and delicately wipes his mustache and beard with a cocktail napkin after every sip. Except for the movement of his mouth pronouncing words, Dick's face remains still as he introduces me to his father. Dick's eyes do not smile.

"This is my father," he says, like lead. "This is Richard."

His father animates slowly, takes my hand, shakes and pats it. Turns to the barkeep and says whatever we want is on him. Whatever we want for this first round. He sips from his glass, wipes his mouth, folds his hands, and looks into his scotch. He watches cubes of ice shrink in his glass.

I see Thomas. I see Harris. They both ignore me. They stare into their drinks.

I'm wondering if henchmanship is a family business. An inherited position. Maybe these fathers were henchmen for another big conglomerate back in the day. Maybe the fathers worked for the president of Sears or Penney's. Perhaps they understand what's going down. Don't want to make like they know me for fear that I might catch on and foil the hit. Perhaps they ignore me now because they don't want to get attached because soon I will be dead. They don't want to feel bad or miss me. Or maybe they were actually very drunk and don't recall meeting me.

Dick and I sit in a booth in a corner of the bar, behind the fathers, their backs lined side by side like gorilla dominos. There are dark curtains hanging from the ceiling and down two sides of the booth. It feels hidden. Dick is the first henchman to seat me over here. He is square jawed and handsome. Brawny, full of muscles. His chest bricks against his shirt. His arms on the table-top look heavy and tight, bouldery like bludgeons.

He leans toward me and says, "See this." He pulls aside the collar of his shirt to reveal a raised band of pink flesh. It's a scar. Tattooed directly on top of the scar are chain links. I haven't looked closely at a tattoo in a long while. I breathe into the bottom of my feet and take a big sip from my drink. Dick pulls his collar looser; the tattooed scar runs a ring around his neck, like a necklace. Most of the scar's about as thick as a lady's finger. It thins out in parts—swoops delicately across the front of his neck, beneath his Adam's apple. It appears wider and blotted in sections around the back of his neck. The tattooed chain links vary in size according to the width of the scar.

He tells me about soap operas and his mother. As a kid, his head on his mother's lap on the couch, she patted the side of his face while they watched soap operas together. She loved soap operas. Loved especially the soap opera actors. Look at all those beautiful men, she'd say. And then Dick would watch the beautiful men kiss and make love to the beautiful women in silky beds, on leather couches, in luxury automobiles. It seemed like quite the life, but sadly it was all make-believe. Then Dick realized that those beautiful men were just actors whose job it was to make out with beautiful women actresses, for a lot of money. The reality of the make-believe, he realized, was also quite the life. It became the life he wanted. He would be a soap opera actor. He practiced on his sister's old dolls that she'd left in the back of her closet after she'd moved out. Dick would line up the dolls alongside his bed and make out with each one of them and then lay them flat in a row along the carpet, take off his clothes, and roll back and forth across the lineup. Their plastic doll parts jabbed his young naked body, left sprays of pink nicks across his skin.

Then his mom's body failed her and she died. Dick was left with his dad who was angry and mean and quickly lost the house—so they were out. But Dick's dad dated lots of women. A different woman each week; Richard tugged his son along to their apartments and houses, where they both stayed, one week at a time. Dick would sleep on the girlfriends' couches while he overheard his dad and whichever girlfriend have sex in her room. The sounds were never like those of the soap operas. The sounds were like burglars ransacking a place—lifting and overturning heavy things while the lady of the home whimpered or moaned. In the mornings Dick couldn't bare to look at the ladies who were not his mom. He kept his head down and ignored them. When his dad would say, "Say good morning to so-and-so, Dick," Dick wouldn't. The girlfriend would inevitably feel mad about this and suggest Richard had raised a rude kid and they should find some other place to stay. Then, with a full-grown man's fist, Richard would clock Dick in the back of his head.

"Every week, the same thing," Dick tells me, his head pitched toward mine in the dark booth. "Ages eight to fifteen," he says looking deeply into the veneer swirls in the tabletop. "Here's some math," he says. "That's seven years. Take fifty-two weeks in a year. Times that by seven. That's three hundred and sixty-four blows to the back of my skull." He says this with the certainty of facts, like there was no plus or minus a few blows—exactly 364.

He says, "Feel this," and takes my hand and presses my fingers against the back of his head, where his neck meets his hair. He moves my hand all the way up the back of his head, through his hair, and around the crown. It feels hard and lumpy, unscalplike. Like an uneven patty of cement dried beneath his skin. "You feel that?" he asks.

"Yes."

He takes a swig of his red wine from a short, stemless glass. "My head produced that in reaction to my father's fucking punches." His lips are wet and dark with the wine. "That was my body trying to protect itself."

I look at his eyes. They've got all of what he just said, plus more, blazing in them. I look at the portion of his chain-linked scar I can see through his loosened collar. He notices and points a big finger at a link in the chain. "This, though," he says, "is from when I was fifteen. This thing"—he quickly slices his finger across the front of his neck, tracing the front section of his tattooed scar—"this thing's from the last time he belted me. He'd cracked me in the head for the last time." Dick's eyes flit his father's way, lance his father's wide back on his stool at the bar. "I was watching soap operas on one of his lady's TVs. The beautiful men were making love to the beautiful women"—he tilts his head and softens his lips and holds up one arm like he's cradling an invisible soap star woman—"and I could just see myself there." Dick's eyes shift. They roll back in his head gently. His eyebrows unknit, his face turns smooth, and he smiles like he's tasting the best food. "I could see myself in there, on the TV, in that job. I could feel it in my body." He glances back over at his dad and the softness leaves his face. "Then my dad and his girlfriend came out and said some shit to me, and I didn't answer, and my dad's fist blew into my head and"—he looks directly at me, his gaze steady as a weight—"that was it. I dove into the TV screen."

He'd thought, in a perfectly still moment, his dad's slug stinging his skull, that he could get there—to the set with the soap opera men and women. That he could step in and start up his life with them.

"Huh," I say.

He stares into his glass.

"When you crashed into it, did you ever feel," I ask him, "for maybe a second, that you'd actually got there?"

His breath comes deep from the bottom of his belly and he answers, "Yes."

The glass from the TV screen didn't mar his head on account of whatever calluses had developed there, but the jagged edges tore a scar all the way around his neck, like he'd leaned into the jaws of a shark. There are 364 links in the chain he had tattooed over the scar tissue.

"One for each of those women," Dick tells me. "One for each fucking crack at my head."

"I'm very sorry," I say, and I really mean it. I drink my whiskey and chew a cube of ice.

Later that night, my clothes in a heap on the floor at the foot of his bed, he stands naked sorting through them. He checks all my pockets, empties them. Lifts and shakes my clothes. "Nothing?" he asks, his voice metallic with anger.

"Nothing," I tell him. And tonight I carried no purse. He throws my clothes at the ground. He looks slowly toward a TV he's got on top of a chest of drawers. He is going to ramrod my head into the screen.

I take my bra off and lie back into his bed, call him over. When he is on top of me, I peer over his shoulder down the length of his prone body and notice how high his ass cheeks rise up beyond his lower back. Steep and solid.

I learn: He growls when he fucks. And during it all, he breaks the four fingers on my left hand. My face down and wawling into his pillow, he tells me to watch the fuck out. I leave quickly. It's still night.

My fingers splinted with chopsticks, taped up white, I hide out in the mushroom field. I realize I didn't check his chest. I recount: I didn't know to check Tom's chest, Harry's chest seemed to be a yes, and I couldn't get to looking at Dick's. Not enough evidence to put it all together, but no matter, because now I am a new kind of scared. I've been expecting to get killed, but I was not expecting to get my face shoved or my fingers broken. I don't know what I am expecting.

I surveil for several days. I ice and rewrap my fingers. I don't sleep. I plan. I decide it is time.

IN THE fields behind Kelly Green's compound, giant mushroom balloons swollen with fungal spores bulge heavily up out of the ground. Wearing a dust mask, I pick the biggest spore ball in the field with my right hand. It weighs a lot. Spore balls are meat heavy, like a fat baby. I hide it in a plastic trash bag behind some wild shrubs. In the night I pad quieter than shallow breath across the field. I've been doing surveillance all day. A car and driver arrived at dusk. Kelly Green ducked into the back seat smoking languorously from the golden cigarette holder, and from the looks of his or her fancy attire, is not likely to return until late in the night, champagne-drunk and sleepy.

I wait till dark. The weather is warm. The window to Kelly Green's study is open. I rig a makeshift catapult with a shovel and bungee cords. I hollow a hole in the earth and insert the handle of the shovel so the shovel stands upright like a scarecrow. I bend the shovel back; the handle is tough plastic and torques like a bow. I secure the bend with bungee cords hooked to tent stakes in the ground. I place the spore ball in the shovel scoop. I say a short prayer for accuracy and release the cords. The spore ball hurtles through the air and splats with a thud just below the window to Kelly Green's study. It explodes on the sill, belching spores all over the room.

Its innards exhaled, the rind drops to the ground by the side of the house, followed by cloudy ribbons of lingering spores. It lies in a heap, moist and heavy as old flesh. Luckily none of the help in the house seem to hear the thud or notice the spores settle a fine silt over all the surfaces in the study. It is wonderful when things that can go drastically wrong do not. I kick dirt into the hole I made and gather the shovel and cords and steaks. I sneak back to the campsite.

I wait. Kelly Green won't go quickly. Lung fungal death is slow. Subtle. It's a creeper.

4.

I meet a fourth. I don't catch his name, but his accent is German. I call him Hefeweizen. He drums his hands against the bar top, catching light on his ring and projecting a reflection of the letters KGH on my blouse. The reflection prances across my breast. I whack my good hand over my heart like I am trying to catch the letters. They dance over my knuckles.

We sit and drink. I can't believe I am on another date with a henchman. I am astonished by myself. My fingers crunched, my wits splintered, and here I am with number four. He approached and I agreed.

"Have you ever been to jail?" he asks me, bold German features barely moving as he speaks.

"No," I say and am sure that if any one of these henchmen decides to rat on me to the police, I will certainly go to jail. I've always been afraid I'd wind up in jail. And for a slow second I think to myself: In prison I won't have to work at Starbucks or Blockbuster. Or date like this. The prospect feels like relief.

"Tell me all the times you've broken bones," he says, looking at my taped fingers.

"My bones?" I ask, "Or someone else's?"

"Wow," he responds, shocked or impressed. "Either."

"Both," I say. And think back to my youth. I take a sip of whiskey. "I broke my arm when I fell off my bike when I was tiny." I think harder. "I broke a girl's rib—two ribs, I think, when I shoved her in an alley when we were little kids." I slow down and watch his face carefully. "And I broke these fingers recently." I look for a glimmer in his eyes, some recognition about the fingers. Do the henchmen converse? Does he know who did this?

Not even a glint. He nods his head, simply listening. We are silent for a moment. He has not introduced me to his father. A lone woman with short, straight, silky white hair and large blue eyes watches us. I have not seen her here before. Maybe she could be his mother. Could there have been henchwomen in the old days? There certainly don't seem to be any in these new days. Not a single young lady sporting a golden KGH on her pinky has crossed my path. But how neat if she would. She would kill me so differently. Maybe immediately. The silver-haired woman smiles slightly and blinks at me. I get nervous and look away from her. Occupy my brain with Hefeweizen's face.

Hefeweizen's face. His eyes are set deep into it, shadowed by his brow. Some dark understanding of the earth shifts beneath that brow. Maybe it is an understanding similar to that which accompanies lung fungal death. Is Kelly Green passing sudden wisdom on to the favored henchman Hefeweizen as Kelly Green dies? Was Hefeweizen born with it?

"What was your first job?" I ask him.

"I was a farmhand."

"In Germany?"

"Yes."

"There are farms in Germany?"

He smiles. His smile is rectangular, exposing both top and bottom rows. "Yes, there are farms. I was a hay baler, weed killer, and cotton stomper."

"I have never known a farmhand," I say. We look at each other. I wait for a story from his past. He tells me none. This is refreshing. This is a different kind of trip to the bar. We drink more.

We leave. The white-haired woman waves as we exit. I wave back, automatically, which surprises me. Hefeweizen notices none of this. We go to his home. He lives in one large room with a tiled floor. In his bed we are naked, lying on our backs, sweaty and a little sticky. It is still night. He lies to the right of me. I drape my right leg over his left. How we arrived in this position at this time,

I am not quite sure. I didn't predict and panic about how he might kill me, because he'd given me no clues. So, I didn't have to distract him from murder. We simply crossed the threshold of his front door and fell naked into his bed, without even the fumblings common to bodies that are brand new to each other, drunk or undrunk. It was seamless.

I tell him about my childhood fear, thinking it's likely he'll fall asleep to the lull of my story voice. I tell him about how I cried myself into many naps as a child, fearing that all the adults in my life would die. I taught myself to make spaghetti, so if they did die, I would not starve. I kept detailed mental maps of my metropolis and knew how to walk home from any point in the city, even if it was far and would take my small legs days. I knew I could find my place and get in and feed myself spaghetti, despite the dead adults.

My story does not lull him to sleep. He nods and blinks at me. And finally I tell him that when I was twelve and all the adults did die, I raised myself on pasta for many years, until some neighbors figured it out and called the cops. They took me away at the age of fifteen and sent me to live in a home at the bottom of the state.

"A child's home?" he asks.

"Yes. And teenagers."

"So you lived alone from ages twelve to fifteen?" he asks thoughtfully.

"Yes."

"How is that possible?"

I turn my head straight toward his and push down the pillow that's puffed between us. I say, "Anything is possible."

"Yes," he says slowly. And when he says this, his eyebrows move up and his scalp moves forward and his hairline shifts a good inch, then back.

"My father used to do that with his forehead and his hair. Move it like that when he was surprised," I tell him.

"Did his ears wiggle too?" Hefeweizen asks.

"No."

"Mine do." He lifts his head off the pillow, looks surprised, moves his whole hair forward and back on his scalp and wiggles his ears up and down.

"That's good," I say, gently touching his ear, feeling it move against my finger. "Can you make them flap like wings?"

"No. I am German," he says and leans firmly back into his pillow. "Legs, not wings."

Who is Hefeweizen? He is number four. Things never happen in fours. He feels extra. Which makes me suspect he's the one that's going to kill me—put me out of my suspense. The other three were prep, perhaps. The beginning part of some larger system of henchmanly restitution.

Beside his bed is a table topped with a cowboy hat, a stack of mail, and four watches lined up neatly. He mentions his compulsion to keep the watches lined neatly, that he gets very nervous and out of sorts when the watches are out of order.

"Yes, very German," I say. His bed is made really tight too. To get in we had to point our toes to slip and slide them between the fitted sheet and the top sheet, like breaking a seal.

In the middle of the night, I wake and mix up the order of the watches. Stick one in the cowboy hat. Toss another to the floor. For this and in the name of Kelly Green I wonder if he will punish me worse? Even after having my fingers busted, a fatal hit, really, is difficult to fathom. I've seen death in my life, but I can't imagine being dead.

In the morning I am still alive. We drive to breakfast. He twists his key into the lock on The Club. It clicks, scrapes, and shrinks off his steering wheel. He holds it for a moment. Suddenly, I think he might bludgeon me in the name of Kelly Green. I hope he doesn't. I don't want to die.

I cannot feel my pinky or my ring finger on my right hand.

They've gone cold and numb. I can't bend them. Now I have two out-of-order hands. And the paralysis in the right is the beginning of a panic attack. This is survival technique. Blood abandons my limbs and pools in my torso, in case my limbs, for example, were to be severed—I might not squirt so much blood all over the place. The body knows to prepare. Hefeweizen reaches over and places The Club behind the bench seat. He starts his truck and pulls away from the curb. I roll down my window. A gust of fresh air dries the sweat that surfaced across my face and neck.

KELLY GREEN develops a cough. A very moist and rumbling cough. So loud I can hear it echo across the field. Sounds like the sputtering chug of a broken boat in the ocean. The drowning sound of a boat that's never going to make it back to land. I spy Kelly Green mostly in silhouette, doubled over, heaving with cough. Lung fungal death starts in the alveoli. There, the spores nest and quietly blossom, first retarding the exchange of oxygen and carbon dioxide. The victim finds himself or herself wickedly fatigued. Short of breath. The fungus then grows too large for the alveoli, causing them to rupture. Fatal concentrations of fungal poisons are released into the bloodstream. They make it to the brain in no time, establishing residence in the limbic system. From here, billions of baby spore balls are born and develop quickly. They take up brain space, squeezing the brain matter for room. I have seen Kelly Green pound his or her head on the desk in migraine agony. I think about the Spanish Inquisition and torture tactics and can't escape my imagined image of some of the inquisitioned with their heads being squeezed in vises, their faces tangled and crying. And I wonder if Kelly Green is thinking of the same thing. Thinking he or she has fallen into a time trap and is suddenly being mutilated for his or her religion. Only in this case, it's not religion, it's business. Does Kelly Green realize this? I wonder if Kelly Green can think at all. I wonder if Kelly Green is having the thoughts of the spore ball. Kelly Green's brain is turning into fungal cauliflower.

Hefeweizen asks me out on a second date. He doesn't dig through my purse. He doesn't story-dump on me. I keep waiting for that, but no. I haven't met his father. His chest appears mark-free, but I have a theory. A markless chest doesn't mean he didn't sample The Floodgates of Love. He quite likely ate them, but perhaps did so as a single guy. Or, ate them with a partner—and has not broken up with her. They might still be together. I might be the other woman. Maybe his lady will kill me.

I accept his invitation. I shouldn't. I should stop with him. Avoid and evade. Run, hide. My job's well done. Kelly Green is as good as mold. I should exit and carry on with the rest of my life, in another place, with other people.

I have this dream: My Love emerges from the bomb shelter. I am sitting in the sand next to the manhole cover. He freezes, looks at me for several long moments like he doesn't recognize my face. He slings his backpack over his shoulder, puts the man-hole cover back in place. Walks away down the road. He grows small in my vision, but I get up and follow him—trailing behind. He walks far, but I keep him in sight. Past tall buildings and short buildings, parking lots and houses, centers of town where errands are run. Eventually he stops behind some places and I hang back and watch him climb a tree and stay there, high up in the leaves. I don't climb up after him. I turn and walk the other way. In my dream I know that he remembers me, but forever we do not talk.

When I wake I am still alive and realize this dream is the first time in a long time that I've thought hard of My Love. I wonder for how long I will think of him. I wonder if and when he will drain from my memory. My acrobat has not. When I blink in the sunshine I see her face that day, underwater, in our room. I remember me with her, and there was none of this. My heart pumped pink and properly, its parts in good order, bloodwashing my brain, so it worked recognizably. I thought My Love would displace her, repack me full, and repair her vacancy. He did not. He moved into his very own room. I evicted him. He left his things and his smell.

I have this small thought: Will another enter, replace their spaces, make them nothing more than facts of my past? Wait and see, I tell myself. It's what I've been telling myself forever. Like with Hefeweizen and his square teeth here. How will he avenge his boss? I should just leave. But my curiosity keeps my legs right here, sticking around, waiting to see.

Hefeweizen takes me to a car show. "When I was a farmhand back home, I also repaired tractors," he tells me as we stand over the shining engine of a very fancy car.

"Huh," I say. He might kill me with a car. Run me over, so I am pasted on the grill of an antique show car. I am petite. I would not damage the frame too much. No doubt Kelly Green has a show car. Ninety-nine percent of persons with surplus funds invest in luxury vehicles. Perhaps Hefeweizen will run me down in Kelly Green's luxury vehicle.

I have been living in a state of anxiety. And marvelment. My mind struggles to juggle it all. There's my life here, hemming shorter every day. There's Kelly Green there, dying by my hand. And the henchmen seem everywhere. Of course, if they destroy me, I'm gone. No more worries.

After the car show, Hefeweizen and I take a drive. He motors conspicuously near the camping park. Fraught, I wonder if we are headed to Kelly Green's. We listen to news radio in his truck. There is a breaking announcement: Kelly Green, president and CEO of Target, has died. Immediately, and for the trimmest slice of time, I can't believe Kelly Green warrants radio airtime. I'd never heard of Kelly Green before I worked with Kelly Green. Then the largeness of Kelly Green's death swells between my ears.

We both stare at the dials on the radio in the dash. The sound from the radio, from the street, from the white noise in the world, goes out like blackness. I cannot breathe.

In my vision, the glowing digital numbers making out the station on the radio are like short nicks, like scars in space. I blink and the light of them remains on the backs of my eyelids. I turn my head, and there is the face of Hefeweizen. I imagine he is remembering his charge. In my mind, I picture the rest of everything will go like this:

His face goes cold. He pulls to the side of the road. He reaches behind the seat, grabs The Club. All in slow motion. He swings the club like an axe and shatters my shins. Right there, in the passenger seat.

I wonder if My Love would feel it. Feel the cold smash sear up his legs, then burn, knotting his stomach in sudden illness. Would he fall to the floor? Throw up? Maybe he is sleeping. Like dishes thrown to the cement at the foot of the futon, would it wake him from a dream? Sweaty and tight, not recognizing the bomb shelter, shaking his red face to focus. Focus.

I imagine Hefeweizen dumps me from the truck. I cannot walk. The skin of my legs does not break, but the bones inside are splattered to a mess. Like granola. Beneath my skin, my calves are soft, loose tubes of granola bobbing in milk. My feet are intact. My thighs, solid. From knees to ankles are limp, unrecognizable, molten.

There is no one around. It's getting late. I'm not far from the campsite. I cannot feel my body. Through my jobs I have health insurance. I could consider going to the hospital. Instead I drag myself to the campsite. Into my tent. The campsite lights will shine through the trees and the tent fabric. Create the illusion of being underwater. I'll take the batteries out of my flashlight, toss them into the woods. I'll pop my bottle of sparkling wine. Glug from it. Elbowed up, I'll look at my flattened calves. Pour some fizzing wine on them. They'll change colors. Brown and yellow and greenish.

I blink again. I am in the truck with Hefeweizen. We are both still staring at the radio. I turn my head toward my passenger-side door in the truck. I flick the lock. Yank up the handle. The door swings open. I leap from it, stumble on the road, fall, scrape, roll. Terrified, I get up and run. I run.

Ions

S HE GOES to the post office to pick up her mail. Blanca Flynn has been on vacation for eight days, with three girlfriends, celebrating a breakup. Mostly she drank. And like her girlfriends, made out with waiters and Jet Ski instructors at a resort on a beach where the sand is red and dusty, the water is warm like her shower, and the cocktails come in colorful plastic tubes as long as her arm.

It is Saturday just before two. There is no line. She walks directly to the bulletproof window. A short stack of envelopes is gingerly handed to her by the old woman behind the counter. She is the oldest, most raisin-wrinkled woman Blanca Flynn has ever seen in her whole life, in person or in pictures.

"Thank you"—she reads the woman's nametag—"Della," she says and tucks the sheaf into her armpit.

As she steps away from the counter and walks toward the door, she gets dizzy. It is so hot and bright outside, and so cool and dim in the post office. Blanca Flynn steadies herself by the stamp machine. She doesn't have to go back to work for another day, and she is glad because she needs to recover from her vacation. She realizes that she may have pushed it too hard this time, tossed one too many empty plastic tubes over her shoulder. She is half proud of this. It was good for her. Heaves and headaches and sunburn included. She'd arrived with a calamity in her heart, but the bright white days on the hot sand, sipping those long drinks, warbled it wet and wavy and far away.

And now she is back. She looks past the stamp machine to the thick door locking away the private parts of the post office. The door clacks open and out strides a mailman. In slips Blanca Flynn. Why? Just because. She brushes against the fist of keys on his belt and makes it across the threshold before the door clunks shut. She hears the mailman shout from the other side of the closed door, jangle his keys. Mail sorters look up from their business in the back and look startled and glance at one another from long tables of bills and magazines and good news and bad news and no news and postcards maybe even from the place she just was and boxes and boxes and boxes, but she glides by quickly and purposefully, and before anyone can stop her, she is out the back way, into the sunshine. She hops from the loading dock and ambles through the parking lot.

She examines her mail: nothing, nothing, junk, a thin and squishy shampoo sampler packet, a letter. It's from him. Her breathing, her blood, her brain—all stop. One two three. She blinks. Focuses. There is his heavily slanted handwriting. There is his name in the upper left corner. There is the stamp he chose to stick. Feelings swell in her chest. They press up her throat, into her head. One screams loudest in her ears: Blanca Flynn is pissed. She pictures him. There is his face, attached to his body, in his bed. And with him, someone else. She sees a naked girl-body in her mind in his bed. She doesn't know who this girl is. She doesn't imagine this girl's face. She sticks a blue dot where the girl's head should be. He fucks her in Blanca's brain in his bed. The girl's blue-dot bobs. Blanca Flynn stares at the envelope.

If she had a bomb she would detonate it here, on the envelope. If she had acid, she would pour it. If she stares at it much longer, she might tear it open with her teeth, rub the pages against her mouth, smear the ink onto her lips.

To the front of her mind slams possible contents: He is sorry. She misunderstood. He was just kidding. The purse she found in his truck was a joke. No, not funny. So, so sorry. Blanca Flynn hears it in his German accent—his mouth full of squatting vowels and sandpaper rubs. He could convince her. It was not an affair. It was nothing. It was work. The girl was a colleague. A sister. A cousin. An aunt. Very undesirable. And for a bright moment—his imagined voice shucking loudly in her head—Blanca Flynn believes her versions of his letter.

She pauses. Rubs her eyes. Looks past the envelope to her toes in her flip-flops. Her toes are very tan. Her feet are tan. So are her legs and her trunk and her face, and they all feel leaden. She wishes she could selectively delete memory: his bed a rumpled mess late in the afternoon. He was a man who made his bed every morning. Quickly and tightly. His golden pinky ring glinting while he folded and smoothed and tucked. Then Blanca Flynn found some girl's stuff in his truck. A clutch containing lipstick and bungee cords and loose change. What a disgusting woman. And the smell on his neck and chest. Not his, not Blanca's, female. All the stupid clues. But if she could scrub her mind clean? If she didn't remember it, did it really happen? Maybe not. For example, Blanca Flynn's girlfriends claim just the other night she danced on a speaker box, peeled off her shirt, propellered it above her head. But she doesn't remember. And there are no pictures. As far as she knows, it didn't happen.

She looks back at the envelope. Her memory, unfortunately, remains intact and still soiled. She considers rolling the letter up, stuffing it in the gas tank of one of the mail trucks, dropping a match in after it, walking away tall, having never read a word. She hesitates for a moment, lifts the envelope to her nose for a quick sniff. She sniffs a big one, but it smells only like paper and envelope stickum. His German tongue licked the lickum on the flap. Her stomach tightens and falls limply into her crotch. And her underwear, suddenly they are a little damp. She shakes her head, sighs, then shushes herself. She reaches for her purse and realizes she's not carrying it. If she was, she'd fish out her pocketknife, flick open the biggest blade, stab all four tires of one of these trucks. Carve his name into the bumper. Blanca Flynn makes a fist and punches the side of her head—quickly, like her wrist snapped from a spring. She does this to derail her train of thought. Sometimes it works. Always it stings. She focuses on the sting until it fades, and for those few moments she doesn't think of him.

She returns her attention to the envelope in her hands. Composes herself. Carefully folds the envelope into a small rectangle and stuffs it in her back pocket like an old tissue. She pats that pocket. Wonders if she might never read it. Wonders if she did, if it would change everything: the course of her life. She'd considered hers with him, now it is without him, but might the letter rewrite him back into it? Could she forgive him? She doesn't know these answers. She thinks she should walk. She walks. Forward. Anywhere.

BLANCA FLYNN walks for some time, thinking. She thinks her German ex-boyfriend is like wet paint spilled on the sidewalk in her brain, and she is without a hose to turn on him and wash him into a blur, so instead she slops through it, ruining her shoes, stamping fresh footprints of old memories everywhere. She met him at the Laundromat when the machines at her place were out of order and her landlord was slow to repair. He was rubbing stain stick into spots on a collared shirt and a pair of navy slacks. He was tall. His shoulders were straight like the crossbar in a capital T. He caught her watching him and smiled, his lips pulling into a wide rectangle revealing top and bottom teeth. Blanca Flynn approached him, looked at the stain-stuck spots on his clothes, asked if it was blood. He turned to her, widened then narrowed his eyes, said "Very good," in his accent that would wear the clothes off her body only hours later.

Appetite grew between the two of them, right there by the machines. Each hurried with the laundry, but tried to appear casual. They dumped their hamper bags, pressed lights and darks into the washer holes, poured detergent, dropped quarters, hit the button, shilly-shallied at each other. He glanced at the washer clock, mentioned they both had some time. They agreed to scoot across the street for a nibble and a sip, why not, why not? They sat at a corner table in a high booth, had cocktails and fondue. Got drunk and randy in the late afternoon. Blanca Flynn speared him in the rib with her fondue fork. He ordered strawberries and a tub of chocolate to go. They both fell into his truck. She pointed this way and then that way, right here, straight there, left at the light, while she unzipped his pants. She pulled his dick through the fly in his boxers, then through the fly in his jeans. Kept it out, like it grew from the gap below his belt buckle. They arrived at her place and she led him by his dick, like a leash, from his truck, across the street, through the gate, down the grass path, and into her bedroom. He giggled and crumbled the whole hundred yards. Grumbled "*Scheiße!*" repeatedly. Couldn't believe her pluck.

Quickly to her bed, then all clothes gone, he dumped the to-go chocolate down her back, rivering it over her ass. He ate it off. They tumbled together. Chocolate everywhere, they were sticky and smudged, caked and clotted. Chocolate dreaded her hair and his hair, soaked through her sheets, stained her mattress, splashed the rug. They took a shower together and the water ran sweet and brown down the drain. She is surprised now by his ease into that mess, given how tidy she'd eventually learn he was. Today she figures, perhaps, it was because they were at her place, not his, making a wreck of her bed, not his.

She wonders if that did it. Was that a sign on night one that she was not for him? Or was it the sexing so soon? Does she believe what they say about sexing too soon? She doesn't think she does. She thinks those that say you shouldn't should go to hell. Where maybe no one has sex. How about that? These days she finds herself mad at people she doesn't know and can only barely imagine. She misses her German lover.

They both returned to the Laundromat in the morning. She'd gotten a parking ticket. He swiped it from her windshield, tucked it into his pocket, shook his head no when she asked to have it. He took her hand and led her inside. She would learn that whenever she held his hand, their palms noticeably wouldn't touch. Instead, she felt a tiny globe of very warm air spin on its axis between the eye of her palm and his.

His load and her load were wet and rumpled lumps in the washers. They ran them again. Slipped to the bench seat of his truck for two more fucks—a washer fuck, then a dryer fuck. It was bright daytime. From beneath The Club behind his seat, he pulled a padded foil sunblocker, unrolled it across his windshield. "For privacy and shade," he assured her in his German voice while he worked her jeans down her legs. She wonders now if he was completely single then. She has never cheated on anyone. She reaches for the letter in her back pocket. Blanca Flynn changes her mind, pushes her hands into her front pockets, still doesn't read it.

Slowly she notices that beneath her slapping sandals, the ground has turned to dirt. And above her, the sun's gone completely green through the leaves in the trees. She realizes that she has never walked so far behind the post office. She stops, looks. It's woodsy.

BLANCA FLYNN does not expect any of what comes next:

A thing falls on her. From a tree. It's a net. It balloons fat and floaty on the way down, like a parachute. She knows this because she heard rustling, looked up, watched it fall—its insides domed wide and round with air. She didn't step out of its way.

When it falls on top of her, get this: The center clings tight to the crown of her head, separates, and scoots over her hair and face. It cinches around her neck and the four corners of the net drop heavily onto the ground, like they are weighted. The corners then skit quickly toward her ankles, leaving short straight grooves in the dirt.

Her head through a hole in the center, the net drapes over her chest and shoulders and back like a poncho. Then it changes. The fibers in the net contract, pulling the mesh close to her body. The holes in the webbing shrink until they disappear into a solid fabric. It clings to Blanca Flynn's body, defining her contours from neck to ankles. It seals itself tight around each arm and each leg. It hugs her breasts and her hips. It becomes one unbroken rubbery sheath, like a second skin. It is red and glossy like candy. She sucks in a quick, deep breath, and the suit gives with the puff of her chest. She bends her arms—they can, like normal. Then the rumpled bumps from the clothes she is wearing smooth out beneath the sheath. Down her arms and out the cuffs around her wrists, liquid the milk white color of her T-shirt runs over the backs of her hands, across her palms, drips from her fingertips. She feels a delicate wash across her chest and back, over her waist and butt and down her legs. From her ankles where the suit ends, a rush of liquid in a swirl the color of her shirt and her pink bra and black panties and denim shorts runs over her feet in her flip-flops and pools in a puddle. All this as she stands there.

She is confounded in such a way that keeps her put, where she is. She doesn't gasp or scream or leave. Her reaction time is slow on account of her vacation, coupled with the thick fog that rolled between her ears and clouded her eyes the moment her German shook his head and shrugged his straight shoulders at the evidence she'd found. It's left her capable of looking up at rustling in the sky but unfit to think to step out of its way. It's left her oddly comfortable with her understanding that her clothes have just melted from her body, beneath this red jellied clinging onesie that was once a net.

She hears "Psst, PSST" from above, and in what feels like the slowest motion, she looks up again.

A curly-headed blond guy leans over the edge of a platform built high up into the thick branches and leaves of a tree.

"Excuse me. Excuse me," he says smiling. He motions for her to come. She doesn't move. His face disappears from the edge and reappears in a square hole cut into the platform near the tree trunk.

"Watch out," he says.

Down falls a chain ladder. It unravels with a jerk and a *ching*, inches from her face.

"Climb it," he says.

Blanca Flynn is baffled by the strangeness of the last few moments but is surprisingly calm. Something sound rolls through her. She feels like she's just heard the first few bars of the best song and is compelled to tune in tightly, wild to catch each next beat.

She decides it is time for things. When presented with opportunities, her German took them, and now today and maybe for the rest of her life, fuck everyone, so should she. She climbs the chain ladder. It twitches and sways with the weight and torque of her slick red body.

At the top she pokes her head through the hole in the platform. The man is still smiling. He offers her his hand and she takes it. He helps her up out of the hole. He has a very sweet face. Blanca Flynn notices it in a way she hasn't noticed faces in what feels like a long while. Not even the waiters at the resort. They all had, it seemed, one handsomish brown face. This guy's eyes squint practically closed when he smiles, but glint sunny like the gold flecks in his hair. She stands with him on the platform, which is like a deck in front of a whole tree home. There are two pots of pink and orange flowers on either side of his front door. She notices she is noticing things. This feels nice. He invites her through the door and into his place.

She has never been in a tree home, but is familiar with other homes and how they make her feel. Sometimes sleepy or short of breath or tall if the ceilings are unusually low. Or fat if there is too much dark furniture. Her German's was so neat. Clinically organized. Like a first-aid kit. It made her feel crisp and ironed.

Sunlight traipses through the window. The room is cool and breezy and made of smooth wood. Immediately she likes his place. She feels awake and warm. She feels like eating breakfast. She smiles at him and stops. She skates backwards inside her head because she thinks she doesn't really see what she thinks she is seeing. She blinks. Focuses. Is floored. At first glance, she saw one big smooth wood room with all the comforts of a home you'd find on the ground: a toilet behind a blue curtain, a stainless steel sink, a small refrigerator, a small work area with what looks like an old-fashioned spinning wheel. More careful inspection, and in addition to those regular home things, she sees some irregular other things she finds hard to believe. But she is standing there looking at them, so is believing.

Several items in his tree home appear to be made of water: the mattress, a small safe, a lampshade, a picture frame, the couch. Pure water. The water is water that apparently holds form—the form of a mattress, a small safe, a lampshade, a picture frame, a couch. No covers, no nothing. Just water in the shapes of things she knows. This is remarkable. Stupefying. Confusing. Staggering. But it doesn't spike her mouth with what or why or no or put a stop to what feels like flower buds blooming in her head.

She is first drawn to the mattress like it is sorcerering her over, but she resists. Defaults to the couch. Takes a good long look at this couch. It is big and cushy and entirely transparent. She can see the grain of the wood in the floorboards—bent and magnified—through the cushions. He walks behind her and crosses the room. The couch ripples when he walks. It ripples when the wind blows through the window. Blanca Flynn thinks it might ripple if she laughed too loud.

Beguiled, she laughs, loud. The couch ripples. She smiles, shakes her head, shrugs her shoulders, looks to him and says, "Wow." It escapes her mouth full of breath.

He nods.

"Can I sit?" she asks.

He swoops his arm out, palm up, in the direction of the couch.

She sits. She floats weightlessly on the cushions. She lays back. When she stretches and shifts and nuzzles herself into the cushions, the water makes soft, smacking sounds, like someone taking a bath.

"Did you make this?" she asks, folding her hands behind her head, relaxing into it.

"Yes," he says.

"From water?" she asks.

"Yes," he says.

"How?"

"Ions," he says and rests his hand on his spinning wheel.

She has no idea what he means. She removes her hands from behind her head. Sits up. She stands up from the water couch. It sloshes lightly.

"Mind if I look around?" she asks.

He shakes his head.

She examines the lampshade. The light is out and water whiffles around the bulb in perfect lampshade formation. He steps close to her. She feels warm. And can smell him.

"You smell good," she says.

"Thanks," he says and steps past her, leaving his scent in the air around her face. He crosses to the small safe near his bed.

Blanca Flynn inhales deeply and detectively and determines he smells like something. Like expensive herbal tea. She breathes to the bottom of her lungs and thinks for a moment he smells like Galliano liqueur. Only not liquory and minus the vanilla. It's a cologne combo she's never smelled before. She likes it.

She watches him at the safe. There is a little red glass vial in the safe. She can see the vial clear through the watered form. A red blotch like a berry, it grows large and small and distorted when he spins the steel combination lock until the safe burbles open. He uncaps the vial and dabs fresh, sweet-smelling oil behind his ears, along his collarbone. She aims her nose in his direction and smells.

"Mmm," she says and wonders if later she might get in close and steal a good whiff.

"What do you do with this stuff?" she asks, smelling him and scanning the water pieces and the basket by the spinning wheel, heaped full of nets.

"I play around with it mostly," he says. "I also sell it to foreign governments and private corporations and sometimes celebrities."

Of all the unexpected everythings so far, this one leaps upon entrance into her ears, startles her. Blanca Flynn wonders, briefly, why she meets men with secrety and obscure jobs. Her cheating German was never entirely clear about his line of work. Often committed to it at odd hours and through the night. Once, over sausage dinner at a beer garden, he said he was an agent. She asked him what kind, and he said an agent in an agency. And when she pressed further, his face iced cold and he spoke something harshly in German like his mouth were built of pumice stones and the words scraped themselves raw on their way out. He pinched the juice from a wedge of lemon and dropped it into his beer.

"Do foreign governments, private corporations, and celebrities pay you visits here?" Blanca Flynn asks him.

"Never," he says.

"How do they get the goods?" she asks.

"They send representatives and assistants in pickup vans to the post office," he says.

She can't tell if this is a lot or a little information.

"So," she says, "you're an entrepreneur?"

He stuffs his hands in his pants pockets, thinks for a beat. "Yes," he says, and his gaze falls on the picture in the water frame on the table by his bed. It is of a woman swinging around a pole. A cap gun snaps fire in Blanca Flynn's gut.

"Who's that floozy?" she blurts. It blows from her mouth and splatters in the direction of his special picture. Immediately she wishes she could take it back. She knows she shouldn't care about his floozies. She tells herself she doesn't. She tells herself the next relationship she is in, she will have a hundred affairs. Quickly she wonders if that relationship might be with this guy, and then she wonders how heartsick he will be when he learns about all her entanglements. And then briefly and meanly, she hopes he'll feel worse than she does now.

He grabs the photo from the table and shakes it vigorously. The water whips off onto the floor and walls. It sizzles on the bare bulb on the ceiling. He shakes away the entire frame and holds a limp still between his thumb and forefinger. He glances nervously at Blanca Flynn, opens his dresser drawer, and tucks the photo under a short stack of T-shirts. She is glad he hides it. He turns and looks at her. She is standing, looking at him, the ghost of her floozy question haunting the space between their bodies. She doesn't know what to do with her arms. She crosses them. Her forearms squeak when they rub against each other. She uncrosses them. They squeak again. Flustered, she places her hands on her hips. Beneath her fingertips she feels the suit he ballooned onto her, and she remembers that she is sleek and rubbery and red.

"You made this too?" she asks, changing the subject and looking down at the suit stretched across her stomach and her thighs and over her knees.

"Yes," he says.

"You knot them and toss them and they gel onto bodies, huh?"

"Pretty much," he says.

She has figured out the sequence. She picks a sparkly, knotted, gray net from the basket by the spinning wheel. She throws it up and watches it float down over his head and body. The net beads away from his head and face, cinching around his neck and falling over his shoulders to the floor. The four corners thunk on the floor, then creep quickly toward his body and cling to his flesh. The holes between the knots close; the fabric shrinks tight and smooth. It contours his calves, his crotch, his chest, his arms. His T-shirt sleeves melt down his arms and drip from his fingers. His shirt bib and underwear and pants slip down his legs, spill over his ankles and bare feet, puddle around them. He flicks his hands dry, steps from the puddle toward the kitchen area. He grabs the broom and a dustpan and sweeps the puddle into the pan, walks to the platform porch. His feet appear dry, he leaves no tracks. He dumps the contents of the dustpan onto the ground below. Blanca Flynn hears it splash in the distance. The spot where the puddle had been looks clean. Blanca sits back down on the couch. He puts the broom away and sits next to her. They both bobble for a minute.

"What is this stuff made from?" she asks and runs her finger along his rubbery gray thigh like it's the shiny finish on a show car. Her German stood her up for a date to the car show. Said he had to work. She believed him.

This guy in gray glances quickly at her. "I keep a flowerbed on the highest branch at the top of this tree," he says. "I grow flowers. The pollen from these flowers isn't pollen, it's sap. I spin that. The sap." He folds his hands in his lap.

"Huh," she says. "You are an inventor?"

He shrugs yes.

She turns to the watery arm of the couch. She jabs her fingers into it. They enter with a splish and she watches them shift fat and thin under the water. She pulls her hand out. It is dry like cornstarch, the arm of the couch intact. She wonders why he didn't just stick his hand into the safe. "Could you have shoved your fingers directly into your safe?" she asks.

"No," he says.

"Why not?" asks Blanca Flynn.

"The combination," he says and leans in toward her and tilts his head and there is his face, right up in front of hers. She sees his eyelashes and the pores around his nose and the creases in his lips. He leans in further and kisses her with an inhale. She thinks her whole self will be sucked out from her red rubbery suit and into his mouth. This is a good feeling. It feels like a long time since she's had this feeling. And like a hot pinprick into the center of her chest, she wonders if her German had this feeling with whomever she was that left her purse and bungee cords in his truck that he should have disposed of before Blanca Flynn climbed into the passenger seat.

He kisses her harder. She kisses back. This goes on for some time until it ends. When their faces pull away, he looks at her for a beat then stands. She looks up at him. He holds out his hand. She takes it. He leads her across the room and onto the mattress. She's been aching to get on that mattress since she arrived, to see how it works. But she thought she shouldn't attend to his bed, not so soon, not this time. Then, oh shit, she thinks, oh well, as she eases backwards into it.

There are no sheets and no blanket on this mattress. It sloshes beneath her, but she stays dry. They bob for a moment. He watches her wobble up and down, then smiles and laughs with no sound.

She smiles too and flips from her back to her stomach, feeling slippery as a baby seal. She looks down into his mattress. Through the clear water Blanca Flynn can see what he keeps under his bed: a barbell, two stacks of magazines (*Science News* and a business something or other), a toolbox, an unzipped duffel bag stuffed with what looks like the chins and cheekbones and empty eyes of masks, a laptop computer case. She wonders if it is dusty under there. She wonders if dust can gather under a burbling water thing that doesn't drip. She decides probably.

She feels his hands on her hips. He flips her back over. The move is so smooth and quick, it's like she is greased. He slips one hand behind her head, the other at her sacrum. He leans into her. Their hips then knees bump, and her rubbery red and his rubbery gray squeak. She giggles and says out loud, "*Squeak!*" because she is embarrassed by the sound. As if her stomach had grumbled audibly.

Now. Beneath him. On the mattress that is water. In his tree home. Two rubbery unitard suits. Here she is. She is with a new person in a new bed. And quickly, like cold air on a cavity, her German shoots to her nerve endings. She swipes her hand across her rear to check if his letter bulges beneath the rubber. No bulge. No letter. She guesses it melted with her clothes. Like that—she feels panic, like she's lost her teeth. She swooshes her tongue through her mouth. Wonders what he might have said in those pages.

This gray guy kisses her again and she snaps to. She focuses on his kiss and muscles aside what she is thinking about until she forgets what she is thinking about. He kisses her again and then again, each kiss longer than the last, each with more gusto. He tucks his fingers into her hair, presses her firmly against him. He rolls her over. Their suits rub against each other and squawk. He rolls her over again. The suits yawp. Blanca Flynn and this man in gray tangle together on the mattress. She wants him. She shifts and pushes her hips to his and wonders how to remove her shiny red suit. She realizes that there are no openings, no zippers, no seams.

She looks at him. Her face is very close to his face. The weight of his whole body on her whole body feels good. She wants to peek at the tent he's pitched on top of her, but she refrains. She moves her hands across his upper back, slides them into the dip of his lower back and follows through up over his butt. There are absolutely no seams in his outfit either.

He plants his hands on the surface of the water on either side of her shoulders. He looks like he might do a push-up over her.

And he does. Only it's quick and jarring and the mattress gives beneath the push, but then springs back up. Together, they are launched from the mattress and into air. Her red suit bounces against his gray suit midair, a few feet above the mattress. The suits squeal. Blanca Flynn laughs. They hit the mattress again with another great squeak and bounce up even higher this time. The mattress ripples with waves and their bodies twine and their suits cut quick, rubbery yips.

They bounce and bounce again. They land on their backs and on their right sides and on their left sides. They kiss and roll in a wad midair. Their suits *ert* and *veep* and *reep* loud and soft. They do this for a long time. The wide thoughts in Blanca Flynn's head narrow to the heavy pressure in her groin, the press of all his parts against hers, squeaking.

THE SUN sets outside. He raises his hands above his head, claps twice, and the light in the lamp flicks on and shines twinkly from beneath the water lampshade. The breeze blows the smell of leaves through the window. Leaves and spice, and she thinks she smells anisette and lemons and salty sweat.

They lie side by side in the gurgly bed, winded. He holds her hand. Their palms touch. He dips his toes and the top of his right foot into the arch of her left. Blanca Flynn thinks the suits must be breathable somehow, because she is very comfortable. He lets go of her hand, gets up, walks his gray rubbery body over to the little fridge. He clinks ice into glasses, uncaps bottles, pours, stirs, returns to the mattress with two thick drinks the color of brick.

"Ooooo," she says, "Bloody Maries."

He laughs, "Bloody *Marys*."

"Right," she says.

He sips and smiles. He tells her, "Mary Bloodies are like drinking meat."

She agrees and tells him, "That sensation is on account of the

Worcestershire sauce and the salt. Mary's Blood calls for meat-related ingredients."

She says very loudly, "Hamburger meat is good to eat!" And she smiles; she is amused by the mishmash of words they've shared, the rhyme she made, and the sound of her big voice in his small place. She feels happy. And sexy. Happier and sexier than she's felt since way back. Since before her German heartbreak. He looks at her and his eyes sparkle darkly. He cups his hands around his mouth like a megaphone and hoots. He laughs and looks shocked.

She elbows up onto her side, lays her hand on his flat gray abdomen, says slowly and with bass, "Good."

He says, "Yes," and slides his arm around her waist, rolls her beneath him again. The rubber *eeks* several short *peeps*.

She tells him she has a secret. He directs his ear toward her mouth. She tells him about the time she wanted to cover her mattress, a regular department store mattress, in plastic cling wrap and take it to the ocean. She tells him she wanted to travel on it to that island in that book where all the little boys went crazy and wanted to kill each other. She tells him that she thought that'd be fun, but that she never did it. He looks surprised and tells her that he did. He adjusts Blanca Flynn onto her back, kneels between her legs, hitches her thighs up onto his hips, again.

IT IS dark outside.

"I'll walk you home," he says.

He walks her to her house.

"That's my car," she says as they stroll past it. She can see her luggage in the shadows in the backseat.

He nods.

"Is this your place?" he asks, looking at the fence and the big dark lawn and the brown door at the end of the path.

"No, this is the front house," she says. "I rent the guesthouse in the back."

"Oh," he says.

She walks with him on the grassy corridor alongside the main house. His rubbery gray is squeaking, her rubbery red is squeaking. She loses her balance slightly and they bump shoulders. The rub makes a small *rrratz*.

At her door she asks him, "How do I get this stuff off?"

"In the bath," he says. "Take a bath." He puts his hand on her hip. She feels the warm pressure of his palm through her suit.

"Want to come in and take one with me?" she asks. He smiles and shakes his head no. She doesn't know how to respond. She expels a huh-huh laugh. It drops from her mouth, lands on her doormat. It was a dumb laugh. Blanca Flynn feels hot and embarrassed.

He steps away from her door, turns, walks. She watches him walk along the path. The grass is long and hides his feet. In the dim night light it looks like his gray shiny body ends at his ankles. He makes a left at the end of the path and is out of her sight. The feeling of surprise and stillness that fell upon her when he dropped his net returns—breaks over the top of her head and nods across the surface of her body. She doesn't go after him.

She realizes she doesn't have her key, that maybe it melted with her clothes and the letter. She digs her spare out from under a fake rock in the dirt by a bush. She unlocks the door, pushes it open, presses on the light, enters the living room. It is clean. There are dark and light vacuum streaks in her brown carpet. She blinks at them and breathes. She feels like her chest is collapsing. Like the seam between her ribs is withdrawing deep into her back, folding her closed like a book. Her two shiny red shoulders might meet and squeak beneath her chin.

She slogs to her bedroom. Slouches toward her answering machine on the bedside table. The light on the machine blinks at her. Messages. She pauses, her finger aimed at the button. She drops her fingertip hard into the button. She erases all without playing them.

A framed picture of Blanca Flynn and her German sits to the right of the answering machine. There he is, smiling his wide square smile. He's got his hand on his hip, and, there, catching the flash, is that ring he'd never talk about or let her try on. It is a white burst on the film. Blanca Flynn's got both her arms around his middle, and she thinks she looks sunny and hopeful in this picture, laughing at something he said in his *schush-scheitz* accent.

She plucks the picture in its frame from the bedside table and shakes it vigorously. The glass dislodges, slides from the frame, and thuds gently against a faded chocolate stain on the carpet. She picks it up. She takes the frame and the glass and the picture and slouches to the kitchen. She puts on a pot of water in the dark. She places the items in the water and turns up the flame. She shuffles out of the kitchen and sits on the edge of her bed. She looks at her ancient telephone. She knows his number. She could call it. Mention the letter. No, no, I didn't get to reading it, she could say. She could ask what might've been in it. What did he write? She wonders if he'd tell her. She wonders if she'd believe him. She hates the hush of being back, alone, in her guesthouse. She hates the letter she didn't read, the messages she erased, the color of her carpet. She hates what feels like clods of dirt lodged in her throat, their mud dripping sickly into her stomach.

She lifts the phone receiver. She presses the ear part to her ear, mashes the mouth part against her mouth. Squeezes her eyes shut and focuses on the dial tone. The dial tone is loud. Her nose breath blows into the receiver. Sounds like short bursts of wind, dial tone in the background. She pulls the receiver away from her face and like it's a hammer, Blanca Flynn smacks the ear part against the side of her head, then rubs the whole receiver down the length of her red thigh. The sequence goes *crack, zeeep-mrrahp*. She returns the receiver to the two hang-up buttons on the phone. She lies back, into her blankets. The side of her head throbs. She wrings her eyes shut. Tunes her attention to the pot on the stove in the kitchen. Listens to it.

PART

2

Freshet

1. Swell

She went on one car date with her older cousin's friend from the army—six months prior to going out with the guy who becomes her serious boyfriend, Talon "T-bird" Blaze. She had a night off from babysitting, and army boy picked her up in his dad's sedan and took her to Shoney's. It is the date place. After dinner, it was night and dark. They parked on the bluffs above the beach. It is the make out place. Music swooned from the speakers in the doors. Army boy put the moves on Janine McQueen.

He felt her up, was technically as far as it went. Her breasts were full for her age. She'd been wearing real bras for two years. Her boobs started growing big in the sixth grade. Army boy liked them the whole night long. At the table at Shoney's he stared at her cleavage. She was wearing a V-neck T-shirt, and the V reclined on her breasts like it'd fallen backwards. He wanted to insert things into the tight line between her breasts. The stem of a fork. He imagined it would stand erect, prongs level with her chin. But mostly he wanted to stick in his finger and his tongue. When she leaned over to take a bite of her patty melt, he imagined pushing his dick between them.

She wore the right bras. This she learned from her older cousin, who introduced her to army boy. The summer before Janine McQueen entered the eighth grade, she saw her nineteen-year-old cousin at the Memorial Day family picnic. They were sharing a smoke on the curb around the corner from Janine's house, and her cousin said, "You got hoots." She tipped her chin at Janine's breasts.

"You gotta show them properly," she continued. Then she explained the importance of the right bra.

"Lift and push," she illustrated with her hands, lifting Janine's boobs, then pushing them together.

"Pull back the neck of your shirt," she said. Janine did.

"Check that out," said the cousin exposing Janine's cleavage. "That's good." Then she took off her own bra, letting her breasts loose behind her tank top. She showed Janine the enforced cups, the wires, the lace, and the bow.

"Also, never again wear anything with a high neck," she said. "Only low necks." She puffed on her cigarette. "I'm serious."

Later, Janine took the bus to the mall and purchased the right bras and a packet of V-necks. And showed hoots from then on, properly.

And it caught on, in no time. Soon all the girls were doing it. Even the flat-chested girls—they rigged their bras and did their best. Junior high and high school–wide, fresh décolletage bounced around campus, attracting sunburns while ohmygodwhatthejesus christholyshits were whispered loudly in faculty lounges.

Back in the car with the army boy, he offed with her shirt and unhooked her lift-and-push bra. Tossed both in the back seat. Then he climbed like a humungous toddler over the front seats and into the back.

"Come on," he said from the backseat. He held out his hand, took hers. She climbed over, topless.

They continued making out, now without the emergency break and gearshift between them. This was her first make out session. Army boy had full, soft lips but rough worker hands. Shotgun-shooting hands, or maybe hands made rough from the rings and ropes in boot camp. The tough patches on his palms scratched her neck, her back, her breasts.

There with army boy, she was introduced to certain elements of making out. She noticed the flat of his tongue on the flat of her tongue while Frenching. Two flat tongues pressed together like palms for a split second, feeling each other, before they tense beefy again and push and slide from mouth to mouth. She noticed nostril breathing. Became aware of her breath in and out of her nose smushed right there onto his face. The smell of his nose pores.

She liked putting her hands on his forearms and his biceps. They seemed huge to her. Her hands could not wrap all the way around. Like palming a football but with no hope of picking it up.

Army boy put the point of his finger in her belly button, gently. She liked this. He ran his finger through a soft strip of blonde belly fuzz, over the waistband of her jeans, and all along the seam stitched across her crotch, applying pressure the whole way. Feeling his hand down there, her scalp behind her ears burned. She leaned into his fingers, and he cupped her whole crotch with his hand, and she felt the heat of his hand through her pants. She liked this.

Against her thigh she noticed his big boner in his pants. He pressed it against her. She'd slow-danced with the boyfriend she had for a day in the seventh grade and felt what she now realized was a smaller boner against her bladder. In the backseat on the bluffs, she shifted her thigh and ran her hand over army boy's slacks and felt it in there. She'd never been this up close to a bigger boner before and was relieved that it stayed covered under his clothes because this was her first date and though she thought army boy was really cute and older, she wasn't ready.

Just below the bluffs, the pervy patrolman was working the traffic beat. He took his coffee and headed up the hill to peep on and then penalize in-vehicle lovers. In-vehicle nudity is illegal. This includes toplessness. The pervy patrolman liked to wear night vision goggles. They didn't help him when the windows were all steamed up, but occasionally he lucked out.

The pervy patrolman parked in the dark, near the sedan on the bluffs. He cut his engine and his lights, donned his night vision goggles. They clicked into place over his eyes. The mechanics in them whirred.

In the dark, through his windshield, he had a decent view of army boy and young Janine McQueen. Until they sunk deeply into the backseat and out of sight. He quietly stepped out of his vehicle and toward their car. Through their rear windshield, cast in night-vision green, he watched. Mostly he watched Janine McQueen's boobs and imagined army boy's hands and mouth were his own. Pervy patrolman thought that if he were that boy in there, he'd do it better. He'd pinch her more, until she winced, made a little noise, or flinched mid-kiss. He'd have her all the way for sure, he thought. In no time she'd be naked and his for sure.

When the windows clouded out foggy, he lost them. He adjusted his starched pants, his belt heavy with gear. He removed his goggles, clipped them to the back of his belt, approached the car. With the backend of his flashlight he tapped the passenger-side rear window. Caught up in the moment there was a several-second delay before the sound registered in the kissers' minds. Janine McQueen pulled her face off army boy's and looked scared.

"Did you hear something?" she asked. On clicked the officer's flashlight, and its beam diffused through the car window and lit up her breasts. The officer pulled the handle and opened the rear door. Army boy had been leaning against it. Out he lurched, but caught himself with his stomach muscles. Suspended as if doing a crunch with Janine McQueen topless on top of him.

"Sir," said army boy, looking at the officer upside down.

Janine McQueen covered her breasts with her hands, climbed off army boy, scanned the backseat for her bra and her shirt.

"Out of the car, son," said the pervy patrolman. He smiled at the girl, his eyes sparkling. "You too, young lady." He winked at her.

She found her bra smashed against the backseat when army boy sat up. She tried to put it on with one hand, using the other and her forearm to hide her breasts.

"Come on now," the pervy patrolman said, "No time for that."

Janine looked at him, face blank, blinked. Shook her head slowly, no way. She found her shirt by her feet. Pulled it over her head. She grabbed her bra, shoved it in her pocket, crawled out of the car. Stood shirted but braless. The pervy patrolman spotlighted her with his flashlight, illuminating her unbrassiered breasts.

"IDs, kids, let's see them," said the pervy patrolman, eyes on Janine's boobs, free beneath her V-neck.

Army boy pulled his wallet from his back pocket, took out his military identification, handed it to the officer. "Army, huh," the officer said and sucked on his front teeth and gums with his tongue. "They happen to teach you that these carryings-on in a vehicle out here is illegal, son?"

"No sir," said army boy.

The pervy patrolman lifted his eyes from army boy's ID and dragged his gaze over Janine's body, from sandals on up. He met her face. "Your ID, miss."

Janine looked at him, smushed her lips into the corner of her mouth and shrugged. Her breasts bounced. Pervy patrolman's pupils followed. In the front seat was her small purse containing one tube of lipstick and a house key. She'd only started shaving her legs that year. She had no ID.

"Driver's license," he said.

When Janine McQueen's age was revealed, pervy patrolman flashed a face at army boy. "Had I'd have found you doing more than you were doing, I'd take your ass to jail," he said to army boy. But inside, he was just jealous and even hornier, missed being

nineteen. Wished the windows hadn't clouded. Wished he could
have watched more, longer.

As he explained the illegality of in-vehicle nudity, he paused,
looked at Janine McQueen, commented sweetly, "Honey, you
look cold and scared. Come here." He held out his arm. Janine McQueen didn't move, so he stepped toward her. Caught
her in a hug. Squeezed firmly. Felt her breasts through his uni-
form against his chest, her hips press against his gear belt. Janine
McQueen pinched her shoulders up to her ears, wrinkled her face,
held it awkwardly away from his body. He kept her for several
strange beats. She didn't breathe. In her mind, she was a flagpole.
A telephone pole. A lamppost. Army boy kicked at the dirt and
coughed and said, "Officer. Sir?" before the officer let go.

SIX MONTHS later, she went out with Talon Blaze. Everyone
called him T-bird. Long hair and a mustache. Narrow hips and
long forearms. He was sixteen and drove an orange van. He lived
with his parents, right next door to Janine McQueen. That's how
they met. Neighbors. They played together as kids. He taught
her how to smoke cigarettes when she was twelve. He always
liked her reddish hair. When he got his van, he asked her out on
a van date. She was fourteen. She said okay.

On her date with T-bird, they drove places around town in the
van. First they drove to Shoney's. They sat at the counter. She
ordered a patty melt, he a bacon burger. They split an order of
fries. She drank a lemonade and he a Coke. They talked about not
much. He told her how he installed the stereo in his van himself,
plus some help from his older stepbrother. She swung her legs and
kicked the brass footrail along the counter bottom. The drinks in
the glasses all the way down the countertop vibrated. She nodded at him, smiled wide. She smiled while chewing. Yammed-up
French fries against her back teeth were visible in the corners of
her smile. They leaned into each other and laughed through their
noses without sound, just nose wind. They talked more when

they were just friends. Now, it seemed they had trouble breathing. Preferred just looking at each other while they chewed. They finished, he paid, and then they drove around more. They drove the winding highway to the bluffs, parked.

In his orange van, there were no regular seats in the back. Instead there was a picnic table attached to the carpeted vehicle floor. For sitting there were benches running along the van walls, parallel to both of the long sides of the table. They were cushioned with planks of foam covered by bumpy nylon weave sleeves. The table could be lowered and two leaves unfolded from the long sides to make it suddenly very wide. The foam planks could be removed so the leaves could rest on the uncushioned benches, making a solid bridge between the two. The foam planks could be placed on top, along with two others that also came with the van, kept in storage compartments under the benches. Now it's a bed. T-bird had prepared. He transformed it from picnic table to bed earlier that day, just in case.

How had Janine McQueen prepared? She wore a hooter bra *and* a snap-down shirt. She kept it snapped low to make him a little crazy, and it did. His eyes fell to her cleavage and struggled to get up throughout the meal. Janine noticed and it reminded her of her last date and so it became part of her date experience. But there was more to her wardrobe rationale. Wearing a snap-down shirt, they could make out hard, and she wouldn't have to take her top off.

On the bed in the van on the bluffs, T-bird started at the front tails and undid her top, from the bottom all the way up. *Pop pop pop pop.* He unhooked her bra, had all access, but she kept her arms in her sleeves. No toplessness. Not illegal.

They made out for a long time. All the windows, even the windshield far away at the front of the van, got clouded out. He unbuttoned her jeans.

"Can I take these off?" he asked.

Janine shrugged and nodded and said, "Mkay."

He offed with her jeans. Then his. He was wearing small under-wear and there was his boner under that cotton. Her eyes wid-ened and she couldn't stop looking. He leaned over her, and now she could only see his face and shoulders and the shallow dawn of his pale chest. He ran his fingers along the elastic waistband of her underwear. She was wearing a sporty pair of underwear. They were not too small or lacy. They were not panties. She had not yet learned about panties. He tugged the elastic waistband over her butt. She said, "Wait—no—the cops," and worried the pervy patrolman would consider this illegal. Bottomlessness. She thought, probably highly illegal. This worried her much more than the sex that she was pretty sure was coming next. She didn't know what to expect with that, but getting busted for in-vehicle nudity, she knew from experience, is unpleasant. But would they get busted if they didn't remove their underwear?

She told T-bird about the patrolman and he cringed a little when she mentioned she was topless with army boy. But then he agreed, said yes, he'd heard about the nudity law too. So he didn't take her underwear all the way off. T-bird pulled the crotch of Janine McQueen's underwear over to the side, against her thigh. Kept it out of the way. Took advantage of the cotton fly space in his.

Now, Janine McQueen had never even worn a tampon. She'd been getting her period irregularly for an entire year and a half already, but hadn't yet graduated from pads. T-bird, long, straight, and pale as a fin, pushed himself against her. She gasped. He stopped, startled. The gasp whistled into the back of her throat, pierced the air between them. T-bird put his right hand on her forehead and brushed away her hair. He looked at her freckles and then into her eyes with his own eyes open wide and his eye-brows high up on his forehead and his left hand down low on her, holding aside her underwear.

He said, "I'll go slow."

Now, he was older and more experienced, but not much older

or even that experienced. His plum had been popped a year earlier by a friend of his stepbrother. She was twenty-three and thought T-bird was young and cute and it'd be a cool thing to do for him—charge his V-card on the Fourth of July. He'd never done it again since.

Janine McQueen held her breath and closed her eyes. He moved in. She felt like she was getting a shot, but the pain was more acute and less pinpointedly localized. The sensation burned through her whole middle body. From the lowest rung of rib to midthigh.

This first sex was a slow process. He pressed his weight into her, and she went: oh. And her face looked like it was electrocuted. He stopped, eased up just a bit, and she went: oh. More electrocution. So she held his shoulders tight, tried to keep him from moving anywhere. Wished she could hit pause.

"Maybe you should breathe," he suggested.

She breathed. He pressed. She went: oh. And squeezed his shoulders. Higher wattage all over her face. Then she breathed again, and he pressed more, and she went: oh oh. He stopped, suspended above her, movementless. She breathed for several seconds. Then nodded okay. He pressed. She flinched, sucked in a breath, said: oh. Her face, a mess of wires. He froze, waited. She breathed.

"Kay," she said. He pressed. In those moments, her underwear like it was, pulled to the side, plus her virginity, and gravity suddenly seemed much, much stronger. They both felt their bodies weighted, as if to the center of the earth. Then, once in, he didn't even get to move around much, because Janine McQueen said, in a dark voice, "Don't move." And in that second, young T-bird's mind launched from the van, rocketed furiously above the bluffs into the starred sky, wailed through the atmosphere. It crashed into the moon and ricocheted back, cometed over the ocean, into the van, hurtled back into his body, demolished him. He barked. Then smiled a lot. Flat against the foam cushions,

Janine McQueen bled a little. T-bird had napkins in his glove compartment. He reached into the front seat, popped it open. Handed the napkins to her, shaky and glistening. "Wow," he said. "Here."

THE NEXT time they do it, it's little bit better. And even a little bit better the next time after that. They hardly even bother with the bluffs anymore—special occasions only. Instead they just pull the van around the corner from their houses on the street neither Janine's nor T-bird's parents ever drive. The picnic table never comes back up. Bumpy nylon weave busts loose. Foam cushion particles stick in their hair, on their clothes, in their butt cracks, dust the floor of the van. Then it dawns on them: a nice couch or even a real bed would be more comfortable. So T-bird drops in while Janine babysits around town.

2. Spill

In the town where all the teenaged girls are babysitters, word gets out that Janine McQueen and Talon "T-bird" Blaze are a serious item. Everyone in the junior high and the high school hears about their rigorous sex life. And because Janine McQueen is the head babysitter, the leader of the girls, the who-knows-why-but-that's-the-way-it-is setter of the action trends, they all copy. In no time, one after another, then whole groups of babysitters pair off, hit the sack with their boyfriends. Junior highers date high school boys. High school girls date junior high boys (they can't believe it, neither one of them). They fuck all over the place. Like a flood it careens through the streets, rushes under doors, saturates carpets, rises to attics, swallows up the town. Teen *s-e-x*.

A contagion, then addiction. The babysitters can't stop doing it, especially while babysitting—a whole house, no parents. Some put the kids to bed, others stick them in front of the TV, others ignore them entirely. Before the parents come home, the babysitters boot out the boyfriends. Sometimes out back doors where the boyfriends run, zipping up jeans, buckling belts, leaping up and over fences, to run across another backyard, through side gates, down driveways, and finally to the safety of a different street where they get into cars or unlock bikes. Ram kickstands with sneakered heels. They haul ass for a few blocks, then hit the brakes, pull over, stop. Breathe. Feel the sex they just had creep around their underwear. Feel heroic.

Back at the houses, the babysitters scrounge between the couch cushions to find bras, undies, socks. They run frantic fingers through their hairdos to smooth out the muss. They mop up spots or hide them under throw pillows. Remake the beds if they've done it there. Push a sponge over the kitchen table if they've done it there. Crack a window to get the air circulating so the brothy smell of wet body parts doesn't hang thick in the space between the babysitters and the parents as the parents count out cash or write checks or ask what time the kids went to bed, all the while breathing deep the odor of what went on, glancing at the babysitters who chew gum, avoid eye contact, their cheeks red hot. They want desperately to get the hell out of there, to go have a smoke.

Some of the babysitters take drugs before sexing in order to crank up the sensations. They have to do all of the above *and* sober up before the parents come home. Eye drops, breath spray, flat shoes. They click on their retainers to camouflage slurring.

An epidemic, it affects their babysitting performance. It puts the kids at risk. Little kids wander out sliding glass doors, into the town, unsafe and alone. Allie Gregg, Adela Cope, Cesar Herbert, Todd Cahill, Elsa Hedrick—lost for days. Finally found in the KidsFun PlayPen at the local fast-food burger chain, eating old fries at the bottom of the slide or half buried in the sinky plastic ball cage. Parents stop hiring certain sitters, call up others. To no avail—they're all doing it.

One mom gets a bright idea: hire boys. A junior at the high school, one of T-bird's friends. He plays football, could use some extra cash, notices the ad in the school paper. He calls the mom, says he's great with kids. He shows up in his football jersey, shoulders broad, butt like a bubble, legs squatty. The mom leaves him cash for pizza and the number to the restaurant. She has a date with her boss. He's recently separated. His wife left him because their kids disappeared in their backyard. He had hired the sitter. He and Mom pull out of the driveway. Football boy orders the pizza, tells six-year-old Nelson Frazier to pay for it with the money on the counter when it arrives. Tells him to brush his teeth after he eats the pizza. Football boy plunks Nelson in front of the tube. He tells him he'll be back. Next door, football boy's girlfriend is babysitting. They have hours of sex in the basement, on the sleeper sofa and the pool table.

All the while Janine McQueen and her T-bird are in love, making love, innovating. She tells her best friend about things to do with sour sugared gummy rings. And another thing with those small tubs of ready-made frosting. Within days, stretched out, half-eaten gummy rings litter carpets. Chocolate and vanilla finger and boob prints mark pillows, cushions, headboards, walls. Everything's sticky. Ants feast. Parents return home to the smell of birthday parties and musk.

Then another thing happens. It's serious. Janine McQueen gets pregnant. Then what? So do all the other girls. The babysitters swell round like buoys. Janine McQueen decides to keep her baby through to its birth, even raise it after. The copycats? They copy. Soon all the babysitters have their babies. Except for the girls that do a lot of drugs. They miscarry. And what about the gay kids? No one knows about them. The rest, though, they have beautiful, healthy, gurgling, bouncy babies. Blondes, brunettes, freckled redheads. These new babies plus the kids the babysitters had been babysitting before they got their own—suddenly it is a town clogged with little ones.

The babysitters are now young mothers. They pledge allegiance to their own babies, not the adult parents' babies. The babysitters are off the market. They're back to being good babysitters, but only to their own kids. These new young parents seem not to mind taking care of their new babies. Don't feel gypped out of life. They quit school. The junior high and the high school are empty except for the drug couples who take long lunches and skip most classes.

And the adult parents? They are fucked up. First there was no one to trust with the care of their children. But trust is a pliable thing. It can be bent around the mind to suit a situation. At least before the babysitters birthed their babies, the adult parents had options. Trustworthy or untrustworthy, they *could* hire a sitter. Now they can't.

The adult parents, each one of them, is overcome. It happens fast, and in several phases. First, it is like the world is beating them up. It starts with a feeling, like strangulation. Like a big fist knuckled into their exposed throats. The bumps and tubes pop and separate. They gag, choke, and freeze. For the adult parents, no babysitters equals life without what feels like movement. These are not the lives they planned. Not how they imagined it would go. They are pinned. Then the world finishes them off. Their futures are slugged solidly upside the face. Sweat, blood, teeth knocked loose, cartwheeling in slow motion, away.

No babysitters, so the adult parents must forfeit essential things: dinners, movies, dancing, drinks, hotel sex. Take, for example, Waldo Hayes. He is not married. He has two kids. No sitter to watch them so he can go out. When is he supposed to meet a woman? When is he supposed to have sex? The adult parents need certain things to keep them cognizant of the fact that their heads are connected to their bodies and down there, on their bodies, are sex organs. Life cannot be exclusively work plus parenting. Because that equals death. Now, the adult parents feel like they're dying. And not dying becomes more important than everything. They love their children, they do. But when freedom is subtracted and death threatens, finally there is war. War in the minds of the dying. And sometimes, in wartime, the best decision maker does not make the decisions. In wartime, right minds are defeated. The adult parents are left to their wrong minds, which run and dive and crawl and shoot while explosions rip ruin across their worlds. War, in the time of so much young sex.

In the rec room at the community center, eyes wild, hands trembling, adult parents spike their coffees with whiskey and Irish cream. They sit in folding chairs. Their kids play on the jungle gym outside, visible through the wide gray window. Those with babies keep them in their carriers, on the floor by their feet. The adult parents sputter, sip, shake their heads. Stare at one another, unblinking as spotlights. One has an idea. He stands. Clears his throat. He begins. His voice cracks. He continues. He mentions the nutritive properties of the ocean. Its riches, resources, extraordinary capability for sustaining life.

He presents facts:

- A single cubic foot of seawater nourishes far more living organisms than its equivalent of soil.
- There's a striking similarity between the analysis of elements in human blood and seawater—so beneficial to sustenance.
- Disease resistance in sea plants and animals is many times better than their counterparts living on land.
- The ocean is a magical solution of sodium and chlorine and oxygen and hydrogen and other elements and trace minerals that act synergistically to rejuvenate life!

The adult parents listen, hushed. They shift in their seats. Here, now, during this time of duress, they share it seems, a consciousness. They, all of them, are getting his gist. One parent clears his throat, pipes in, "Sound travels great distances. In there—in the ocean." A few mmm yes and agree.

"It does," says another.

"And underwater," contributes a single mother, "it is quite easy to pick up things that are too heavy to lift on land."

Someone mutters, "Right, yeah, that's a plus."

"Not to mention the ocean sensations," says a fat bearded dad. "The heft of relief when your body floats in water."

"And when water bumps against your skin," says the mother with the thick glasses. She takes her husband's hand. "The press of it against your abdomen," she says. "The pressure of it to your cheek, under your arms, on your eyelids," she pushes her glasses up her forehead, places the heels of her palms against the sockets of her eyes and says, "It's a release. It's like—"

"The brain can stop braining," says the mom in the long dress. "The rhythm of the sea particles," she says. "And there are colors under there." She looks dreamy. "Soft swaying tall grasses, sea leaves—"

"The gentle coo of the ocean jungle," murmurs the father who teaches piano.

Ahhh, they mumble.

"It's a glinting place of hidden cities where everything is blue and diamonds," says the mom with the triplets, looking for the first time in forever less exhausted. Yeah, yeah, the adult parents nod and agree. Smile like their faces are cracking. They continue, one after another.

"Don't forget about the friendly fish and dynamic dolphins."

"The watchful whales, mild-mannered manatees."

Right, yes. They gain momentum and enthusiasm.

"A live fish in the open ocean never stops growing!"

"The bluefin tuna can move faster than a horse!"

"Bowhead whales can sing two notes at a time!"

"Dolphins sleep with one eye open!"

"Beluga whales play tag!"

These creatures, the parents confirm, would be excellent influences and companions. Not a single parent mentions sharks or gills.

That's all it takes. Their lives, as they'd seen them—in the golden era before the babysitters started having sex—seem closer,

possible. They decide. They decide the ocean's better than teenaged girls with babies of their own. They decide the ocean's better
than them, the adult parents as they are now—their minds all bat-
tleground. The ocean, they understand, is undefeatable. It seems
like such a good idea: Turn the children over to the sea. They set a
date: tomorrow. They down the creamy dregs in their paper cups,
stretch, sigh, toss their cups in the tall trash can by the door. They
shake hands, bow their heads, feel briefly light and safe. Peaceful.

The next day, the high worn off, but their resolve intrac-
table, the adult parents corral their kids, bundle their babies.
Their minds, singularly focused, like the inside of a copper
pipe. Their nerves, their appearances, wrinkled and frayed, they
drive their kids to the beach. It is dusk. A procession of family
wagons snake into the beach parking lot. Pull into the spaces
facing the ocean. They park.

The adult parents get out, open back doors for the kids. Children climb out of the vehicles. Salty wind off the ocean blows
into their small faces. They squint and catch their breaths, push
hair out of their eyes with their little hands. The kids glimpse the
other kids. Excited, some climb on bumpers, race toward one
another, jump from the short cinderblock wall separating the
sand from the parking lot. They throw sand. Run and roll in it.
Those still in the parking lot waiting for permission squeal and
fidget and chomp like Christmas Eve. The adult parents hand
the larger children the babies in carriers. The parents point to
the ocean and nod. "Go," they smile. And the kids bound and
tumble across the sand. Twenty, thirty, forty of them in a pack
jumping and falling over each other like puppies. Screeching and
laughing at the beach.

A few nervous ones glance back for their parents. Five adult
dads, six adult moms wave and smile assuredly as they gulp deep
breaths of ocean air into their lungs. The adult parents are light-
headed, sick. "Go ahead," they shoo. Even the pervy patrolman,
in civvies, stands with his wife. The wind lifts her hair off her

neck. Her shoulders hunch. Her hands shield her eyes like a visor. They watch their kids romp toward the sea.

Some parents stay in their cars, can't get out. Driver-side windows rolled wide open, adult parents hang their elbows, arms, heads out over the doors like rags. The breeze carries wafts of talcum powder and diaper dumps and the almost-nothing soft scent of kid skin. Slowly the adult parents pull themselves off the doors and sink deep into their seats. They watch their children through windshields. The kids gather like seagulls on the sand in front of the waves. Throw pebbles, shells, seaweed leaves into the waves, at each other. Some hug. The adult parents lean into their headrests. Grab the skin between their eyes at the tops of their noses and pinch. They shut their eyes, rub their foreheads and temples with their fingertips. The waves crash below a low sky the color of guts.

The kids gather close. The tide rises. Rolls over the sand. Waves stretch and stand high, then break and crumble and foam over the kids. A few are knocked over. They splash into the spume, flop and turn. Some stand, slip, fall again. Upon withdrawal, wave water cradles the spilled kids, rocks them clear from the beach and into the sea. Some kids notice. Point, grunt, perplexed, until they capsize and are slipstreamed away.

Sets of waves from way out rush the beach and tumble over the sand, toppling more little kids, trawling them into the ocean. Shrill children screams and yips are swallowed by ocean rumble as they are sucked into the salty sea and the beach is washed bare. In the darkening light, baby shadows shift in silhouette inside the faces of tall waves, then disappear. The children are coddled out, pocketed by the deep. One, two, three at a time. Until the sky is black, the sand is black, the sea is black.

In the parking lot, adult parents loll on their sides, on their backs, on their bellies on the asphalt by their cars. They are like the tops of their heads have been lopped off. And the bottoms of their hearts lanced open. Their brains slaver out of their skulls.

Porridge exposed to wind, sand, salt, flies. Their hearts empty and drain over their intestines, collapse against their ribs.

Just inland, up on the bluffs, Janine McQueen and T-bird are parked in the van. Their little baby naps in its baby boat seat-belted to the passenger seat. Janine McQueen and T-bird make out on the van bed. They feed their baby. They make out more. The moon slices a silver gash across the ocean. They stay all night.

Hangdangling

———

S AILOR IS building a boat in her bedroom. Sailor's dad is all for projects. Especially woodworking. He is a carpenter and taught Sailor everything he knows back when she was in middle school. For her thirteenth birthday she wanted a live/work space. Her dad thought that fine and moved her into the large garage with the peaked ceiling. It's smaller than a barn but much bigger than the average two-car. He scraped and sprayed the oil stains off the cement, insulated the dry wall, bought her a Murphy bed to save space and to protect her bed linens from sawdust or paint. Then several years later, now seventeen years old, and for months and months, she set to work on a twenty-two-foot clinker-built double-ender—a version of a nice one she'd seen at the docks. Sailor's dad jokes with her, says her interests and her timing couldn't be better—the weather's been so grisly. Torrential rains, flash floods, vegetation everywhere has gone from deep green to putrid. Everyone's got high, heavy stacks of sandbags around their homes. Sailor's dad says she'll have to save them all. But she doesn't want to save anyone. She envisions just herself sailing off in the boat she built, tasting away her days on the big brine. World-wise and capable and bronzed. Docking and talking to folks, meeting their eyes directly, looking closely into the lines across their faces. Then off, hoisting sails, tying hitch knots, carving oceanic froth around the globe.

She's in love with a boy named Whaler. They've got similar-sounding androgynous names that are also nouns, but don't confuse them. Sailor is the girl. Whaler is the boy. Think: Sailor is a *she*.

Sailor and Whaler are both in high school and work part-time at the aquarium, when it's open. Sailor tests all the tanks for salinity, with kits and vials, drops and tabs, and a colored chart. Whaler feeds the sharks, from white buckets of blood and scales, bones and fins, meat and fat. He does it with his bare hands. Sailor thinks this is tough of him, macho. His hands stink like sea guts, always.

One time, mid-feed, Sailor slunk by Whaler with her salinity-tester attaché, en route to the sea lions to test their waters. It was a rare day—hot out and sunshiney. Sailor's shorts were short, and she even wore an impractical pair of kitten heels because she'd recently realized they made her legs in shorts look good. She and Whaler had not started dating, but she had a big bright sneak for him; the sight of him was like cellular pyromania, starting in her groin and quickly conflagrating through her whole body. And she was pretty sure he liked her. They'd smile and stare and get sweaty and mumble Hey, Hi, when passing at work or in the hallway at school.

Sailor heard the sea lions barking from behind acrylic demi-walls. She noticed the sunlight crinkle across the surface of the tide pool exhibit. She saw Whaler, spotlighted with his white bucket of blood, up on the shark deck. She slowed to a saunter, caught Whaler's eye. He had a soaking handful of fish parts poised above the surface of the shark tank, ready to chuck—when the sight of Sailor stopped him stupid. She grinned and waved, sweet cheeked and rubbery. Whaler smiled wide, tipped his chin her way, hiked his eyebrows high for hello. A shark head broke the surface of the tank water, swum its wide-open jaw directly over Whaler's fist full of bloody fish, and shut its chops at Whaler's elbow. Witnessing this, Sailor screamed. The scream filled the whole dome of her mouth on its loud way out. Whaler's eyes, all terror and shock, exploded open across his face. His free fist sledgehammered up over his head and came pounding down on the shark's snout. The shark's jaw released, popped like a trunk. Whaler yanked his arm from its mouth, scraping it on several rows of teeth. His arm came out torn and bleeding. Shark fin flicked water like sparks into the air and disappeared.

Whaler was gauzed and hauled away into an ambulance. Sailor watched its lights whirl. She worried a lot, hoped he'd be okay. Hoped he wouldn't die before they had the chance to make out. She'd been daydreaming and nightdreaming a lot lately about making out with him. She cut work early, was too upset to finish her shift. She ran directly to the beach, kicked off her heels, charged across the sand and into the surf. She tossed and wambled in the waves while Whaler got gassed, pricked, swabbed, sewn, and swaddled at the hospital. Later, chilled and dripping, Sailor called the hospital from a pay phone. Found out he was safe. She returned home dried stiff and salty. Told her dad she'd been splashed by the orca at work.

Whaler's arm turned out okay. Turned out he was attacked by the aquarium's really old shark. So old it only had half its instincts left—to lunge at food, but not to chew. Whaler recovered and wasn't even afraid to return to the blood and the bucket and the sharks. They started dating right away. Maybe because they got to suffer trauma together—were up close and intimate with mad-dog terror and mortality. Sailor had read somewhere that this is good for love—peril and adversity. It brings lovers closer together. This, and the mean pink scars that burrow streaks down his arm (she traces them with her pointer finger, sometimes wishes she had them too—that thing about love that makes you want to be *like* your lover) makes their love intense.

They're also very secretive. Not with each other, but toward the world. This is one of the best aspects of their young love lives. Secrets, particularly love secrets, sauce and fatten the love soup. Both Sailor and Whaler coincidentally and fortuitously share this notion. So Sailor and Whaler keep their love deeply undercover. Even at school, no one knows. They watch each other around campus. Beam and wink at each other from behind the drips that drop from the hoods of their slickers. When they talk in groups, they prattle in easy and offhand ways. Not too much eye contact. No touching. They blab about assignments, television, teachers, sinkholes. No one suspects that they are furiously in love.

They chomp into and through the make out phase of their relationship early on and then make the most of their free time by practicing sex on each other. They do it at the aquarium, after hours, in the jellyfish room. The jellyfish room is their hiding place. Not only is it dry, but it is dark. Barely lit—just the few tank lights in black tanks casting a faint glow in a black room. The jellyfish—floating nowhere, their filament glowing in the tank lights—look like clouds and smoke and silky strings. Slippery and undulant. They are Sailor's favorite part of the aquarium.

During work hours, Sailor watches the jellyfish rapturously. When she tests their salinity, she blows them kisses. They don't look like creatures with stingers. They look soft. She likes to imagine they are stingless. Then she likes to imagine one plopped on her face. The cool, wet, jiggling weight of it smothering her.

At night, the burbling filter pump hushes the sounds of Sailor's and Whaler's heaving and breathing as they press hard into each other in the darkest corner of the jellyfish exhibit. The natural scent of the aquarium conceals the scent of their wet sex. He stuffs his hands up her top and down her bottoms and rubs and grabs all over. She stuffs hers up and down his and does the same. They squeeze and fuck and squeeze and fuck, hot enough to bust. When they kiss, sometimes their teeth gnash.

Afterwards, their aquarium uniforms rumpled and stretched, they catch their breaths against the jellyfish tanks. Leaning their

sweaty foreheads into the glass, funneling steam from their nostrils, they watch the sexy jellies.

"That one there," she says, "the way that one looks is how the
inside of your cheek tastes on my tongue."

He smiles. She gently strokes his scar arm. Feels the new pink
ridges bump across the palm of her hand.

"You know," she says, "I'd like you even if that shark weren't
senile and you'd become a one-armer," she tells him, their faces
inches from the other, and both pressed against the tank glass.

"Thanks," he says and kisses her on the mouth and squeezes
her ass.

MEANWHILE, THEIR parents. There's Sailor's dad and
Whaler has a mom. Both single parents, they are of particular
note because they happened to have been babysitters, back in the
day. Technically Whaler's mom was a babysitter, Sailor's dad was
a boyfriend. Of course they were not a couple then. It is coincidence that they both happened to take part in that particular
moment in history, at that particular place, in that particular time.
It's coincidence when they, all grown up, find themselves in the
same new town, with the children they'd conceived as teenagers.

Dad and Mom had been lonely. Burnt out on life on one of the
few clear and sunny days, they each left work early, hit the beach.
He went surfing, she went tanning—both trying hard to recap-
ture their youths. On their ways home, separately, they stopped at
the boardwalk fish shop to purchase scallops. Sailor's dad entered
within minutes of Whaler's mom. They were the only customers in the shop. They smiled, nodded, noticed each other. Each
thought the other looked distantly familiar. Hello, how are you,
scallops too? They small-talked, swapped recipes. Then, A cup of
coffee? They took their scallops and went next door, stirred milk
into their cups, sipped and chitchatted. Revealed sections of their
pasts. Turned out turned out turned out, they were at the same
place at the same time back then, just as now. Miraculously, they

never knew each other then. Thought perhaps, once or twice, they'd probably passed in the hall. Turned out their kids went to the same high school. Turned out their kids both worked at the aquarium. Turned out neither parent had dated in a very long time. Turned out Dad and Mom had so much in common. So they embarked on a relationship. They had no idea their kids were on one too.

About the grown-up babysitter parents: Most of their youth was lost to parenthood. For this, now grown up, they experience a sense of loss. Take Whaler's mom. Little Whaler was the adorable baby she'd conceived on an air hockey table in the attic game room of one of her babysittee's houses. Back then, during the great babysitter sex-heave that swept the town, all was peaches for the babysitters until, one day and perhaps for some if not all of them, it wasn't. Once grown up, for example, Whaler's mother reflected upon her life and determined that the blazing noontime of her youth was not the best time to have a kid. For obvious reasons: What the fuck happened to the sexy afternoons, twilights, and evenings of her youth? They got gone—they set like the sun and extinguished into the infinite deep of motherhood. This casts a shade of grief over her adult life. But it is a peculiar lament. It is not for the sex she had then—she doesn't regret those babysitting shags. She remembers them fondly—while the kids were downstairs playing in the kitchen or hopscotching the streets, those shags were worth it. Particularly those still, swollen moments right before. She and her boyfriend, their body heats fanatic. She remembers her arousal zapping from her and meeting his to hiss and braise especially tinglingly along the swath of skin between hipbones, the stretch of side between hipbone and ribs, the breastplate between shoulders, their foreheads. Those flush and moiling moments of almost touching or just touching that seethe with a locomotive chug toward sex, Whaler's mother remembers, were richly best. Sometimes even better than the sex itself. Actual youth sex, Whaler's mother muses in her adulthood, happened in an alien-abductive way: Another power obtrudes, seizes your body whole, and, in the distant hovels of one side of your mind, out creeps the notion that this oughtn't be happening. From the other side glows the awareness that what is happening is truly miraculous. And between the two she remembers her lungs, filling with water. She breathed from it so deeply she rumbled.

So she pines for what she considers misplaced time. And in that time she imagines a kind of life: the kind that comes between having parents and necessary schooling—the youth of that, and being a parent and necessary working—the adulthood of that. She's misplaced the time of life when you, as your own person, own your life. When the whole thing is all yours.

Had she not had Whaler so young, she imagines her twenties: She would have some kind of job. Mind-numbing probably, or oddly houred. Perhaps she would sell things. Colorful T-shirts. She'd fold and refold them around a plastic slab, making the sharpest angles. She could have been a coffee jerk or a night watchwoman at a building owned by a large corporation, while car washing on the weekends. The pay would be poor but just enough to cover her. Rent for a place for her. Food for her. Carefully selected items of clothing, all for her. And then there's off-work hours. She could eat crackers or smoke cigarettes for dinner. She could find, know, and forget lovers. She could enter parties as the sun sets, exit as it rises. She could drive through the wet night if she couldn't sleep or if she just wanted to see the streets lit and glossy under the tall lamps. She could think and walk and work and play in a thick and solitary haze of all herself.

She considers this time misplaced because she's not convinced it's lost, it's just not handy. So while trying to locate it, she does things like skip work in order to tan at the beach. She's even done it in the rain. No matter what, it feels right.

Sailor's dad has his own, man version of this kind of longing. Therefore, their shared actual experiences plus their adult perspectives on those experiences equals a lot in common for Sailor's dad and Whaler's mom, and while some may think opposites attract, so do sames. And their regrets about their particular choices as youths don't color their parenting in ways one might expect. They don't encourage their kids to go out and have sex or anything, but they don't forbid it or exert any kind of mind ownership over their kids about it. They just let them be, practice good-tempered indifference to their children's private lives.

Still, Sailor and Whaler keep their relationship from their parents too. Not because the parents would disapprove and bring their love to an abrupt and treacherous halt. Sailor's dad wouldn't even ground her or sit her down for a talk about the responsibilities one takes on when one does all the things one's body wants to do. It is simply thrilling for both Sailor and Whaler to keep their richly embroidered love and sex life secret. It keeps it tickling in their minds and bodies at all times. And for those moments home from work when Sailor's dad asks, How goes it at the aquarium? Sailor can say fine. And when he asks, what'd you do today? She can say, nothing, same-old same. When in truth, ripe all over her skin and dancing wildly through her thoughts and underwear is the fact that she's just had delicious jellyfish sex with the person who is the breath-filching favorite of her life. She can keep her face expressionless and still while the frictive memory of all of Whaler's parts buzz on and in her. And she can slip to her room, pull down her Murphy bed, lie on it, smell Whaler all over her mouth each time she breathes deep. This is a joy of her youth.

MEANWHILE, SAILOR'S dad and Whaler's mom get serious. They decide it's time to tell the kids. One night, Sailor's dad fixes dinner, sits across from Sailor, clears his throat, mentions his new girlfriend.

"I'm seeing a woman," says Dad. He smears butter on his bread. "I have a girlfriend."

"Okay," says Sailor, not particularly interested but tuned to the sound of his voice. It has the sound of serious talk, which she hasn't heard since she was little and they lost track of her mom.

"You might know her son," he tells her, "from school and the aquarium."

The muscles in Sailor's stomach buckle. She balls the napkin on her lap.

"His mother told me he was bit by a shark there, working at the aquarium," her dad continues.

Her potatoes, moving down the tube from mouth to stomach, stop bluntly and change directions. She takes a gulp of water. "Yeah, I think I know that guy," she says, struggling to sound casual, "from the aquarium." She feels pale and sweaty, her napkin damp in her fist. "And from a few classes I think," she shrugs.

"Think he's a nice guy?" Sailor's dad asks.

"Probably," she says. Her voice is a placemat.

Eventually, Sailor's dad schedules an introduction. Sailor to meet his new girlfriend and her son, they to meet her. Hey, hey, yep, I've seen you around, the kids say at the restaurant, each trying to breathe steadily and keep the color out of their faces. Sailor hardly notices Whaler's mom at all, doesn't care about her dad's new girlfriend, is too distracted by the blood zinging through her veins at the sight of her Whaler in his T-shirt and jeans, his hair combed neatly to the side. The two families eat fish-and-chips on big plates, served by a waitress in a lady swashbuckler's costume. On a previous date, Sailor's dad had heard from Whaler's mom that Whaler is an ace carpenter in woodshop. Dunking a chip in some ketchup, Sailor's dad looks at his girlfriend's son.

"I hear you're handy," Dad says to Whaler. Dad pops the chip in his mouth, chews. "Maybe you two can work on the boat together." He smiles at Whaler. "You can come over and help her with the boat," he says. Then to Sailor, "You can finish building that boat."

Like flash burn over her whole body, she's scorched and feverish. She's thrilled by the prospect of seeing her Whaler more.

Licking the lengths of his arm scars and breathing deep the smell of his sea-gut hands as he moves them across her face and neck, under her shirt. *And*, she feels a shift, a surprise, her brain flipping over in its brainpan. Suddenly, the prospect of sexing in her room becomes especially rousing. Sailor looks down at her plate, pokes her fish with her fork, tries to calm her body and keep all sizzle off her face. She sighs, says, "Alright," trying to sound indifferent. She glances at Whaler. He is looking down at his food. His forehead looks moist. She has a hunch he's been thinking what she's been thinking.

"Sure," he says dully, "I'll help."

Sailor slips her socked foot out of her muddy shoe, carefully stretches her leg out under the table, points her toes, gives him a little push in the crotch. They both jolt and twitch, briefly. She is surprised by herself. He is surprised by her. They try not to laugh. They are both, at the table in this restaurant, their two dating parents by their sides, flabbergasted by the situation. They try to keep their faces plain as foam.

MEANWHILE, THE weather is really rebelling. Unpredictable as always, but lately it's cudgeling out of control. While the kids pretend to be nothing more than aquarium co-workers, schoolmates, boatbuilders, outside pounding rain rain rain rain rain scores the white noise for all the inhabitants of the town. Even the aquarium is shutting down more frequently because the exposed tanks overflow, and Corporate is afraid the seals, sea lions, whales, sharks, and dolphins will hop the gush and swim away, only to tragically and inevitably wind up beached somewhere in the streets surrounding the aquarium when the glut subsides.

One afternoon when the aquarium manager has called Whaler and then called Sailor to tell her not to come in, to take care and keep dry, Sailor dials Whaler and whispers to him over the phone. "Do you think it's our love secret? Do you think it sends direct

energy to the atmosphere and is making the weather nuts?" Out
of his mom's earshot, Whaler laughs and tells her it's possible.

Aquarium hours freed up, they work on the boat. Whenever
his mom visits her dad, Whaler tags along, acts casual. "I just
want to say hey," he says. "Help Sailor out with the tiller and the
transom." Then they all eat dinner together and when the plates
are clean, Sailor says, "We're gonna hit the garage, tinker with the
grab rail, the turnbuckle, and the companionway."

Dad says, "Great, good."

Mom says, "Build hard!"

Whaler blinks at them. Sailor says, "Okay."

The parents are still naively confident they are the only daters
around, and/or they are just totally distracted by their own new
relationship and the blinding excitement and fear that accom-
pany it.

So the kids don their slickers and race across the backyard to
Sailor's bedroom garage. Plunked in the middle is a beautiful
boat, pretty much done. Whaler's help helped a lot, and they've
whipped through the finishing touches. *Zip zip zip clap smack,*
they dust their hands on their thighs. Now they use the boat for
sex practice. Special-gear-on-the-sex-rig sex. Because one of the
best parts of sex is inventing it.

Sailor and Whaler figure out how to wangle sailing accoutre-
ments to make a sex thing. Like this: They start with body fittings
and equipage. Sailor knots wristbands, ankle shackles, and two trunk
harnesses from leather parceling. Each band and shackle wraps three
times around the wrists, three times around the ankles, and is tied
off by a butterfly knot with artillery loop. Through the eye in each
loop she screws U-bolts and shanks. The trunk harnesses are knotted to fit over the head, strap across the shoulders. The leather parceling crosses in the center of the chest and in between the shoulder
blades. She ties the harness off at the backside cross with another
butterfly knot. Through that loop, another U-bolt.

As for the boat apparatus: Into the deck just below the mainsail,

Whaler secures extra O-ring line feeds. Through pulleys in the mainsail mast beam he threads nylon cordage—able to heft up to three tons dead weight—hardly necessary for young Whaler and Sailor, each only weighing a buck plus, but they appreciate the tender elasticity of the cord. To the ends of the cordage running through the pulleys they secure snap hooks. Whaler runs a main line through the pulleys and fixes a tensioning cleat to the deck.

They hoist and unfurl the jib sheet sail, for nautical authenticity and dramatic effect. They turn down the lights in the garage, light up a few candles on the deck, flick on the stereo, not to music but to ocean sounds—sounds that occur naturally outside Sailor's window, now reproduced and amplified, unnaturally, inside. Gulls gackering, waves breaking, steamers honking, whales whinnying, echoey, underwater. Plus the deep background sound of real pounding rain—so constant these days they hardly hear it.

Amorous lighting, ocean sounds, stormy backdrop, their harnesses, the chord fed up the mast beam, their parents unaware over in the house—and Sailor and Whaler are set. They start with their clothes. They take them off and toss them below deck. This part makes Sailor nervous because she's still not used to total nudity in front of the love of her young life. At the aquarium, they kept their clothes on, and it's so dark there. Standing here naked on the deck of her boat in the middle of her room, with Whaler naked too, she feels bashful. They ready the rig, sneaking peaks at each other, blushing.

"You have a high belly button," Whaler tells her.

"I do?" she asks.

"I think so."

"Oh," she says, worried.

"I like it," he says.

"Okay." She blushes. "Thanks."

She puts on wet suit gloves and booties, he puts on wet suit gloves and booties—to protect their wrists and ankles. Over the wet suit, she wraps her wrists and her ankles with the knotted

bands and shackles. Then she wraps his wrists, including his scar
arm—heartily healed and rugged looking—and ankles. They pull
on wet suit vests to protect their chests, so the harnesses don't
tear their skin. Not so naked anymore. The wet suit smashes her
breasts flat against her chest. They both look like skin divers that
forgot their bottoms. She helps him pull his harness over his head.
She tugs on the knot between his shoulder blades to tighten. He
does all of the same for her.

Now they clip the snap hooks from the cordage ends to the
U-bolts on each of their wrist and ankle bands and their chest
harnesses. *Click. Clack. Cluck. Clink. Chink.*

Locked in, they face each other on the boat deck. Whaler
squats and feeds the main line connecting all the pulleys through
the tensioning cleat on the floor by their feet. Sailor notices his
balls sway just a few inches from the deck. She feels her face get
warm and looks away. He winds the end of the line around his
fist. Stands. "Up?" he says. She nods. They climb onto the boom,
constructed specially to hold their body weights. They both balance on the boom, facing each other. His foot her foot, his foot
her foot. They are belly to belly, steadying themselves by keeping
a hand on the mast. Whaler looks directly at Sailor, smiles.

"Do it," she whispers, arms out, feet apart.

He pulls hard on the main line. The cordage springs taut,
yanking them at their wrists and ankles, at the U-bolts between
their shoulder blades. Instead of the mainsail, Sailor and Whaler
are hoisted up the mast, several feet off the boom, which is several
feet off the ship deck, which is several feet from the garage floor.
Their arms and legs splay wide and open. Whaler gives the main
line a quick jerk and the tensioning cleat locks it tight.

They are face to face, belly to belly, groin to groin, so close,
nearly naked, strung up and suspended midair in her garage room
at her dad's house. The elasticity in the cordage gives them a little
bounce. They can lean into each other, touch body with body,
but they can't use their hands.

For a moment imagine your hands. Take the right and the left and flex them so the fingers are spread, and palm faces palm. Keeping fingers taut and flared, like your pinkies are noosed and tied in one direction, your pointers in another, your thumbs in another, bring the hands together. Fingertip pads toward fingertip pads, but no touching. Slowly close the space between your palms, but still do not touch. Notice the air bang warm and tinglingly between the balls and heels of your palms. Now imagine one hand were Whaler and the other Sailor. And imagine one whole hand was Whaler's genitals and abdomen and chest and the other whole hand were Sailor's genitals and abdomen and breasts. And there's that hot pocket of livening air between. This is what they are like up there.

Today they find barely touching outstandingly more tantalizing than touching all over. They are strapped and stuck, an inch of air between them, except for down there where he pokes up at her. They don't put it in though, not for a while. That's part of the thing about the rig. It's about restraint. So sometimes he pokes past her inner thighs and Sailor thinks it is like a bridge between them. Sometimes it's high up, its tip toward her belly button, and then it is more like a wedge between them. Whichever way, she is at all times aware of it down there, on her, looking a little bit strangled even though it's the single thing between the two of them that's not bound or tethered.

They breathe slowly, inhaling the scents from each other's necks. For Sailor, the smell of wet suit occasionally defeating Whaler's sea-gut skin.

Up here, suspended, so close, no hands—their attention is pulled tightly into the slim space of air between them. Like a high-pitched quiet. Sailor is aware of the thin cushion of it. The layer of wavy heat that wraps Whaler's body like gauze. And her own, which if she really concentrates, she can feel bounce slightly, softly, against his.

Her hipbones graze his, the small knobs of them. The hairs

on his thighs twiddle against hers. All of their skin, up and down each of their bodies, crackles. She breathes deeply and thinks she can hear his heart beat in her lungs.

Sailor is flushed and light-headed. Sex rigged, jimmied high, floating, and on fire—she feels like whatever stilts prop up her brain and keep its tubes together in her skull are kicked out—so the brain and all its pink hoses and ducts spill down the inside of her neck. They catch and tangle and detach her muscles and organs from their spots, drag them down the inside of her body, behind her skin. Down through her thighs, past her knees, down her shins, out the bottoms of her feet. Drained. Here, with her Whaler. All the room in her cleared for him.

Why? Why do they do it this way? Because barely touching sucks from the whole sky and the whole earth the simmering sense of *soon* that swells in the body to make all of everything in life feel worthwhile. Because to capture and suspend those moments of barely touching is a marvelment of love.

Strung up and hangdangling. Outside the rains hammer against rooftops, wreck down on trees, collapse bridges, while Sailor and Whaler start to shift and bounce, slowly from the rig. Down there he nudges her. She is slippery; so is he. Their breathing quickens; their muscles throughout their bodies flex and contract. This is when they give up on some of the restraint part. This is when they have aquarium-style sex, only near naked, aerial, strung taut like a sail, pressing back and forth.

There are moments during their rig-sexing session when Sailor and Whaler achieve a pitch-perfect grace. When the tension in the cords plus the particular torque on the points of attachment plus gravity's interminable power and the miraculous just-right movement of their bodies together—for short-held breaths—catch sublime turns of glory. They both feel it. Their whole bodies, light and permeable. It's like their bodies have disappeared, but of course are very much there—shuddering into each other.

This just-right grace can exist for only an instant. Most of the rig sexing, while a hoot and delight, is hardly so refined. Most of it is clinking and clunking and bumping. Awkward and clumsy. Splayed out, Whaler and Sailor giggle and *hmmphmmmp* a lot up there. They feel off balanced, new to what they're doing. They'd gotten so good at aquarium sex, but up here, no hands, no legs, they're starting over. But they are full of pride for their invention—that instead of the mainsail on their boat, they've hoisted themselves in its place. And it is a place for sex. Their consciousness of this is like helium filling their skulls, seeping through the seams in the bone. Their faces so close, they dig in and kiss deliriously, and while they kiss they smile widely and laugh.

MEANWHILE, OF course the big rains are still falling slaughterously, the winds are blowing belligerently. The grim storm's strength explodes suddenly. From severe weather system to nature danger—in a snap. Dams burst. Trailer homes dissolve into vinyl sheets and planks that surf the melee across the town. Cars, trucks, trees, pets, chairs—all in it. The local government sounds the city hall alarm. It wails dimly. The wind and rain outshout it. The streets fill deep.

In the kitchen Sailor's dad and Whaler's mom watch through the window, stupefied. He turns to her slowly. Looks nowhere for a long moment. "Today is not the anniversary of the day all those parents dumped their kids at the beach?" he asks. "Is it?"

She pauses, swallows, drops her eyes to the sink, like her memory of everything is there in its basin. She breathes, looks up. "No," she says. "It isn't."

Sailor's dad and Whaler's mom watch the backyard turn from swampy to lakelike. They grab their galoshes and plunge into the backyard to get to the garage, to get to their kids, to get them to the main house. Dad and Mom slip and slide and struggle toward the garage. They arrive at the back door drenched and muddy. They sling open the door. In careens a wave. Sailor and Whaler are loving on, hoisted high up the mast. They hardly notice the disturbance. Sailor's dad and Whaler's mom look up. There are their kids. Together and contrapted. Dad and Mom experience the kind of shock that is shock plus not shock. When impossibility and inevitability collide. They clap loudly against each other in Dad's and Mom's skulls. And just before the echo in their heads subsides, before Dad and Mom can gather their wits enough to make any kind of parental move, this: The wind rips the roof off of the garage. It tumbles and bashes away through the neighborhood, smashing into other ripped-off roofs. A rogue wave of terrific height and violence gushes through the garage door. Sweeps Dad and Mom off their feet. Knocks the boat off its blocks. Sailor and Whaler bounce and swing daredevilishly on their rig. The rush blows out the large garage door, tearing the front of the garage wide open just in time for the wind to catch the jib sail and set the boat coursing down the driveway. Dad and Mom splash and slip along the deluge in the downpour. They lunge onto the barbecue deck off the back of the house, scuttle up the trellis, climb onto the roof of the house while the boat and their kids careen down the swamped road toward the ocean.

It would be picaresque if, while they sailed away from the garage and their parents and home, they managed a long moment of that pitch-perfect ballet. Moving just so, suspended and lovemaking, under a low gray sky, thick and heavy as whipping cream, guided by a slender wind puffing the jib sail taut, the two of them refined and fluid and elegant. But they don't manage that. This whole sequence is messy. Shocked by the roof and the wave, the parents and the exodus, Sailor and Whaler continue their communion, but are absolutely arrhythmic while they go. Carried away.

Once their sloop hits the harbor, idyllically, the rain lets up. The wind continues to blow directly, seaward. They stop sexing and just hang. Whaler's back bears the brunt of the wind. And while their surface areas are small and their masses great by comparison to the canvas of an actual sail, their bodies function inefficiently but nonetheless as a main sail. And not until they are out at sea, their hometown behind them and mostly submerged, does Whaler bite the release chord he affixed to the collar of his wet suit vest. His right arm snaps free, unfettered. He uses it to undo his left arm and ankles and finally reaches behind himself to unhook the chord clipped to the ring between his shoulder blades. He drops to the deck of the boat. He pulls Sailor's mainline from its cleat, lowers her gently down. They take the two steps below deck, find their pants and shirts, put them on. Return to the deck, attach and raise the canvas mainsail. They sail. The boat works great. They make a life on it. Careening here, careening there, weathering storms, standing in perfect stillness at the bow, the sun highest in the sky and sizzling over a sea so calm, Sailor daydreams she could strut across it in spiked heels, each step clinking.

Cataplasms

––––

DANGUY WECK is twelve and small—thready and frail. He has interests: science and anatomy, swirly doodle drawings, his neon tetra fish, and a type of meditation he calls *hatching*. And for some time, until one grim day, he enjoys the trampoline in the backyard over at Budweiser Dad's house.

Danguy Weck's got a twin called Little Sis because she came out nine minutes after Danguy, making him the oldest.

Danguy's dad is a whaler named Whaler. He's always at sea. Once, wondering about his dad from the shore and peering through his favorite telescope—a nineteenth-century three-draw mahogany barrel maritime optical, a gift from his dad—Danguy Weck studied the sea line for fourteen hours. He sat in the sand, a safe distance from the water's edge, from daybreak to dusk. Just as the sun slipped around the other side of the globe, in the red moments before the sky seeped plum and the sea glassed black, Danguy Weck was sure he spotted his dad creaming across swooping orange combers, his knee braced in the notch at the bow of his ship, a smoking pipe between his teeth, salt and wind tangling his beard, the shaft of a live iron in his fist, poised lancelike by his ear. Danguy jumped, then shivered. Gasped and caught his breath. He ran home. Through the sand, across the road, down the sidewalk, past the alley, over the fence, across the lawn, up the porch, through the door, through the living room, down the hall, and into his bedroom. He slammed his door and sat on his bed and closed his eyes. His dad through that telescope was the best picture in his head he's ever seen in real life. He sat quiet and still, so it would stick.

Whaler had a love of his lifelong days, a sailor. They'd been kids together, seaside sweethearts, runaways. They navigated the earth's seven seas in their schooner. Journeying under the night-dome of the sky, they dreamed of raising a family on that very boat, of every day all of them together. The ocean there. The sky there. Them here. Then Sailor died overboard, hit by the boom in a storm days after delivering the twins. His first mate lost to the briny deep, his heart ransacked, and the equation he'd taken for granted, ocean plus loved ones equals eternity, was annulled. Confident in his own maneuverings over the world's waters, but frightened of losing his babies to the heaving deep, he took them ashore, swore for good and all to keep them on dry ground. Landlocked, safe—off of, out of, away from the sea.

He brought his babies to the house of the Great Aunt by the shore. Not his aunt, but someone's. Someone's Great Aunt. Herself a widow, she took one long look into Whaler's eyes and got it. His grief like mist on his eyelashes, but behind them, in the pools of his pupils, she recognized something ruptured and was moved. The babies in their bassinet below deck, the Great Aunt and Whaler spent a night anchored on his boat, drinking the last bottles of basil booze in honor of his Sailor, talking, drinking more. Whaler trusted the Great Aunt and told her his honest life stories. When it came time for him to get out of Dodge and head back to sea, she offered him her help and he offered her his. She'd look after his children; he would send money always, also gifts.

DANGUY WECK'S favorite time with the Great Aunt was when, for his eleventh birthday, she fixed herself some cocktails and told him the story of his parents:

Sailor and Whaler were young and industrious. Some time after they'd left home, they sold for a pretty penny the boat they had built together. They bought another and in it they opened *The Sea Boozer*. It was their boat bar. They built the bar down below, on the lower deck. It was small, dark, smoky. Eight barstools long, each bolted to the floor. At one end was a jukebox with many decent selections. At the other end, a dartboard. There was no room for a pool table, and there were drunks who complained. Whaler told them, "Sorry, but no pool at this bar. This bar is for bingeing and camaraderie and travel."

They didn't advertise. They got known in a murmuring way. *The Sea Boozer* became a thing heavy drinkers in seaside towns around the world knew about. They knew about its irregular cocktails. About its young owners. According to whispered legend, it was a place to go when the place you were in was not the place you wanted to stay.

They picked up drinkers at night only. When word rippled that *The Sea Boozer* was dipping by, those interested peeled themselves from their barstools on land, hoofed it aboard—hushed and hurried. They were always old men. If they were not actually old, they looked old. They lounged on the upper deck by moonlight while Sailor captained the ship out of whichever harbor and into the rhubarb sea. Once land disappeared behind them, the drinkers were invited below, bar's open. There they remained until *The Sea Boozer* touched land again, and Sailor would hustle them out. Sailor and Whaler then resupplied with whatever was available locally. They accumulated inventory all over. For example, off the coast of a smattering of islands in the South Pacific, they purchased several cases of basil booze. The dock dealer told her about the white family that moved to the island to do research and brought with them basil seeds. The youngest son tossed the seeds in the backyard and the seeds made home in the exceptionally nutritious soil. The plants heartily flowered. The wind blew basil sperm across the land and new basil plants planted. And due to the particular conditions of the place, in a few years those basil plants had grown into enormous trees, trunks and all. Dark green leaves, the size of umbrellas, kept shade for the islanders and scented the wind. Special liquor was made from juiced leaves. It could be shot straight or sipped over ice. When fresh tomatoes were available, Sailor liked to shake it with tomato juice and salt and pepper, serve it with an avocado wedge. It tasted like a whole delicious meal that also got you very drunk. It was one of her specialties.

Drinks were served in deep glasses and filled one-third the way up. The bar coasters bound the base of the glass to the bar top to keep drinks from spilling when the boat lurched and wobbled and turned over swells. Those drinkers that preferred not to remove their glass from the brace at each sip pulled their liquor from a flexi-straw. Ice was hard to keep. Whaler and Sailor loaded up on land, and when it ran out, drinks were served neat.

Sailor had a coconut shaker. It was fat and round. The top lopped off and the inside scraped dry and fruitless, she filled the coconut shell with ice when they had it, poured boozes over the ice, upended a pint glass and stuffed it in the coconut hole, sealing it shut. With two hands she shook the mix. The ice against the coconut and against the mixing glass and back into the coconut clonked woodenly. If he was also behind the bar, Whaler liked to step behind Sailor, place his hands on her hips, prop his chin over her shoulder, press his body close against hers, and they'd move their hips in unison to the shake. He'd breathe deeply the smell of her hair, which he said always retained the smell of her, despite the sea smell in the air, the booze smell of the men, the leather and oak and fruit smoke from the pipes and the stale cigarette smoke that milkied the cabin. The Great Aunt told Danguy Weck that when Whaler told her this part of his story, his face smoothed soft and his eyes shimmered.

There was a thing about Whaler and Sailor when they were together. An incarmined crackling between and around them. It was kind and sexy. They liked each other so much. A glimpse of their brightness together was affirming. Their customers experienced this, sipping on their side of the bar, blinking at the lovers through boozy eyes. They were startled happily by it, found themselves liking to be around Whaler and Sailor, considered them good kids. One of their customers revealed this to them—a skinny old guy who'd been a banker in his day, made piles of money, hated his job, built a bomb shelter during a war, hid in it, and wrote poetry until it became too much to bear, so he gave up and hit the bars. He told them he hoped they'd always get along. He told them they wouldn't, unless they died young, but he told them he'd hope.

Other old guys liked to look at Sailor. "Oh, pumpkin juice, come here," some heavy-lidded scraggle-bearded drinker would say. Sailor would scoot to his end of the bar. "Would you reach that blue bottle behind you, up on the second shelf," he would request slowly because her shirt would hike high and scraggle-beard wanted a peek. She would reach for it, grab hold of it above her head, behind the safety wire. Scraggle-beard would pipe, "Good goddamn, where is your belly button?" And because the old drunk couldn't see her high belly button even as she stretched to reach the bottle, he thought she was born without one. "I had it removed in high school," she'd tell him, sending his mind spinning.

Sometimes the drunk drinkers raised their voices and talked threateningly to one another, often about who had made more money in his life. At which point Sailor would step in and draw their attention to the fact that their incomes and life choices had brought them to exactly the same place at exactly the same time, so shut up. She'd tell them she kept an electric eel tazer beneath the bar. They'd blink drunkenly at her. She'd tell them she was serious. Maybe they believed her. Then Whaler would step in and explain that they reserved the right to refuse service to anyone, and if a drinker gets out of hand, he gets eighty-sixed. Which meant he was bobbing on a lifeboat in the middle of nowhere. These rules were already known, though—were included in the gossip about *The Sea Boozer.*

Whaler and Sailor had their own place to sleep. A cavelike sleep space in the hull. The drinkers crashed out on the upper deck, if the weather permitted, in the booths if it didn't. Some stayed up, drunk, talking. When she and Whaler retired to sleep, Sailor locked cabinet doors that closed across the back of the bar, kept the liquor tight.

They did fairly well. Were paid in many ways. Sailor accumulated stacks of jewelry boxes loaded with the sparkling adornments of drinkers' late wives. Or some oldies unloaded the last of their savings on that boat bar before drinking it slim and then coming ashore on some island somewhere to build the end of their days from pineapples or lie flat in the hot white sand while warm green waters lap away their lives.

There were those customers with deep and silky singing voices, who lay on deck and crooned sounds like wind over reeds. Familiar or unfamiliar tunes, it didn't matter. They sung a mix of notes and words that made a listener instantly full and empty.

The Sea Boozer had a big grill that hung over the starboard side of the ship. On it they grilled fish caught and sometimes red meats purchased in some harbor.

"I love cooking meats with you," Sailor would say to Whaler as he stood by the grill, long fork in one hand, long tongs in the other.

They ate lying out on the deck, meats in a pile on a plate between them, smoke curling from the grill into the sky that, above the ocean, always appeared domed. Like the inside of a blown black balloon.

The Great Aunt doesn't tell Danguy Weck this part of Whaler's story, but she likes it: One time, late afternoon, idling over sauntering rollers while all the drinkers happened to have passed out cold below deck, Sailor and Whaler rigged the ropes and pulleys, the clips and things—for old time's sake. They stripped off their clothes and hoisted their bodies high. They were older and deeply familiar with the freedom to be with each other whenever, so that teenaged luster had faded. But they experienced something newly different out of the garage and on the water, where the view all the way around was ocean. The gray look of it up close, with its white frothed ribbons and its bits of things floating beneath shining surface planes. Then long stretches of green and blue beyond. Then the dark line separating the bright sea from the light sky. Looking, the line between ocean and sky wound all the way around them like a ring, and they were alone in the center of it. The wind was mild and blew at them agreeably. This was really something, Whaler had told the Great Aunt, the middle of the ocean, strung up above it, that sea wind on their suspended nude bodies. He remembered especially the breeze ribboning against his armpits, through the tiny valleys where inner thighs end, across the bottoms of his feet. The wind on the pads of his feet.

THEY CAME into a lot of money when Whaler grew into his name. An ancient whale fisherman, wrinkled and brown, mostly out of work for decades on account of various moratoriums on whaling, his arms like logs on the bar top, had been drinking on the boat for weeks and was plumb out of cash, couldn't settle his tab. So instead he closed out with a set of sterling lily irons and suggested Whaler give the irons a go.

One day Whaler did. There were disturbances on the surface of the water not far from the boat bar. Whaler pitched the smallest of the irons and, first try, nailed a walrus. Hauled on deck, it made a wet mess. The next time the boat docked, a whisper here and a whisper there, and Whaler was in touch with clients interested in purchasing. Turned out it was a rare walrus. He sold its walrus parts—not cheaply—and decided such was the life for him.

His sharp eyesight and powerful upper body made him an adept whaler. And relatively humane—with his impeccable aim, he never failed to harpoon his target in just the right spot, causing a quick death. When Danguy Weck heard this, his small face pulled pale and he stopped the Great Aunt. Worried suddenly, he asked her if his dad was bad. Gently, in her balmy way, she explained that he was not. That his whaling techniques are much better than the sloppier whaling practices that often leave maimed whales alive for hours before they finally bleed out and die. He is also a light harvester. His operation is small: one great mammal per kill, one kill just every so often. His environmental impact is minimal. And he sells mostly only to those who, because of religious prohibitions, or an industriousness of thought and procedure, use every part of the animal. Where the olden-day whalers rendered the fat from the carcass, saved a few bones, and dumped the rest overboard, Whaler divvies up the whale parts, finds a market for all of them. He gets the biggest bucks, she explained, for endangered species. Danguy's mouth dropped open. The Great Aunt shrugged her shoulders and told him that's what keeps him and his sister clothed and fed. When the horror didn't fade from his face, she assured him his father is a good man and loves him very much.

SOME SECRET things happened on *The Sea Boozer*. The Great Aunt fixed another pitcher of screwdrivers and told Danguy he was now old enough to know and to keep the secret: Some drinkers boarded *The Sea Boozer* to die. To drink away the last of themselves.

There was an old, bent man that seemed in every way about him broken. He ordered the roughest elixir, downed more of it than his organs could tread. He drowned himself in melon-headed whale brandy—made from the urine found remaining in the bladder of a dead melon-headed whale. He even ate the ear fipple at the bottom of the bottle. It's the hard waxy plug found in the ear canal of whales. Scientists count the layers in the plug to determine a whale's age. A drinker who makes it to the fipple may not come back. Sailor warned him. Told him all about what to expect. He insisted. So this old man drunk down to the fipple, swallowed it whole. From stumbling drunkenness to sudden, seeming focus, he experienced a surge of lucid sobriety—an effect of ingesting the ear fipple. His reflexes and sensibilities briefly and unexpectedly sharp, he rose from the bar stool, strode to the upper deck, sat at the bow, eyes wide, face fraught. He was watching something hard play out in his head. The folklore behind the ear fipple is that it recounts for the eater a mind movie of his or her life. And at the end of the film, the hallucinator decides whether the rest is worth living. This guy watched. He stood. He closed his eyes, leaned his hips into the railing on the bow. Whaler witnessed his muscles go slack from his head down, like his power was cut off from somewhere inside him. His limpness toppled forward, overboard. He sunk directly beneath the boat and fell deeply. Whaler dove in after him but the old man descended too quickly out of reach.

The old man had left his sack of stuff by his stool in the bar. Sailor and Whaler sorted through it. Turned out he'd been a patrol officer in the little town their parents grew up in. They wondered if their parents had ever known him. Had ever been written a speeding ticket by him? In his wallet was an aged photograph of two baby kids. The blacks and whites of the print were mostly gray and the edges were scalloped and timeworn soft.

There were others too. Accidental deaths, maybe. Drinkers too drunk to stay aboard. Sailor and Whaler tried to keep an eye, but at night, when they retired to their cubby, if a still-drunk opted to stroll around the gangway and lose his footing, they woke to a missing person and tragedy dripping damply across the deck.

ONE DAY, Whaler was made an offer. Turned out, the way petroleum replaced whale oil and contributed to the collapse of the olden-age whaling industry, current research indicated that whale oil, when refined according to certain conditions and in such and such a way, burns a million times better than gasoline. So good that a single tank of whale gas could keep an average-size passenger vehicle running for a whole year, sometimes more. This was a top-secret discovery that displeased the government considerably. So the government schemed a secret mission to eliminate all the whales in the ocean. Ears to the underground, they finally managed to hear about Whaler. They were surprised and impressed that he'd been doing what he'd been doing without ever registering on their radar. They thought he would be a good man to have on board.

An undercover government agent, in the disguise of an old drunk fisherman, boarded *The Sea Boozer*. Then twilight, several drinking days in, the agent staggered updeck to find Whaler at the bow of the ship, in a strong and stable lunge, panning the sea through the narrow zoom of a mariner's telescope. The agent straightened his posture, focused his eyes, shed the guise of the old drunk, and revealed his true identity and interests to Whaler. Assured him that he and Sailor and any children they might ever have would be taken care of for their lifetimes. Assured him that the whaling crimes he committed thus far would escape charge. He pledged that the Bureau of Alcohol, Tobacco, and Firearms would never hear a peep about the unlicensed boat bar, nor would the tax commission, nor the bureau of missing persons and their affiliated departments of prosecution and incarceration. Apparently the agent had gleaned a lot of information regarding the ship's goings-on while he drank and yakked with the boys at the bar.

"And if I'm not interested in the offer?" Whaler asked, threatened and deceived by whom he thought was just a sad old drunk but who now looked unexpectedly dashing and important.

"Oh, you and your bar mistress can count on dreaming of the high seas from prison. Separate and forever."

SAILOR AND Whaler sunk *The Sea Boozer*, with the government agent in it. They made their break in two rescue vessels—one for them, the other for the small clutch of old drunks. They loaded Whaler's prize irons and sacks of their cash savings on their lifeboat and stocked the drinkers' boat with cases of booze. The drinkers were serious ones and thanked them and assured Sailor and Whaler that they'd be fine, not to worry, and the business about that agent in that sunk ship was, is, and will forever be as if it never happened. Hard living on the sea—bar keeping and whale hunting and the communities and experiences those life-styles brushed up and against and all over them—made the couple great judges of character. And these witnesses, Sailor and Whaler believed, were men of their words. That, and they'd boarded to drink aggressively toward death. Several rounds in, they declared such to both Whaler and Sailor. Sick of this trend in her establish-ment, Sailor replied, "Not on my clock." To which the drink-ers complained about business policy and how it shouldn't be changed so abruptly. The government agent probably pricked up his ears and took notes in his mind while Sailor short-poured the whiners.

Officially on the lam, they purchased another boat from an undisclosed purveyor at an undisclosed location. Whaler's ille-gal whaling provided him intricate connections to fringe markets where the paperless exchange of goods and services are all done by the black of night. Finally, barless but sailing, whaling and together, they made their new ship their new home, and laid low on the high seas. To Danguy Weck, this last bit feels like a post-card sent to him from wherever they are. He keeps it tacked to the wall in the room in his mind.

UNLIKE HIS parents, Danguy Weck hates the ocean. It fright-ens him—the blue unbridled bigness of it. The animals in it. Swimming. Contained water, however, he enjoys all right. For example, his fish tank. He keeps his aquarium stocked full of neon tetras and especially loves to mesmerize them.

He's a drawer. Seated at his desk, his narrow shoulders hunched and a marker squeezed tight between his fingers pressing hard, he draws swirlywhirlycues in black ink on plain paper. Sometimes just one large paper-size swirl—like what the sideshow hypnotists spin to get the hypnotized to take off their pants or bark like a dog. Other times he draws many small swirls, a hundred on a page, taking up all the space. The tetras respond similarly to either. He holds his swirly doodle to the front face of the tank, pinning it from behind with the eraser end of a pencil. Then he spins the page around this axis, creating a spellbinding effect for the fish on the other side of the glass. They swim out from behind the lava rock right up to the gyre. The whole school of them—a clump the size of a fat fist. Their pointy fish faces focused, one by one, in response to Danguy's drawing, each tetra follows the twirls, spins in place. Like drill bits on slow-motored, low-batteried drills. Like if they actually had drill capabilities and were to push into the glass, they might gore teeny tetra holes clear into it, making a round of leaks that would sprinkle over his dresser like a showerhead.

Danguy spins his sketch and through the side of the tank watches his shiny tetras turn, transfixed. Their slick silver scales catch and toss the sunlight that beats through the window, through the tank glass, through the water, and sparkles off the twisting tetras in a carousel kind of way.

After spinning the swirls and entrancing his tetras for close to an hour, he stops. Crumples his drawing, trashes it. He pulls the curtain, darkens his room, sits back on his bed and waits. The tetras stop turning. They don't swim at all. They flip sideways and float around the tank, pushed by the bubbles rumbling from the water filter. Then, one by one, the tetras leap from the tank. They break the surface of the water and go. Where do they think they're going? Danguy has no idea, but what happens is they tend to leap out the back side, closest to the wall. More often than not, they hit the wall. And because the wall paint has a dry matte finish and the tetras are so light and wet, they stick to the wall. Like spitballs. They die and dry, stuck to the paint on the wall behind

the tank. For a short time they remain shining, the whole clus-
tered exodus of them like mirrored bits. Then they dehydrate and
shrivel. Their scales waste away and what's left on Danguy's wall
but tiny tetra skeletons with hollowed-out eye holes. The spine
down the length of their bodies is like a thin toenail clipping.
Danguy Weck is fascinated. He figures his drawings have direct
effect on his tetras' neurochemistry. His favorite shows are docu-
mentaries about science. His hypnosis, he judges, disrupts the
chemicals that pass information to the cortexes in their little tetra
brains, affecting their decision-making capabilities. A risky move,
such as jumping out of one's natural and intended habitat, the
tetras perhaps misinterpret as an ambiguous move. Their instincts
for survival are retarded; the result is death on the wall.

Danguy Weck misses them when they're gone. He scrapes
their brittle flakes off the wall into an envelope, tucks the envelope under his mattress, dodders next door to Budweiser Dad's
house to jump on his trampoline. Maybe mention the dead tetras.
More often then not, Budweiser Dad will say something like, "I'll
bet you miss 'em, sport." Then, "How 'bout I run over to the
store in the mall and pick you up a fistful of new ones." Danguy
Weck will stick around Budweiser Dad's backyard and bounce on
his trampoline—very springy and the size of a small swimming
pool. Danguy Weck works on his flips, can almost land on his
feet. Budweiser Dad returns in no time with a twist-tied plastic
baggie bloated with water and a small school of neon tetras swish-
ing nervously nowhere. "Here you go, kiddo. Go put them in
your tank."

Budweiser Dad's well regarded in the neighborhood. Smiles
and waves when he mows his lawn. Only Danguy knows about
the Budweiser. He caught a peek into his recycling bin once when
he was jumping on the trampoline. Budweiser Dad had left the
lid off, and to the brim were crushed and crumpled red and white
cans. Danguy's never seen him drink the Budweiser. He doesn't
act like guys Danguy saw on that special about alcoholics—falling

around and yelling. Danguy thinks he's nice. He's a respected, powerful official in the community. Many years as an officer of the law, then on to councils and committees and occupying various offices, bureaus, agencies, and headquarters. Numerous plaques and badges with engraved honors and awards line the wall of his back room where he keeps a cooler stocked with grape soda, mostly for Danguy. Budweiser Dad invites Little Sis over for jumping, but she never goes. She does all right with friends, has playdates all the time.

Once, sipping on his soda, sweaty from the trampoline, Danguy got a good look at Budweiser Dad's special recognition things. Lots of veneered wood and gold-colored metal. All very official looking with emblems and insignias. Even a framed photograph: Budweiser Dad standing rooster-chested with the president on the lawn in front of the White House. They both look like they are about to laugh but are trying to keep it serious, as though they're best friends forever and posing for photos is such a riot.

Budweiser Dad noticed Danguy noticing his awards of distinction. He explained to him the mightiness and authority they imply. Budweiser Dad's never had to pay a parking ticket or registration renewal fees on his vehicle, never been summoned for jury duty, can park in handicap spots even without any handicaps, never had to pay a cent of alimony to his ex; he gets big tax breaks and gigantic tax returns; he can't ever remember what the letters in DUI stand for.

"Recognize that guy there?" he asked, jerking his thumb at the picture with the president. "He's a real good friend of mine." Budweiser Dad dipped his hand into his back pocket, pulled out his wallet, flipped it open, extracted a black card with a gold stripe below a gold star. He explained that it's a special pass. He never has to purchase gasoline. He runs it through the credit-card swiper at any pump, fills up for free. "Not even members of the Supreme Court have one of these," he told Danguy, his eyes glistening. "My buddy there's always got my back," he said, referencing the picture again. "I could safely get away with just about anything," he told Danguy Weck with a wheezy laugh. "Seriously," he continued, "if you ever find yourself in any trouble, come to me." His eyes looked pink and wet and heavy and proud. Danguy nodded his head, wondered briefly if Budweiser Dad might have ever known that government agent his parents sunk in their old boat. Danguy tipped his head back and drained the rest of the contents of the purple can. With his bottom teeth he bit and sucked the grape soda mustache off his upper lip.

"You know if you go for a jump on the tramp now," Budweiser Dad said, "a few bounces and you'll belch like you have a blowhole." Danguy Weck thought quickly of his father. He imagined Whaler pitching a lily iron into his neck as Danguy Weck jumped highest on the trampoline, breaching the tops of the houses, his burp echoing through the neighborhood like thunder.

WHEN HE is not messing with his tetras or over at Budweiser Dad's, Danguy Weck practices deep monks-in-the-mountains-style meditation. He'd seen a special on those monks on TV when he was nine. Remembers the long scene of the small bald monk sitting cross-legged in the snow, the snow melted into a brown circle around his body. Danguy remembers the monk's voice talking over the picture of himself poised in the dirt. Danguy remembers especially the monk talking about his beating heart. The monk said he puts his ears on his heartbeat and then his brain and his breath are free to exit out the back of his head, to go wherever. This made sense to nine-year-old Danguy Weck. Later, in his bedroom, he practiced sitting like the monk and listening to his heartbeat. Two years later, he could exit out the back of his head pretty easily.

Like this: A little bit of calm, that breathing, and those heartbeats, and Danguy Weck, his whole him, becomes tiny and can stand inside his skull, which is a dark and empty round room. Pinned on the wall toward the front of his head is the postcard from his parents. In the curve along the back of his skull is a small porthole window with a combination lock knob. The window is clear. He peers through it and sees an inflatable moon bounce that goes on forever. The moon bounce is nice, fat, pillowy tubes in red and orange and purple, and it is the entire groundscape. Above the moon bounce is the sky-scape, which is just blue like sky. And cutting a plane through that sky is a thin floating layer of tree leaves. All fresh, single leaves, no branches or tree trunks. They are damp and bright green. Like the leaf ceiling of the rainforest jungle, only leaves only, no other tree parts. Everything is sunned up bright and warm and the leaf cover is just dense enough to cast the light between the moon bounce and the leaves an airier shade of green. And there are small holes in places between leaves that let long sticks of sunlight beam through at all angles, making the space between the moon bounce and the leaf ceiling a crisscross of sunlight bars. From the window in his skull, he gets the full three-layer view. The thick blue-sky band that goes forever. Then the green leaves canopy. Then, and this is his favorite site, there is the sunbeam space in the green light between the leaf ceiling and the moon bounce.

He spins the knob on the combination lock. It whirrs around and makes fast, slick ticking noises like it's oiled up. He doesn't even need the combination. Once it eases to a stop, the porthole smoothes right open. He climbs up into the window and has the option of jumping up and out into the blue sky and onto the green leaves, blustering a hole through them, and landing on the moon bounce like fluff while the scattered leaves flut-ter back together to close the hole above him. Or he can jump directly onto the moon bounce and toss and turn and fling him-self through the yellow bars in the green light. He can leap and bound any which way he wants. He never lands on his head or bites his tongue or the inside of his cheek or knocks his knee into his teeth or turns his ankles. There are no other kids to clunk into or poke him in the eye or jump on him when he can't get up. Little Sis is nowhere to be found. Each bounce is perfect. If he jumps high enough he can break the leaf cover with his head and get a face full of blue sky before tumbling back into the bounce, the sound of leaves rustling above him.

◊

TODAY THINGS change. It is the last day of school, the first afternoon of summer. Danguy Weck and Little Sis are walking home. When they arrive, Budweiser Dad is mowing his lawn. He cuts the engine, smiles, and waves. "Danguy, my boy," he says. "Last day of school?"

"Yes."

"Shoot, let's celebrate! Get over here and hit the tramp!" And to Little Sis he says, "You too. I've got cold colas. Put your books away and come on over!"

Little Sis shakes her head. Danguy tosses his bag into the house, turns to head over. "Have fucking fun," whispers Little Sis.

ALL JUMPED out and full up on grape soda, Danguy Weck hangs his legs over the edge of the trampoline. Bats away from his face the little summer flies that are already buzzing circles in the twilight heat. Budweiser Dad pokes his head out the back door to his garage, waves Danguy over.

He is standing on the step up to the door inside his garage. He pushes the door open wider, invites Danguy in. Danguy stands on the step next to Budweiser Dad, looks out into the garage. Budweiser Dad shuts the door behind him.

Danguy has never seen inside this garage before. The floor is completely covered, wall-to-wall, with empty and crushed Budweiser cans. Feet deep. Danguy suspects if Budweiser Dad opened the wide electric garage door, the cans would rush out and clatter across his driveway. Spill into the street. Cause an accident. In the middle of it all is a big leather chair. Like a small island in a red and white crushed can sea.

"Come on," says Budweiser Dad, and he and Danguy wade through the cans to get to the chair. The cans clack and shangle and turn over warm, sticky beer breath as Budweiser Dad and Danguy Weck make their way through. The chair, when they get there, is big enough for two. Here, Budweiser Dad does bad things.

Bad things? What bad things? The basics. The regular old bad things that Danguy's seen so many shows about, he didn't even see it coming. Bad things so brutal they're boring. And not the point. Never the point are the things. Always, it's what comes after.

DANGUY WECK walks swiftly and tight-legged to his house and directly to his room. Little Sis is kneeling in front of his aquarium tapping the glass and scaring his neon tetras. Danguy stands behind her. Feels the heat from Budweiser Dad's hands and body impressed on his skin. Feels too warm. Even the button and the zipper on his jeans feel red-hot. As though they've just been pulled from a fire, attached to his pants, and are now scorching his skin. Danguy wonders if it's his own body producing this heat, if he's having an exothermic reaction to something.

Budweiser Dad's hands were fat and rough but moist. Danguy knows moist equals sweat. Sweat is composed principally of bodily H_2O and mineral salts like sodium chloride, urea, sugars. And in Budweiser Dad's case, likely a lot of Budweiser. Perhaps too much Budweiser for Budweiser Dad's body. Perhaps, thinks Danguy Weck, there was a malfunction in Budweiser Dad's body's processes. Something could be very wrong in his liver. The Budweiser, thinks Danguy, probably refermented in Budweiser Dad's broken liver, so his liver is excreting poisonous by-products that escape through Budweiser Dad's sweat glands. It's this poison that's irritated Danguy's skin all over, making him too hot. He feels fevered. Short of breath. He's still standing behind Little Sis, who still doesn't notice him, hadn't heard him come in, doesn't notice his reflection in the tank glass.

Danguy thinks about his breath. He is panting, quietly but quickly. He knows panting, through the process of respiration, evaporates water from his body—important water needed to cool his internal organs so as to keep them working properly. But breathing like this, it escapes too fast. And he is already so hot.

He panics. He thinks he might die. He's worried his enzymes will denature. He's certain his enzyme molecules are becoming too agitated with kinetic energy from the heat. This will cause their bonds to break, their shapes to change. Then his enzymes can't do their jobs, can't carry out the basic biochemical functions in his body necessary for survival. He is convinced he is about to die.

He takes the deepest breath he's ever taken. His legs bent, his chest swollen to pop, he gathers his voice from somewhere deep—a place below his feet, maybe in the ground beneath the house somewhere, or from the center of the earth. Then out it goes. He roars into the back of Little Sis's head: "GET THE FUCK OUT OF HERE!" Locks of her hair blow in his wind.

She seizes, jerks, jumps as she slaps her palms over her ears. Her little limbs clang like a stack of pots knocked over. Her elbows bang into the tank, agitating the water, disrupting the gravel, unburying the plastic plant roots and tossing a loop of tank slime to the floor. She whips around. Her eyes are blasted enormous. She screams. It vibrates the bones in Danguy's face. He notices the shrill pierce of her scream echo through the empty house. Little Sis rumples her mouth and slits her eyes. Slowly removes one hand from her ear. She balls it into a small fist, holds it out in front of her brother's face, and extends her little girl middle finger. She pumps it twice into the air at him, glares, leaves.

Danguy Weck slams his door shut. He is sweating profusely. He pulls off his T-shirt, unbuttons his jeans, pushes them down his legs. Pushes his underwear down his legs. Steps out of the heap around his ankles. Bolts to his window, flicks the latch, slides the frame high, climbs out of his window. He jumps the few feet to ground, lands in the dirt in the side yard. In Danguy's mind: textbook images of enzymes—like puzzle pieces, contoured for an exact fit. But he imagines his, now, shapeshifting in the too-hot heat of his body so the substrates can't attach, no reactions can be catalyzed. He's certain his body functions are on the brink of arrest.

But he gets to the hose, twists it on, holds it over his head, and showers himself with cold water to reduce his fever and save his enzymes before death stamps him dead. Blinking beneath the deluge that drenches his eyelids cool and heavy, through the slim spaces between the slats in the fence dividing the properties, Danguy Weck thinks he sees Budweiser Dad in his kitchen window, angling to glimpse the small boy shape of Danguy Weck, sputtering under the hose, naked except for socks.

THAT NIGHT, burrowed deep in his bed, his pillow over his head, Danguy Weck can't sleep. Too loud in his ears is the sound of shangling empty beer cans. He pictures a couple, just married, driving off with paper flowers, a soap-signed rear windshield, and a billion strings tied to their bumper tugging along a trillion bouncing metal cans. When they lean out the window to say goodbye, the couple has no skin on their faces or hands. They are wet muscles—all thin red lines and pink meat and bendy yellow joint linkers that keep the parts together as they smile and wave in tux and gown. Through the night he lay with his eyes pinned wide.

The Great Aunt is back in the morning in time for breakfast. Danguy Weck is not hungry. Little Sis eats cereal at the kitchen table, slurping it from her bowl. When she chews, her face twitches like circuits are exploding behind it. She pauses mid-chew, presses her hand to the right side of her head where her jaw and ear meet. She winces. Scowling at Danguy and with a mouth full of wet cereal, Little Sis growls, "You fucked me up." Danguy glances at the Great Aunt who is over by the sink, pouring coffee in her mug. She turns, smiles absently at the kids, takes a cigarette from the pack in the bread basket on the counter, scratches at her whalebone lighter until it catches. She takes a long drag and plunks down next to Little Sis. The Great Aunt notices Little Sis's ear. "Is that blood?" she asks. Danguy stands, pads quickly to his room.

WHEN THE Great Aunt asks Danguy Weck what the hell got into him that he'd do a thing like that to his sister, he doesn't want to answer. His mouth falls open with a dull pop, but nothing comes out. He doesn't know how to answer. Blinking at the Great Aunt, dumb-faced, slack-jawed, he experiences a kind of freeze. The picture screen in his mind flickers and goes dark. The pipes connecting his brain to his voice box to his mouth feel black and blocked completely.

Nothing.

Then, calmly, two words arrive in his mind, clear and cold as blocks of ice: NO ANSWERS. Meaning, he never wants to answer a question ever. He closes his mouth, fixes his face stiff as a brick. The Great Aunt frowns, huffs, clears her throat, presses him, wants to know why he yelled so violently into the back of Little Sis's head. Tells him he very well might have busted her eardrum. Why the *hell*? She waits. He locks his jaw, slits his eyes, stares clear through the Great Aunt's eyeballs. She waits a few beats longer, sighs forcefully, and sneers, "This silent treatment business is not going to fly, Danguy." She tilts her forehead toward him, snaps her eyebrow high and pointy. He flinches but keeps silent. She turns, exits his bedroom. He folds his arms across his chest and sits on his floor. He devises a two-part plan.

FOR DANGUY Weck on his twelfth birthday, his father sent him a diamond-blade pocketknife. A special something Whaler picked up somewhere, traded for illegal whale parts off the coast of a place known for diamonds, maybe Africa. The blade is actual diamond—100 percent pure gajillion karats of diamond in the shape of a pocketknife blade. Like a shard of glass, but incontestably better. There is a lustrousness to diamond that exists simply in the shiver of the molecules composing the matter. Because of the quake of the electron configuration and its refractive index, the diamond scintillates. Makes glass look old and homeless by comparison. Danguy Weck takes it out of its velvet box and places it gently on his desk. From the bathroom he grabs rubbing alcohol, cotton balls, a washcloth, gauze pads, bandage tape, and a package of adhesive sutures the Great Aunt keeps in the first-aid kit under the sink.

Alone in his room he waits for the sound of the Great Aunt's car backing out of the driveway. He hears the door thump shut, the engine turn over, the tires roll on the grit and gravel. He's got a mirror propped up on his desk next to his diamond knife and supplies. Seated cross-legged in his desk chair, he swabs his neck and the knife blade with rubbing alcohol. Then he closes his eyes and slowly starts in on the monks-in-the-mountains breathing. Deep and deliberate enough to fill his head with the sound of his heartbeat.

He is in his skull. The knob lock spins. He exits out the porthole window. Dives into the blue, then *poof*, through the leaves. It is bliss. His actual body still in his room, operating according to plan, but his consciousness and its associated registry of pain is bouncing on the other side of the porthole window.

A very delicate operation occurs. His hands, working their mission, make an incision in his throat just below his unpronounced Adam's apple. The diamond blade slices through skin effortlessly. The right hand pushes the point of the blade into the short, clean gash, intending to pluck out the voice box with the tip of the knife, like an olive on a toothpick. The knife blade gently fishes right, left, up, down, angling for the voice box. The left hand holds the washcloth at his collar, to suck up the blood. The right hand removes the knife. No olive. Tries again. No dice. Once more and the tip sticks. However, the incision is too small to extract the voice box. But it is deep. Something busts. Perhaps the pressure from the prodding diamond tip has damaged and collapsed the voice box. Tumbling across the moon bounce, Danguy Weck notices a sound from somewhere outside his mind space. A squealing. It distracts him, snaps him out of it. Like the him in his head is on a tether that's suddenly yanked. He's lashed through the knob-lock porthole window, out of his brain, and back to reality, to the whole of his real and present body.

A knife in his throat, and he is in white-hot-nightmare-burning pain while Little Sis does a single-member marching parade with her clarinet up and down the hallway outside his room. Danguy screams in agony, and no sound comes out. Just a gurgle.

He is pained and bleeding. He mashes the washcloth to his throat—one part panicked, two parts thrilled. No sound, no voice box. No voice box, no speaking. No speaking, no answers, no questions. He swabs the incision with alcohol. It burns. He pins the small slice shut with three adhesive sutures. They butterfly tight. Gauze pads, then tape, and he notices all the while that he is breathing and can swallow. He didn't mangle his air tube or his food tube. His lungs aren't going to fill with blood. He did a good job.

The pain, however, is vicious. He feels sick to his stomach and does not want to throw up. He tucks his forehead to his knees and passes out.

DANGUY WECK heals fairly quickly and well. He keeps to his room for several days. The Great Aunt is out mostly, and Little Sis away on playdates. Except once when she catches him shuffling around the house. "What the fuck's wrong with your neck?" Little Sis asks, staring at the gauze and white tape. Danguy Weck can't answer her. He blinks, shoves her, walks to his room.

Danguy Weck thinks about Budweiser Dad and part two of his plan. He thinks about the tin can ocean. About how Budweiser Dad's breath smelled a little like garlic bread. Danguy Weck thinks about all that Budweiser. That's a lot of Budweiser. That's really bad for Budweiser Dad's liver. It's undoubtedly what made his sweat toxic, which nearly killed Danguy Weck. Danguy worries about Budweiser Dad's liver. Thinks it should function better, purify his internal fluids better. Just in case some other kid comes by and Budweiser Dad gets his hands on him. Or even his hands on Danguy Weck again. Danguy doesn't want Budweiser Dad's poison sweat to denature any more enzymes. And so his idea: Budweiser Dad needs a liver transplant.

Danguy goes to the pier. He rents a pole, buys some bait, spends an afternoon holding the railing tight, the pole jutting out over the sea, the line dropped deep into it. He catches a brown fish. Reeling it in, Danguy agrees with what he'd suspected: It looks like a liver. And those gills gacking in the sunlight, Danguy is confident they will work as purification slats and function in a liver way. On the hook at the end of the line, the fish flexes and snaps its steaky body. Danguy Weck unhooks its mouth, round like a penny, drops the fish into a bucket, puts the bucket in his red wagon, wheels it home. The liver fish swishes around in there, but after several hours in the bucket, its movements slow to none, except for those gills that fan and collapse aggressively. He stashes the fish in the bucket behind the bush near the fence in the Great Aunt's backyard. He packs a backpack with his first-aid supplies and a pair of rubber gloves from under the kitchen sink.

IN THE night Danguy Weck slips out his window. He moves like a shadow, careful not to wake Little Sis in the bedroom next to his; she would ruin everything. The Great Aunt is out again. Danguy thinks she might have a boyfriend or something. Sloshing the fish bucket, Danguy sneaks into Budweiser Dad's backyard. The backyard garage door is unlocked. He finds Budweiser Dad passed out in his big chair, a can of Budweiser in his hand. He is snoring, rumbling like a motorboat. Danguy wades through the Ocean of Can. It makes a ruckus, but Budweiser Dad doesn't stir.

KO'd. Danguy ranges around the back of his chair. He dons his rubber gloves. Doesn't want to touch Budweiser Dad's skin and get his poison sweat on him. Danguy pushes with all his might against the back of Budweiser Dad's shoulder. Budweiser Dad slumps forward. He exhales gustily. Danguy tramps to the front of the chair. He takes hold of Budweiser Dad's big forearm. He braces his foot against the chair. He pulls with all the strength in his arms and stomach and back. He extends his braced leg to manage some extra leverage to get Budweiser Dad out of his chair. It works. Budweiser Dad lurches forward and slumps from his chair to the sea of cans. He snorts, but doesn't wake. He's likely drunk a lot of Budweiser. Danguy Weck is lucky.

Budweiser Dad is facedown in the cans. He can breathe through the crumpled spaces between them. Danguy places one gloved hand on Budweiser Dad's shoulder, the other on the side of his hip. With all his strength, plus some he didn't know he had, Danguy Weck flips Budweiser Dad over. He is still deep asleep. Danguy takes his diamond knife from his backpack, slices and tears Budweiser Dad's undershirt. Swabs his knife and Budweiser Dad's abdomen with rubbing alcohol. Makes a clean entrance into the liver area of his stomach. The diamond knife parts skin like it is melting it. Carefully poking around, he locates the liver. Still no change in Budweiser Dad. Still passed out cold. Danguy can see a sliver of his liver through the fine cut. It looks awful—pale, milky. Danguy works his small finger under it, lifts it a little. Works more of his small hand in there. Grabs hold of it. Lifts and pulls it out. With his other hand he grabs the fish from the bucket. It is barely moving. The fish in his left hand, the liver in his right, he notices they weigh about the same.

The liver fish is pretty flat and slippery. Danguy angles it into the incision. It slides through the gap and into the hollow liver space. Budweiser Dad has lost some blood. The washcloth is heavy and shining and red, all the way through. Danguy uses thirty adhesive sutures to mend the slice. Then he gauzes and tapes like Budweiser Dad's a fragile package to be sent overseas.

Danguy packs his things, flushes the liver and his gloves down Budweiser Dad's toilet, scurries back home, and climbs through his window.

TWO DAYS later: "Danguy," the Great Aunt stands in the living room between him and the TV, holding a white trash bag containing a wad of blood-soaked clothes. "Whose blood is this?"

He looks at her, a small tight knot of gauze taped to his throat. He shrugs.

"Whose is it?" she asks again.

He shrugs again, makes how-should-I-know eyes. Leans left to see the TV behind her hips.

She looks at him for a few beats. "Is it yours?" she asks gently, "from that business you did to your neck?"

He looks at her, lifts his shoulders, tilts his head, raises his eyebrows: maybe. He feels a sheen of sweat gloss his forehead and nose and cheeks.

"Are you okay?" she asks.

He feels queasy and doesn't want to talk about it. Then he realizes he can't, which is tranquilizing. He wipes his face on his sleeve. The Great Aunt's eyes flick to the front window above the couch behind Danguy Weck. She squints and looks harder. Danguy turns to see.

A pack of official-businessiers tromp around the driveway, across the lawn, and in and out of Budweiser Dad's front door. Some have badges and belts and vests and are stretching yellow Do-Not-Cross ribbon around the property. There's another with a gurney and a long black waterproof bag with a zipper all the way up the front, and another in the driver's seat of a white van with whirly lights on top. Then about four men in dark suits and white shirts and dark ties and very short, clean haircuts arrive in a black town car. Danguy Weck and the Great Aunt watch.

Danguy suddenly remembers a thing from that show about alcohol and how it thins a person's blood and impedes clotting.

He looks at the bag of bloody clothes in the Great Aunt's arms and he recognizes there is quite a lot of blood on those clothes. They are still sticky wet and glistening with it. And the veins in the Great Aunt's forearms are popping out because the bag is so heavy. Danguy remembers that perhaps Budweiser Dad did bleed a lot. Danguy's heart slams around his chest.

Panic creeping up his esophagus and dizzying his head, he turns to the Great Aunt whose expressions shift across her face like time-lapse photography. She looks at Danguy, then to the bag in her hands, then back out the window. Her face gets very pale and then looks even more wrinkly. Danguy thinks she is connecting the dots in her mind and has come to a dreadful quadrangle of understanding:

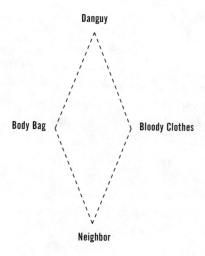

Her voice like a lead pipe, the Great Aunt says, "Go pack your things."

Danguy looks up at her.

"NOW," she says.

He hustles to his room, pulls a duffel bag out of his closet, hears the Great Aunt open the door to the basement and yell down the stairs at Little Sis who is probably roller-skating in circles on the cement floor. She tells Little Sis to pack her shit now, pronto.

"What?" he hears Little Sis say.

The Great Aunt repeats herself louder.

"Why?" he hears Little Sis ask.

"Your brother's in trouble," she shouts.

"So."

"They might take him away," she hollers.

"Good."

"I'm radioing your father."

Danguy hears her skates clomp up the stairs, double time.

IN THE dark, dead middle of the night, Danguy Weck, Little Sis, and Whaler sail far across the bounding main. Danguy positions himself in the middle of Whaler's boat, trying to keep the sea on all sides as far away from himself as possible. In the belly of the boat, he's set his tetra tank—emptied but for a few inches of water and his school of neon tetras darting around close to the gravel. He sits curled in a ball. His hands locked around his shins, his forehead on his knees. Little Sis is unafraid and is skipping along the gangway in the moonlight. Whaler couldn't get her to stop and doesn't have a life jacket. He put a harness on her and leashed her to the mast to keep her from falling overboard. He curses at himself because here he is, after all these years, careening across the ocean with his kids.

"Had wanted you two safe and landside," he says. "Forever."

Danguy lifts his head and stares at his dad behind the ship's wheel. It's hard to see him in the dark, but when the sail catches the moon it casts a deep shadowed light over Whaler's face. His beard is trim, and above it, his face looks like stiff leather. Danguy thinks he should feel more things, here, finally, with his father he's never known. But he doesn't.

"But when the real shit goes down, kids," Whaler continues, "sometimes you gotta fuck it and split. Hit the ocean." He takes one hand off the spoke handle of the wheel and rubs his forehead. His fingers leave a dark smudge. "I sure as hell don't need the government on my ass. In my line of work," he says. His voice is salty. He looks at Danguy, sighs, says, "I'm sure he deserved it, Danguy, but the *president's* old buddy?" He shakes his head slowly and whistles.

"Where the fuck are we going?" asks Little Sis sweetly.

Whaler tells them about the Plexiglas Russian Safety Pod.

A few years ago, Whaler'd done a good deal of illegal trading with the Russians. Sold them the heart of a blue whale. "Largest whale on the planet," he tells his kids. "Its heart is the size of a compact car. A small child could crawl through its aorta."

Upon delivery, the Russians didn't have all the money that had been agreed upon. But before Whaler could return to his boat for a harpoon to hurl into the much littler human heart of the Russian kingpin, the Russian offered Whaler something else: knowledge and use of a top-secret hideaway in the sea. For relaxation and/or protection. "Whatever your needs," the Russian boss said.

The blue whale heart up on a lift in a warehouse on a dock off the Bering Sea, the Russians, with their large pale heads and big shoulders, imparted their information to Whaler. They gave him the latitude and longitude of a place in the ocean. At this particular intersection of down and across the planet, all is undetectable. Radar proof, hard to see from air and sea. Unfindable by any geographic positioning system. For all intents and purposes, invisible.

"Everything you can need it has," said the Russian. "For times for fun, also safekeeping!" He filled glasses full of vodka. "Best use of it only!" he said and lifted his glass, slugged it down. "Like summer cottage!" he bellowed, his lips glistening. He laughed heartily and slapped Whaler square in the back.

THE PLEXIGLAS Russian Safety Pod is a very large bubble in the middle of the ocean. Entirely blue transparent Plexiglas, it's situated at the surface of the sea, about half submerged and secured on stilts sunk deep into the ocean floor. A giant hollow ball, Plexiglas thick as tires are wide. Several feet above the bottom arc of the orb, a level Plexiglas slab establishes the floor. Two main intersecting blue Plexiglas planes, which separate the inside of the Pod into four rooms, divide the rest of the sphere. Two bedrooms, a living room, a kitchen. Part of the kitchen is divided off by another Plexi wall for the bathroom. Cut into the walls are archways for ins and outs within the Pod. There are no doors. In the living room is a rubber-rimmed porthole window. It is positioned higher than your average window, so a few Plexi steps unfold from the porthole into the living room. There are notches on the outside of the Pod beneath that window to secure boards for entrances and exits from boats. When Whaler dropped them off, Danguy Weck and Little Sis walked a plank from his ship to the living room window. When he left, Whaler dislodged the plank, took it with him.

Because the outside is visible all through the inside of the Pod and the bottom half dome is submerged, when Danguy stands and meanders through his new home, the surface of the ocean is level with his neck. This feels to him what it must be like to be decapitated and still alive. It is awful. So he prefers to look down, where in the space between the floor and the bottom of the bubble, in what he guesses is the basement (accessible through a hinged Plexi hatch in the living room) are boxes of supplies. From the floor of the Pod, the basement supplies block some of the view of the ocean beneath. Danguy likes to look at them and pretend he is on solid ground.

In the supply boxes are blankets, an inflatable raft—the kind that inflates automatically when you pull the cord, goggles, fins, medkits, a few bottles of pills labeled пилюльки, a Russian-English dictionary. He uses it. The pills are sleeping pills.

In the kitchen there are Plexi cupboards filled with chromey cellophane-wrapped packages. Black-inked across the wrappers: еда замены аварийной ситуации. And in them:

Applesauce, noodles, rice, or mashed potatoes
Pound cake
Beverage powder
Wheat bread snack pack
Yellow bread spread
Packet (coffee, creamer, sugar, salt, napkin, wet nap, spoon)

Next to the packages are cans of beef and Sterno heaters. In similar but squishier packaging is water. вода in black across the wrapper. Danguy presumes this is backup water because there's a device in the sink in the kitchen—a distiller. It draws in seawater, distills it through a network of pipes behind the transparent blue Plexi doors beneath the sink, and dispenses it from the tap. In another cupboard, bottles of booze—plain white labels with водочка boldy stamped across, which Danguy supposes means vodka, he doesn't bother looking it up—and several cartons of cigarettes: сигареты.

Other plumbing? Attached to the bottom of the toilet is a wide, pie-size tube that extends out from the bottom of the Pod and disappears into the deep. The flusher is pressurized. Danguy figures it shoots it somewhere. So they flush trash in there too— wrappers, napkins, empty Sterno cans—because they don't know where to put it, haven't figured out where the Russians meant the trash to go.

More on the bathroom—like all the other rooms, it's transparent. From anywhere in the Pod, visibility is 100 percent.

"That's fucked," said Little Sis standing in the archway to the bathroom as she and Danguy wandered their new home. On the other side of the Plexiglas, Whaler's boat was shrinking to a speck in the distance. "There's no way I'm watching you shit."

Danguy taped blankets to the three bathroom walls visible within the Pod. He left the one that faces out bare, for a view.

LIFE IN the Pod is really boring. Danguy already hypnotized his tetras. They leapt from the tank, hit the Plexi wall, and didn't stick. They slid down the wall and piled up in the angle where floor and wall meet. They stayed wet, then rotted. He can't replace them. They're freshwater fish.

"Your room smells like ass," says Little Sis standing in the archway between their rooms. She turns, cuts across her room and through the other archway into the living room. She digs into the basket by the coffee table, selects several glossy Russian magazines, jumps into the couch. There is no TV.

Danguy thinks of the words to the flag pledge, the way they say *one nation indivisible*, and he thinks of how that works in this place. Microscope style, it is his and Little Sis's nation in the ocean. And it's fairly indivisible because its divisibility doesn't very well divide, on account of the transparency of the dividers. He thinks it's more like invisible divisibility, which he thinks sucks, because most things right now suck. He wonders what Whaler has in mind for them when school starts.

"I'M GOING for a dip!" Little Sis yells from the living room. She has found a way to pass the time. She ties a sheet to the leg of the couch, pops open the porthole window, stretches the sheet through and out the window. She puts on fins and goggles. She climbs out the porthole, down the sheet. He hates it when she does this. The sea could suddenly swell high, rush the window, drown him dead. And he can't ask her to stop. Even if he could scream into her good ear, she wouldn't listen. One time he wrote her a note. *Please don't* it said. He held it up in front of his face. She snatched it, crumpled it, bounced it off his forehead. Outside the porthole entrance, she lets go of the sheet and falls backwards into a roller.

She is wearing a skirt and shirt. They billow big all around her body. Danguy thinks she looks like a jellyfish. She skims, glides, kicks, pushes, grabs, tumbles, and somersaults all the way around and beneath the Pod. Silver bubbles like shimmering ropes lasso from her nostrils.

Watching her rolling in orbit around the Pod, there is a moment when he wants to tell her things. He wants to tell her the story of their mom and dad. She was celebrating her birthday with friends from school when the Great Aunt sat him down. He wonders if she knows the story and thinks if she doesn't, she should. She swims and turns gracefully out there. And from some small space in his heart, he wants to tell her that he thinks she's a pretty gutsy girl for doing that so fearlessly. That she must have high levels of iron in her blood or something, which has galvanized her mind in a way that has made her courageous. He would like to ask if he could stand next to her and put his arm around her shoulder and pose for a picture, looking proud. He opens his mouth, but no words can come out. He pushes air through his vocal chords, makes a sound like the bleat of a kazoo.

Danguy gets a paper and a pen, draws a swirly whirly. Holds it to the wall inside the Pod. Spins it at Little Sis. She swims by, seems to notice he's doing something in there, at her. On the other side of the Plexi, in the ocean in the middle of nowhere, she flicks him off and keeps swimming. She does not get eaten by a shark.

She climbs back up the sheet and in through the window just as the Pod goes dark. Drenched and squeaking against the Plexiglas, Little Sis closes the porthole window and descends the Plexi steps. Danguy looks up. Weather changes fast on the ocean. The clouds, suddenly, are thick and look like piles of charcoal. The sea stretches and jerks, whitecapping like it's got rabies. It's storm time. When the sea swells, the Pod gets splashed and slapped and disappears completely into the boundless wet.

Green sea, blue Plexiglas, and the darkened sky that weighs

heavily over the wrestling waves. The Pod's completely submerged. Little Sis over there loves loves loves it. She is standing on the couch dripping all over it, watching with her arms raised like a conductor. There are fish outside the bubble—beneath Little Sis and Danguy, eye level with them, above them. The fish don't seem to notice the storm. They're accustomed to complete submersion. They twiddle their little fan fins next to their gills and burp their round mouths and don't blink and appear very calm even though their whole bodies sway many feet one way and many feet to the other according to the push of the water.

They are largish fish. Larger than the liver fish, Danguy notices. And despite being in the middle of the sea, surrounded by its fish all the time, he thinks rarely of Budweiser Dad, dead or alive. Perhaps because the fish in this particular area of the ocean, for whatever reason, are remarkably colorful, have little resemblance to livers. But right now because the sky above the surface is gray, visibility down here is poor. Light that illuminates colors is cut and so the fish appear dark and more liverlike than ever. This causes the collapsed voice box in Danguy Weck's throat to ache. It is distressing, and in his brain sounds the sound of cans, and behind his eyes appears the face of Budweiser Dad, and in his nose lingers the scent of him.

Danguy Weck sits in his room, breathes like a monk, and tries to hatch. But it's not working anymore; he can't seem to breathe slow enough or get into the room in his head where he can exit out the porthole window in the back of his mind. Sick to his stomach, he watches the white flat belly of a manta ray undulate around and up and over the top of the Pod and disappear beyond it.

◊

WHEN DANGUY Weck is a grown-up, he will ride the subway with his wife and encounter the one-eyed glass-eyed man. The one-eyed glass-eyed man will stagger in from the rear of the car, cursing and drooling and popping every passenger in the back of the head with his cane as he lurches up the aisle. At the front of the car he will turn and face all the passengers, holding his cane like a spear, and shout "Money for the blind man! Money for the blind man!" He will hold out his hand and totter and wobble in his old shoes like he's on a boat in a storm. When no one responds and the men and the women turn to the window or look at their feet, he will grumble, "No? NO?" And spit-lipped, a rolling wetness in his voice, he'll slur, "Come on you flying fucking fuckers!" And he will bring his fingers to his eye, press them hard into its socket. He will cluck his tongue and remove his eyeball. His eyelid will wither and sink. A little girl several seats up will burst and cry and it will sound like waves crashing. Her mom will scoop her arm around the girl's face and tuck her daughter into her chest.

"It's glass, motherfuckers," the man will sputter, balancing his eyeball in the middle of his palm.

From his seat, Danguy Weck will wonder about this man's life. About his parents, about his schooling, about his jobs, and the lovers that plundered the territory behind his rib cage. He will think about the shitless portion of the human heart—that small space leftover from when you're born. Before everything. He will put a protective arm around his ladylove, tip his face toward hers, lift his hand and sign to her, *don't look at him.*

Honky Sticky

IN HER new life she's called Honky Sticky. She got this name from the fat black girl at school. She was once known as Little Sis, back when she lived by the shore. Before eight-year-old Rat Face, who would become her new kid sister, found her washed up on the rocks—her lips blistered, her calves scabby, her raft half deflated, empty bottles of vodka, empty cans of beef, cigarette butts floating in unclear puddles of water in the belly of the boat. Before Foster Mom agreed to carry her to the car, to drive her to the desert, to nurse her well, to raise her up. The name Honky Sticky stuck when on the first day at her new school, Fatty Black Girl flung it at her. *Honky* because she's white and has kind of large front teeth. *Sticky* because she's skinny.

On the playground at recess Fatty Black Girl approached Little Sis from behind. She leaned in and grumbled into Little Sis's bad ear. Little Sis felt the girl's hair poof into her neck. Little Sis froze. "Where'd you get those tusks, Honky?" whispered Fatty Black Girl. "Tusks for teeth, sticks for legs!" she snarled. But Little Sis couldn't quite make out what she was saying. She felt breath on her neck and the vibration of sounds and jumbled words, which she would sort out in a minute but was just then experiencing a processing delay. She turned to get a better look at the girl. She felt a bit overwhelmed by her height and size and hair. "You got a birth defect, Honky Sticky?" the girl sneered.

"Born without a stomach!" Little Sis looked her up and down, agitated by her violent approach. "You deaf too?" the girl shouted. And by the time she registered everything Fatty Black Girl was saying, the girl was done. Had turned. Was lumbering away and jerking her thumb over her shoulder behind her, bellowing loudly across the play yard, "HON-KY STICK-Y! HON-KY STICK-Y!"

In that moment Honky Sticky realized what had gone down and shouted loudly at Fatty Black Girl's back, "FUCK YOU, YOU FAT FUCKING BITCH!" But it was too late. She didn't fight back soon enough. And the art teacher happened to be walking by, just then. She heard Honky Sticky, was deeply offended, gave her detention for her first whole month of school.

That same day, while Honky sat in detention, Fatty Black Girl took to prank calling Honky Sticky's home, asking to speak to Honky Sticky, saying she was an old friend from her old school. She convinced Rat Face, who then convinced her mom, that Honky Sticky is definitely the real name of the girl they'd found. This was easy because both found it hard to believe anyone could simply be known as Little Sis.

When she walked in the door after clocking one detention, Rat Face and Foster Mom greeted her with a cake and a big sign glittered with Rat Face's second grade craft supplies. It read WEL-COME HONKY STICKY!

"You're fucking kidding me," said Honky, subtly, under her breath. But she was also kind of touched by the celebration of it all. The cake looked plush and heavily frosted and Foster Mom looked friendly in her apron and Rat Face's pointy face seemed less pointy and Honky thought for a minute that she was now Rat Face's big sister, and as such resolved she would be willing to beat anyone's ass who made fun of Rat Face's face. And on the sign above the door up there, the glitter was a kind of blue that reminded Honky Sticky of the ocean, in certain shades of sunlight. In that moment, she decided she could make a life here.

SHE TRIES. She used to be good at making friends, but she's not having much luck in this new town after word spread all the way over to the junior high that she socked a third grader in the gut over at the elementary school for making fun of Rat Face's lisp and horrible nose. The girls in Honky Sticky's class avoid her. Much like they avoid Fatty Black Girl. But neat for Fatty Black Girl that she always has older girls with long and brightly enameled nails pick her up from school in long cars shining in shimmering metallic-flecked paint. The cars roll slowly through the school parking lot on small fat wheels with sparkling gold spokes. Fatty Black Girl climbs into the passenger seat, which is always purple or red or green velvety fabric. She says, "See ya, suckers," to the whole lot of kids who watch, hushed. Honky Sticky still thinks she is a fat bitch, but is a little envious of her effect on a crowd.

So Honky Sticky joins the asshole Girl Scout Cadettes because that's what all the girls in her grade do. But Honky sniffs out some bonuses: All members are appointed an automatic best friend for the first four months of membership, and Honky Sticky hears you can earn a badge for swimming. Both things seem all right. She doesn't mind the green dress. It's short, but comes with green bloomers, so if she had to run and hop a fence, only the bloomers would show, not her actual underwear. And the sash feels military-like. Like it could be a thing that could carry a railroad track of bullet ammunition across her chest if it were a different kind of sash and there were a war happening she had to fight in.

When she finds out her appointed best friend is the troop leader's daughter and is the worst kind of ballet girl—the prissiest kind, the kind that doesn't have it in her to watch her toenails fall off, to suck on rocks to keep from eating, to quit school, to move to the city—Honky Sticky's disappointed, but keeps it to herself. Tells the girl she would love to attend a recital. But then on Girl Scout Cadette swim day, when it turns out to be swim *lessons* for the bunch of losers who don't know how to swim in the first place, Honky Sticky goes ape shit. She laps tidal waves around the stupid girls in her troop. Crosses the pool twelve times, underwater the whole time, there and back, no breaths, swimming with her eyes open. She cools it however, when the drain in the floor of the pool catches her eye. She notices a glimmer of something from inside it, but doesn't dive down toward it. Doesn't want to attract all the other scouts' attention to it. She keeps on swimming, calmly and with good form. At the end of the day, she gets a badge, but is told by the troop leader that being a show-off isn't a Girl Scout Cadette value.

Then there's the disabled kids. Honky Sticky is supposed to sell bars of chocolate to earn money for the Girl Scout Cadettes to take a field trip to the disabled kids' home and teach the disabled kids how to crotchet coasters and hats. The disabled kids' home is far away. The Girl Scout Cadettes will have to stay in a hotel overnight, so they need to earn their hotel money. But Honky Sticky doesn't sell a single bar. She eats them all herself. A whole box of bars of chocolate. And when the troop leader finds out Honky Sticky is out of chocolate without a dime to show for it, she is livid. She pulls Honky Sticky into the kitchen next to the banquet hall in the community center. She tells Honky Sticky she should feel ashamed about her behavior.

"How could you?" she screams. "How selfish!" she shrieks. Honky Sticky thinks she is overreacting. The troop leader shakes her head and spears Honky Sticky with her small dark eyeballs. Honky Sticky notices the woman's eye shadow has clumped in the rivulets in her wrinkly upper eyelid. She imagines putting the troop leader's face on an ironing board and with a tiny iron, the size of a kidney bean, pressing those upper lids smooth over the bump of her eyeballs. She imagines the sizzle when she first presses the iron down.

"It's enough to make me sick!" shouts the troop leader, one hand to her forehead and the other laid flat on her stomach, as though she might actually get sick. Then she stops. Drops her hands. Tells

Honky Sticky to lift her Girl Scout Cadette skirt and pull down her Girl Scout Cadette bloomers. She whaps Honky's tiny ass with a spatula four times—two solid smacks on each cheek.

Honky Sticky feels prickerfish in her underwear the whole walk home. She thinks the Girl Scout Cadettes is crap. She thinks crocheting and community service is a crock of shit. When she arrives home and walks into the kitchen, Rat Face is sitting at the table. Foster Mom grates cheese onto a plate on the cutting board. The cordless phone is directly next to the plate and has some orange cheese gratings on it.

"The *whole* box?" says Foster Mom without looking up. She says it in a way that reminds Honky of a hangnail caught on a wool sweater. Honky grits her teeth and shakes the sound out of her head.

"That chocolate wasn't yours to eat," Foster Mom continues, still without looking up. Rat Face sniggers, but nervously. Her little laugh-breaths pump quickly from her pointy face. Honky Sticky catches them in her good ear, whips her head over her shoulder. Her hair shakes. She glares at Rat Face. Considers shoving her off her seat.

After dinner, but before she heads out to work, Foster Mom calls back the troop leader and agrees to pay $25 for the box of chocolate bars. Then she grounds Honky Sticky from dessert for a month. And tries to make Honky Sticky believe that $25 is blowing an irreparable hole in the family savings. But Honky Sticky's seen Foster Mom's purse gaping wide and stuffed full of cash bills mornings after working all night at the place in town.

That night, from the bottom bunk, Honky asks Rat Face about Foster Mom's job. Hanging her head over the edge of the top bunk, Rat Face explains, "Downtown there's this place called Club Fantasia where nice-looking ladies who can also dance work." Rat Face's lisp is significant and Honky Sticky has to turn her good ear Rat Face's way to catch it all. Also, her voice always sounds like her nose is stopped up. "Mom goes there and lines up with the rest of the ladies against a wall and over in a part of the place is a board with all the ladies' names and the men sign up for slots to dance with them."

"Dance how?" asks Honky Sticky.

Rat Face leans further off the bunk. "Like this," she says and holds her arms out—one up like she is presenting a big prize, the other bent like a hook, like she is holding a bag of groceries to her chest. "She dances with them like this for some songs," some spit rains down from Rat Face's mouth, "then they say thanks and give her a tip or ask her to sit down and have a conversation. They're nice, Mom says. She says they're important businessmen from China and Japan and they take good care of her."

Honky Sticky wonders if the Girl Scout Cadettes might have dance lessons one of these days. And if they do, if they'll ask Foster Mom to teach them. And if she does, if Foster Mom will ask Honky to help demonstrate the moves because she would catch on quick. And after demonstrating well, Foster Mom could lay her hand on the top of Honky's head and squat down to look her in the eye and smile and say, *Great job!*

THE FOLLOWING morning Honky Sticky learns the troop leader has trash-talked Honky Sticky to her daughter. Told her Honky Sticky is a bad kid, an unsavory character—pigging out on the chocolate that was intended to help the disabled. She tells her Honky Sticky is surely no Girl Scout Cadette with those kinds of values. She tells her that Honky Sticky, displaying that kind of impulsive behavior at such a young age, will likely get into smoking and drinking and drugs and sex with boys and bad grades next. The daughter relays all of this to Honky in the yard near the swing sets before the first bell rings.

Then she hands Honky Sticky a note and says, "Here. Read this. It's from my mom." The note disinvites Honky Sticky from the troop meeting that afternoon and every afternoon in the world for the rest of her life.

"I'm fired from the Girl Scout Cadettes?" Honky says slowly.

"Yeah," says the appointed best friend. She unlatches the golden half-heart Best Friends Girl Scout Cadette pendant from around her neck and says, "And we have to break up." She holds the pendant in her closed fist in front of Honky Sticky's face. Honky stares at it, confused. The girl shakes her fist and rolls her eyes. Kneading two syllables into it, she says "He-re."

"What?" says Honky.

The girl makes an annoyed sound in the back of her throat, opens her fist, and lets her half of the golden heart and chain fall to the ground in front of Honky Sticky's boot. The class bell rings. The girl turns pointedly on toe and walks speedily to class. Honky Sticky stares at the half heart and chain glinting from the ground. "Oh man," she says to the ground. "Oh shit." She bends over to pick it up, suddenly feeling like she might cry. Even though the appointed best friend was a pain-in-the-ass pansy ballerina, she was her friend. Honky Sticky sucks in a breath and holds it. Jams her sadness into feeling pissed. She picks up a ripe, wet cactus fruit the size of a human heart and wails it across the yard at the outside wall of the music room. Her pitch is so rigorous it hurts her ribs. The cactus fruit bursts into splatted pink bits.

Honky Sticky turns away from the classroom building, cuts through the playground, past the last water fountain, and heads into the cactus woods. She trudges in deep, finds a spot under a monstrous cactus. She sits in the dirt and sand while all the assholes in school sit in class.

She thinks about how she guesses she shouldn't have eaten the chocolate bars. About how she should have bought her own chocolates with money she could earn doing things because she's not totally disabled. She starts to feel a little bad. Then she stops and thinks the kind of thinking she is doing is boring. What the fuck are disabled kids going to do with crocheted coasters and hats? She stands. Dusts her ass, still a little tender from the spatula. The appointed best friend was a pile of shit too. Kept telling

Honky not to cuss and then cried during the swimming lesson when Honky grabbed the girl's ankles under water and yanked them.

"She tried to drown me!" the girl blathered. Honky whispered into the girl's soggy ear, "Shut your fuckin' face." The girl probably told on her for that too. Now she never has to go to her recitals.

Honky chucks the girl's pendant way over her head. It flashes through the sky and catches on some cactus spikes. She removes her half of the pendant from her neck and chucks it also. She walks over to a muddy puddle a few feet from the giant cactus, where another cactus had broken in half and leaked its water supply onto the ground. She drops the note from the troop leader into the puddle. It floats. It looks like a blurt of whipped cream in a nasty spill of cocoa. She steps on the note. Drowns it. Smashes it with her boot tip into the soft mud and wet sand beneath the puddle. She admires her boots. They are beluga-skin cowgirl boots with stacked whalebone heels. A gift from her dad. When she grows out of them, she's considering getting them bronzed. Or resined so she can still look at the beluga skin and the layers in the heel. Her brother Danguy packed them in her supply bag, along with her goggles and her fins, when he sent her floating.

She can't be totally sure, but slooping across the sea, she had the time and mind space to piece it together, and here's how she figures all that happened: That night Danguy Weck prepared dinner. Little Sis has admitted to herself that she is grateful for this—his cooking. Now, in her memory of him, the fact of his cooking feels nice. She has in her head framed a picture of her brother, fixing dinner like he would. She sees him there, through the clear blue wall separating the living room from the kitchen. He is cast in blue, as small as she is, standing and facing the sink and the blue Plexiglas counter with the sink pipes and bucket of Russian cleaning products visible through the counter doors. He is wearing shorts and a T-shirt and his knees are like hers; the inner knobs of them touch. From out of his shirtsleeves poke his elbows. She remembers his pointy elbows, which appeared to Little Sis even pointier than hers feel. She remembers thinking that they are twins and that they are different. And that his pointy elbows looked shaky and nervous as his hands did things like peel back the tin pop-top lids on the cans of dinner meat. From this picture of the back of him, she can't see the scar on the front of his neck, but it is in the picture because of her memory of it. It is a pink knot resembling an inny-outy belly button right there on his throat.

She sits in the desert dirt digging her heel into the cactus puddle. Stops doing that and pounds her heel on dry dirt, knocking the mud off her boots. She pulls her knees to her chest and rests her forehead on them. She smells her shirt. It smells clean. She remembers catching Danguy Weck leaning over the laundry machine with bandages on his neck, right before they got sent to sea. His silence was rotund. Something about his silence topped the volume of his scream that blew out Little Sis's left-side hearing. She had several nights of drowning dreams after that scream, each morning waking up with spots of blood on her pillow and brown crust around her ear. The Great Aunt took Little Sis to the doctor who peered into her ear through a small tube with a tiny light and a magnifying eyepiece. The doctor whistled and shook his head and patted Little Sis's knee and said, loudly and with elastic lips, "I'm sorry, damage has been done." Then he showed her pamphlet diagrams of inner ears. Then he drew over one of the diagrams to show what happened to Little Sis's inner ear. He drew what looked like a porcupine or a fireball stuffed deep in there.

Some night after that, Little Sis dreamed at last that she was amphibious and finally didn't drown in this dream, but while underwater and from the center of some ocean, she flicked her forked tongue, and what stuck to the end of it but the entire shoreline, which she pulled back toward her mouth drawing miles of continental crust deep into the sea. Then in her waking life, the

Great Aunt found a sack of bloody clothes behind the dryer, and Little Sis and her brother were hustled in the night onto Whaler's boat, which glossed far away from the shore, and not until all land had disappeared and except for their one onboard lantern, everywhere around them was black, did he hug both his kids, one at a time. Whaler's face, up close to Little Sis's, smelled like wood and smoke and wax and pepper.

In the Pod, Danguy Weck kept his eyes sprung wide. His small self hummed without sound, like an appliance that is plugged in and always on. How she wound up here in the desert, today, dismissed from the Girl Scout Crapettes—she's convinced it started when Danguy Weck made their last dinner together. The Russians kept pills in the Pod and Little Sis had spied her brother studying them in their bottles from time to time. Perhaps that night he crushed a few and stirred them into her food. Probably her mashed potatoes. She remembers: They were creamy but bitter. But she ate them because she was hungry and they were not too bad. And all those packaged foods tasted familiar but strange. Like a recognizable sentence, *hello how are you*, but written backwards: *uoy era woh olleh*. She ate them and some beef and a slice of bread with yellow dressing, sitting next to her brother on the couch. Of course they didn't speak. Little Sis looked out and watched a storm pass and the ocean settle into night around the Pod. She carried her empty plate to the kitchen, and on her way back to the couch she felt like she was wearing a necklace of heavy rocks and a hat made of bricks and a giant pair of glasses with concrete frames and fisheye lenses as thick as dictionaries. She thought, or maybe said out loud, "Holy shit," and remembers wanting, so badly, to tip her head into something soft. And when she reached the couch and finally did, breath went out of her fingertips.

She imagines the rest of the night like this: From the basement her brother pulled the inflatable raft. He climbed the steps to the porthole window and nervously unhooked it. The sea was

probably flat and velvety. He shook the raft open. A length of
rope was threaded through a rubber eyelet hook at one end of
the raft. He probably tied the rope to the latch on the porthole. Then he yanked the air chord. The raft hissed and swelled
aggressively, like a giant marshmallow in a giant microwave. It
probably bonked against the Pod and shook and puffed like it
was in a race with itself. Ballooned taut, the air stopped and a
nice cushy lifeboat floated calmly by the Pod.

Danguy packed a bag of meals, packages of water, a blanket,
a med kit, bottles of vodka, a carton of cigarettes, a change of
clothes, her boots and ocean accessories. He probably pushed the
bag out the porthole and into the raft.

Then he went to the couch. Stood in front of it. Little Sis
was probably breathing loudly through her mouth. Whenever she
wakes up, her mouth is dry. She was probably lying on her side,
her good ear pressed to the pillow, her bad facing up. He probably clapped to check on her level of outness. She is sure she didn't
stir. Can't remember any disturbance after she'd hit that couch.
He probably scooped his arm underneath her armpit, hooked his
other around her waist. He pulled her up. Her head, heavy on
her loose neck, probably rolled backwards. He stood her up and
shimmied his grip lower around her waist and heaved her over
his shoulder. Danguy Weck and his sister, over his shoulder. She
is skinny and light like sticks. But Danguy probably found her
pretty heavy. He carried her up the steps slowly, maybe stumbling
a little. He leaned cautiously out the window. He probably tried
to let her down easily, but there were his pointy elbows versus
gravity and all its strength. Gravity's stronger. She flumped into
the raft, one leg over the side of it. This is a fact that she can be
sure of, because she woke this way, out there, the Pod gone from
sight. Then Danguy untied the rope, leaned as far out the window as he could. Probably gave the raft a little push.

And now she is here. Living this life. And Danguy Weck is
where, she wonders. Still in the Pod? Lonely? She wonders if he

feels lonely. The Great Aunt once told her about how her parents built a boat when they were teenagers and during a flood sailed away from home and never saw their parents again. She told her that Whaler and Sailor would think about their parents. They fantasized that their parents had made it safely out of the flood. That they were in some other house in some other place cooking together in the kitchen—imagining, often, what happened to their kids while their kids, oceans away, imagined about them. The Great Aunt told her that when talking to someone is unmanageable, it helps to think about that person, hard and often. Did Whaler return to the Pod and get Danguy Weck? She doesn't bet he did, but the prospect of the prospect of that yanks directly at her heart. At its tubes and valves. Jerks them away from the main meat of the beating muscle. She taps her fingertip against the point of a cactus needle. She taps lightly a few times, then harder. It pierces the tip of her finger and stings. And it is so hot out here. She could use a drink.

Foster Mom's got nothing, is a nondrinker, and is probably home right now anyway. Honky gets up and hoofs it through the cactus woods and exits into a quiet part of town on the other side. She passes a bar with no windows, just an open padded door beneath a sign that says BAR. A drunk guy stands in the doorway, smoking a cigarette. He waves at Honky Sticky. She waves back. Wonders for a second if they'd serve her a drink. Thinks not, keeps walking. Steps into the diner next door and takes a seat at the counter. A different drunk guy sits a few seats down. His head hangs over the counter as though in a sling, and his eyelids and his lips droop and sag. But his stare is screwed tight on the lady refilling the napkin dispensers. She is a pretty waitress. She smiles at Honky Sticky. Honky Sticky, right away, loves her face, thinks she is the greatest waitress. She hands Honky a menu, says, "Hey there."

"Hi," Honky whispers, suddenly very shy.

The pretty waitress wears black pants and squishy black shoes. And her shirt is very short. Honky Sticky wonders if she buys shirts for short people. People with normal length legs, but foreshortened torsos. Maybe they have a whole store for that kind of people and the pretty waitress shops there for tops that show off her flat brown breadbasket. Honky imagines the waitress at a store, thumbing through the racks of what to her are half shirts but to the shorty-guts are ultimate coverage items they can tuck deep into their pants. Rat Face could shop there for a shirt, and on her it'd be a dress.

"Thirsty?" the waitress asks.

"Yeah."

"How about a Coke?"

"Okay," says Honky, feeling a little dumb and without words.

The waitress gets the Coke and sticks a straw in it and sets it in front of Honky Sticky and winks. Honky blushes. "Hungry?" the waitress asks. There is a sign posted above the coffee maker listing the menu items that they are out of for the day. On half a piece of lined paper, handwritten, it says: *Sorry, all! No cheese grits, chimichanga, pecan pie today!* Then two dots and a downward curve to make an unsmiley face.

Honky says quietly, "I'd like one chimichanga, some cheese grits," she tries not to smile, "and a slice of pecan pie." She points her face toward the counter, but kicks her gaze up at the waitress from beneath her eyebrows, twinkles at her through her bangs. The pretty waitress laughs, puts down her order pad, leans over the counter, takes Honky Sticky's cheeks in her hands. Her hands are warm and soft and smell like soap. She squeezes Honky's cheeks just a little and says, "You!" through the neat gap between her two front teeth, "are number one!"

Honky is startled and feeling warm. She glances at the drunk down the counter whose drippy eyes look surprised. Honky shrugs at him. The waitress says, "I'll hook you up with something good, sweetheart." She turns and shouts through the window to the cook, "A strawberry French toast." When it arrives it is Honky Sticky's favorite, crispy and sweet.

HONKY STICKY walks on. The French toast was delicious and the waitress was so pretty and Honky can still feel her hands on her face. Honky Sticky is experiencing a kind of gladness and delight. The retarded Girl Scout Cadettes and her shitty appointed ex–best friend and this rinky-dink town that's so far inland that she thinks she might choke and so has been caught by Rat Face more than once standing in the backyard screaming at the sky, begging it to split open and drop a flood, anything—all that shit right now feels shrunken and far away. Even her brother, whose memory causes a quiet commotion in her nervous system, is probably, she thinks, somewhere and doing fine. This thought goes down creamy and cool.

She spots a boy sitting on the curb in front of the corner mart. He wears puffy suede sneakers and janitor pants and an old white T-shirt. He is smoking a cigarette and wearing big square sunglasses. She thinks a cigarette would be nice about now. She'd smoked a carton of Russian ones on the raft. Taught herself how to blow O's while lying back in her lifeboat, staring up at the sky, trying to ring stars and planets that seemed larger and closer and brighter than she'd ever noticed before. Under her head, beneath the raft, the sea slapped the rubber and echoed through the vessel like a drum. Honky thought it sounded a little like someone chewing a mouthful of wet food. She approaches him. "Hi," she says. "Can I have a cigarette?"

He looks up at her in a diagonal kind of way and pulls his sunglasses down the bridge of his nose a bit so he can peek at her with one eye—the whole move looking like maybe he's practiced it. He keeps that one eye on her for a still beat, then half smiles. His lips are big and his teeth are small. He says, "Okay," and digs into his pocket and removes a pack. He jerks the pack and out slides a cigarette. They sit on the curb and smoke.

Then, "You like vodka?" he asks.

"Yeah," she says. "I like Russian vodka from Russia."

They walk to his house, which is a few blocks from where she stays with Foster Mom and Rat Face. He walks as though music is playing somewhere. At his house no one's home. The place smells like oranges.

"You like oranges?" he asks. In the kitchen the walls are yellow and on the counter is a basket stacked high with oranges. Honky Sticky likes the combination of the yellow and the orange in this room. Any time of day she thinks, the colors here suggest morning. He grabs an orange from the basket, holds it up level to his face with his arm bent. He drops it and quickly straightens his arm so the orange bounces off his elbow pit and pops up above his head. He catches it with a flourish and smiles at Honky and makes a *click-click* sound inside of his mouth. Then with a knife from the drawer he slices smoothly all the way around the orange and unwinds the peel in a single curly ribbon. She thinks of the ride to the Pod in her dad's sloop. He filleted a fish. Whaler wielded the knife straight down the fish belly and across some other important parts, so the fish fell easily away from the bones, in steak formation. He dug his fingers down its middle, gathered up the guts and chucked them over his shoulder and into the sea. Her new friend holds the orange twist up and bounces it a few times before whipping it into the trash beneath the sink. He hands her the whole round inside of the orange. She bites into it like an apple. It's sweet and tangy and juicy. She shoves the whole thing in her mouth. It's a lot and difficult to chew. Juice squirts out of her mouth and dribbles down her chin. He grabs a paper towel from the roll under the cabinet and holds it taught under her face like a circus net. It catches the juice. In her head, the sound of her chewing, and for a second, in her stomach, she feels back on the raft. He watches her finish chewing.

"Whoa," he says.

"I can also fit my fist in my mouth," she says, swallowing.

"Let's see."

She swallows the rest of the orange and balls her fist, opens her mouth wide, stuffs it in. She gags a little and wraps her lips around her wrist.

"Wow," he says, loudly and from his throat.

She pulls her fist out, gagging again, just a little. "Thanks," she says.

"Let's retire to the den," he says.

In it there's a big TV with all the movie channels. They drink vodka and limeade, which tastes so much better than the straight pulls Honky took from the bottle those days and nights on the raft.

"Is this Russian vodka?" asks Honky Sticky, taking a sip of her cocktail and then holding it up to the light and examining the glass.

"I don't know," he says and holds the bottle up to the light, similarly. Then he looks closely at the label. "I think it's French," he says.

"Ah," says Honky.

DUKE ADAIR becomes Honky Sticky's new best friend. He is fourteen and used to live with his dad and now lives with his mom who is rarely home because she works in sales for a vodka company and is often traveling to cities selling vodka to fine dining restaurants, while keeping the cabinet at home stocked with free samples and jars of plump olives. Honky Sticky strolls over to Duke Adair's house every day after school. They never hang out in school because Duke is two grades older and those grades are in another building on the opposite side of the far-away faculty parking lot. They are both skilled roller skaters and enjoy skating circles and figure eights in the driveway part of his backyard while sipping martinis from big cone glasses. Honky and Duke neither spill nor fall. They get drunk and fling olives at each other. Roll over and mash pimentos into the cement.

Duke Adair is the first person Honky Sticky does some things with. On her thirteenth birthday, he gives her her first kiss. On his driveway they sit, their heads bobbley and their eyeballs red and wet from the vodka cocktails. He tells her to open her mouth

wider because her teeth are long and he can't get in. He knows
to whisper into her good ear. She goes to bed that night, having done kissing, feeling older and proud. Just before wandering
into sleep she wonders what her brother got for his birthday. She
hopes it's something good.

Honky Sticky and Duke Adair kiss every day after that, after
school, after drinking and skating. They press their bodies hard
into each other and push their hands all around. Mauvy Pinker is
what Honky Sticky calls her virginity. Once, when they come up
for air after kissing for a very long time, Honky Sticky looks into
his hooded eyes and says, "I've still got my Mauvy Pinker." He
nods and seems to understand what she's talking about. She likes
that about him. She says, "I like you a lot, but I think I should
hang on to my Mauvy Pinker."

"Okay," he tells her, and they go back to kissing more.

Then a few days later they go ahead and do it. "Bye-bye Mauvy
Pinker," he says like he is talking over the sound of horses gal-
loping through his body. Honky holds her breath and the sensation is not unlike the time she dove beneath the Pod. She swam
directly below it, spread her body flat against the bottom of the
orb. The entire ocean pressed against her back and there was
the Pod, solid against her front, plus a slippery layer of film that
clung to the Plexiglas. Her breath kicked into the place in her
neck where she feels like air is pumped slowly through her body,
even though she is not breathing. She stayed until she thought
her lungs might catch fire.

SCHOOL SEEMS better since she's been hanging out with
Duke Adair. Fatty Black Girl's still a cunt and the Girl Scout
Cadettes still file off to their meetings every Tuesday and Thurs-
day in their green uniforms with the green sash. Honky gives
them all the finger as they scurry by. Then she tromps off campus
to Duke Adair's house.

There's something about him that reminds her of Danguy

Weck. His hands look like Danguy's, only a little larger, on account of Duke Adair's older age. And now Honky Sticky's read books about how people think about things but disagrees with what they might think about her thoughts regarding the similarities between Danguy and Duke: She does not want to be her brother's girl-friend. It is not a hidden thing in her brain or in her desire.

She thinks some more. She and Danguy are twins. She looks at her own hands and they are Danguy's too. Or his are hers. They're probably the same size still, now, wherever he is. So there's something about Duke Adair that reminds her of herself.

One day after school, over cocktails and cigarettes and after sexing against the side of the shed in his backyard, she explains to Duke Adair how she misses water.

"I can dive deep," she tells him. "The damage in my ear helps because my ruptured drum blew my eustachian tube wide, so now I have only one eustachian tube to clear when I'm free div-ing, and it's my right one and it's pretty amenable. Listen." She pushes her right ear flush against his left ear and squeezes her nostrils shut between her thumb and her finger. She presses her lips shut and then blows air up into her nose, which can't escape her nostrils, and so doubles back into her ear canals, making the faint sound of an air leak. "Hear that?" asks Honky.

"Maybe," says Duke.

"What'd you hear?"

"Like a parrot fart."

"Fuck yeah," says Honky. "That's my gift!" She holds up her hand. He slaps it five. "I got another one too," she says. "I think I've got a vestigial gill mechanism." She waves her hand in front of her neck. "In my neck."

He blinks at her. Asks, "What do you mean?"

"When I'm underwater," she says, "it feels like I can breathe. For a little bit."

He looks at her like she's TV.

"I miss it," she says.

He takes a sip of his vodka root beer. He suggests they go night-dipping.

HONKY SLIPS out of bed while Rat Face sleeps. Even Rat Face's breathing has a lisp. Honky puts on a one-piece bathing suit and socks, for silent stepping. She steals down the hallway, through the kitchen. She creeps through the pantry, crawls out the dog door because the front door creaks. The dog the door's for died a few years ago. Rat Face still cries over it. On the back step, Honky ties on her sneakers and runs through the yard and through the back neighbor's yard, to the street, then to the corner two blocks over. Duke Adair is there.

They share a cigarette. He says, "I like your bathing suit."

She says, "Thanks."

They cut through alleys and across the park. At the community center, Duke Adair hops the gate surrounding the pool. Honky Sticky slides her body through the bars. This is where the Girl Scout Cadettes took their lessons. Tonight, the whole area is dark except for the one sousurface pool lamp illuminating the water in ways similar to certain patches of the ocean Honky Sticky slopped over in her raft on those pitch-black nights. Sort of enchanting like that. Honky just stands for a minute and looks.

Shoes off, standing by the deep end, she asks Duke, "Where's your suit?"

"I don't swim," he tells her and climbs onto the diving board and lays belly down.

"Oh." Honky sits at the edge of the pool, points her toes, and slides soundlessly past the surface of the water. It feels wonderful.

Under there, she does what she does in the water. Staying down long without air, she slips and turns, streams bubbles from her nose. Feels like she did back then. Rolling weightless in the community pool, she closes her eyes and sees the Pod. And Danguy running around inside, looking the opposite of how she feels.

She wishes he could sometimes feel better. She swims low and below and pressure increases against her chest, but it is like being squeezed, and she doesn't mind. She thinks about the noise underneath and inside the sea. In the ocean back then, she liked to think she could hear the stem post and the keel of her dad's boat carve its course across the surface of the sea—splitting the waters around his bow, folding them back together in the spume chasing his stern, out there, wherever. She opens her eyes and she is slinking along the tiled bottom of the pool. She slides over the drain, feeling the raised striations of the grate better than she can see them. But behind the grate she thinks she sees light. The deep green blur of the pool is a yellow blur in that drain. When she surfaces she tells Duke Adair she'd like to return tomorrow with goggles, fins, and a screwdriver.

TWO SHORT screws secure the grate to its drain. Honky Sticky removes them easily, pulls up the grate. She thrusts it away. It drifts toward the shallow end. The drainpipe on the pool floor is a little bigger around than a cantaloupe. Near the opening, a post crosses the diameter of the mouth of the pipe, dividing it in half. Bright light from down the shaft shines up on both sides of the post. In her goggles, Honky squints. She reaches her hand in and takes hold of the post. It feels like a handle. She lets her fins and her legs, her trunk and her free arm float up and away from the drain—like her body is a helium balloon tethered to the drain post by her stringy arm. The light from down there blazes a cylindrical beam straight up and into the pool. It is as big as the drain around, as steady and strong as a grand opening spotlight, the kind that slings a phosphorescent shaft back and forth across the sky. Only this spot is still.

Honky Sticky hangs on, upside down, underwater, in the middle of it, feeling lit up all around her edges, swaying just slightly. She's got her eyes locked on a sight deep in the drain. She focuses harder and looks closer. Like she's looking through a peephole, she sees kids on the other side. Some toddler kids and babies swimming around in what looks like the ocean but is visible in this drain, in this pool, hundreds of miles from the sea. Honky Sticky recognizes the sight, has seen it before. Drifting in the raft someplace between the Pod and the shore, she glimpsed a glow in the water over the side of her vessel. Across a section of the surface of ocean, light shavings tinseled, illuminated from a source down below. Like the sun through blue stained glass, only it was night, the sky above the raft was black, and Honky Sticky was looking down into the sea. She put on her goggles, leaned over the rubber bumper, broke the surface of the ocean with her face. It was sparkling and lucent like daytime. Little kid butts, soft and round and propelled by little kid legs kicking point-toed through seaweed stalks and in and out of rock formations, crossed in and out of her field of view. Back then looking into the sea, like now looking into the drain, Honky watches what looks like the kids just going about their lives. A few of the bigger-looking kids hold the babies. Cradle them and go, move through the space of the sea.

Honky Sticky feels the thing in her throat kick in, feels like it's pushing a kind of air around her body. She doesn't need to surface just yet. She looks harder into the drain. Wonders if and then wishes, for a moment, that she might see Danguy Weck. She doesn't know why she'd see him in there, she just hopes she does. Wants to watch him dribble by smoothly and unshaken, finally comfortable in the water. Maybe he would look at her and could read her thoughts. Her thoughts would be complicated. If he intended for her to die at sea, she didn't, and for that she's got fistfuls of middle fingers to erect at him. If he intended to save her, she's safe. For that, she is calm and pink and thankful. For his throat, she might hug him. Plunk her chin on his shoulder and breathe a long breath in and then let it out. Then she would pass him paper and a pen. She would read his notes.

Her brother does not swim by. Just other little kids. They look calm enough, but she worries maybe the kids are stuck. What if their environment got lodged somehow, between here and the deep sea? Honky Sticky gives the handle a twist. The post makes a complete revolution and sinks several inches into the drain. A wide gap opens on the inside lip of the drain tube. Pool water swirls in. First slow, then spinning rapidly. Suddenly cyclonic. The water hurricanes down the drain, is sucked away. Honky feels the roar of the draining water on her wrist and her hand, her hair and her neck. She lets go of the post, kicks forcefully to the surface. Duke Adair hangs his head over the diving board, smiles with all his teeth when she pops her head up and grabs onto the edge of the pool. She is gasping for breath and coughing, but louder than her sounds is the rumbling whoosh of water charging through pipes. The pool is shrinking shallow, quickly. They run.

HONKY STICKY doesn't get the chance to tell Duke Adair about the kids in the drain. The cops pin it on him—trespassing, defacing public property, intentional breach of desert county drought laws, which are strict and apparently very important to the people in charge. They find out his mom's never home. And something about contributing to the delinquency of a minor. They send him away. Maybe to his grandparents'. Honky learns he was on juvi probation when he lived with his dad. She thinks everyone in charge is overreacting and their aggressive decision making is shit because there he goes, out of her life. But she doesn't speak up, doesn't take any fall for it. She doesn't want to be sent away. She reserves a place in her head where she feels bad about this for the rest of her life, for letting him get sent away. It shrinks slowly over time. She tells me now it's about the size of a cranberry.

I MEET Honky Sticky in a bar in the summertime. The bar is outdoors. I spot her paused by the giant speaker between the patio plant and the fountain, a few steps away from the long bar where men in black shirts scoop ice and upend bottles. She is shaking her hair to the music. I watch her and feel my ribs splinter in my chest, making room for the sight of her.

We meet and it is miracle time. Every day for days on end. Like The Floodgates of Love have dissolved into our tap water, our beer, her saliva, my sweat. We meet and marry right away, in the way that can happen. She is my wife.

I tell her my secrets. I tell her about Kelly Green, for whose death I preserve clayey and clotted human remorse in my gut. "You feel a little like My Love did," she suggests, piecing my life together in her mind. *Ahhh* is how that feels to me. And she promises me we could find the Pod if need be. Hide out in it if the business of Kelly Green's death ever comes back around. She assures me she doesn't think it will, but we could go if it did.

I tell her about the acrobat and her eyeballs glitter like the tinfoil skin of the sea. She holds the back of my head with her hands and smiles and says *Mmm* and *Oh* and *Shit!* in ways that sound like cake. She asks me if in an X-ray my heart might look like soup in a sack. I tell her it's likely. I tell her about a thing I don't think of—hate to—practically ever. About a kid in the public pool a long time ago. She doesn't think I'm a horrible person.

There is something about her face. In it I see features of the faces of every television and every movie person I've ever watched and loved. Every crush. Every friend. Which makes me feel like I grew up with her. But I didn't. So when she tells me about Honky Sticky, I like to imagine myself there. I would have liked to have been there.

Before she returns from work, sometimes I go to the beach. Sit as the sun sets and the sand gets cold. I watch the waves and through binoculars grope the horizon looking for an old ship captained by an old man leaning on a harpoon. Everywhere else I maraud the faces of men looking for one that looks like her, but silent, with a pale splotch of a scar on his man neck. And other times, I scour features for big lips and small teeth. Is a Duke Adair out there? I want to lean softly into her good ear, to say one day to her as we walk around together, "Is that him? Do you think that's him?" We are holding hands, looking.

ACKNOWLEDGMENTS

If I could dress thank yous in great outfits and send them to the homes of Geoffrey Wolff and Michelle Latiolais and Caitlin Flanagan and Aimee Bender—and the thank yous would dance well and be funny and miraculously make every day magical and happy for them all, I would. Because thanking them for their encouragement and guidance and interest and friendship and time doesn't cover the gratitude I've got busting out the bottom of my heart.

Gargantuan thanks to my agent Claudia Ballard and my editor Roxanna Aliaga and the crew at Soft Skull and Counterpoint. Outstanding thanks to the Fiction Writing Workshop at UCI for their sensitive readings, shrewd comments, and contagious and nourishing love for and celebration of language and moments on a page. Very special thanks to Matt Sumell. And to the Dorothy and Donald Strauss Endowed Thesis Fellowship, which granted me deeply appreciated funds and time to work on this book.

Thank you to my family, and their good natures and nurturings. My wise brother Ethan Peck, my mom Francine Matarazzo, my dad John Schumann, my stepmom Beth Schumann, my stepdad Steve Peck. And where friends and family overlap and are best—tremendous, chest-swelling thanks to Heather Kinlaw and Melanie Beard.

The daughter of a painter and a linguist, Marisa Matarazzo grew up in Los Angeles. She attended Harvard-Westlake High School and pursued acting as a teenager. She earned her BA from Yale, where she received the Wallace Prize for fiction writing, the Jodie Foster Scholarship, the Arthur Willis Colton Scholarship, and was a two-time recipient of the Elmore A. Willets Prize for fiction. Earning her MFA from UC Irvine, she was the recipient of the Dorothy and Donald Strauss Endowed Thesis Fellowship. Her stories have been published in *Faultline* and *Hobart*. She lives in Los Angeles.

Printed in the United States
by Baker & Taylor Publisher Services